TRIPPING ON A HALO

BY ALESSANDRA TORRE

Digital ISBN: 978-0-9997841-6-7

Print ISBN: 978-0-9997841-7-4

Editing: Marion Archer

Proofing: Angie Owens, Erik Gevers, Perla Calas

Front Cover Design: Perfect Pear Creative Covers Image: Wayhome Studio

1

I had a giant penis in my purse. I'd let a bit of air out of it so I could squish it down, its plastic inflatable body contorted into odd angles, bits of it poking out of the top. I've been carrying the thing around for three days now. Yesterday, I needed to find my Smoothie King rewards thingy in the bottom of my purse, and I'd had to haul the penis out and lean it against the counter in order to find the teeny purple swipe card. The guy behind me chuckled, and the cashier looked horrified, but that was probably due to the two kids who had just skipped in, a frazzled soccer mom in tow.

I'd apologized to all involved parties and struggled to get the penis BACK in the bag, which was a time-consuming struggle that led to me being banned from Smoothie King. I know what you're thinking. Extreme, right? I mean, BANNED? It was a five-foot inflatable dong. Give me a Sharpie and squint a little, and I could turn it into a snake. Or a really tall mushroom. It didn't even have balls, for piglets' sake.

I kept my arm clamped down on the humongous bag and rounded the corner, hoofing it a little to keep Declan Moss in my sights. He was a dozen yards ahead of me, his suit fitting on that tall frame like it was custom. It wasn't. Three weeks ago, I saw him pick that pinstripe number out at Men's Warehouse. My playlist had been disrupted by a painfully annoying 90's song and I'd almost missed his exit, his steps clipping out the food court and toward his truck faster than a Supermarket Sweep contestant.

My headache, which had started two hours ago and was peaking upward at an alarming rate, spiked, stopping me for a brief moment. I struggled, my panic rising, and continued forward, increasing my speed. I glanced at my watch. Normally he was in the office by now, my attempted entrances routinely thwarted by the brunette bitch at his front desk, who was a ninja at keeping me out. Declan approached the cross street at Madison Ave and I craned my neck, right, then left, looking for oncoming traffic.

A dump truck barreled from the right, toward the intersection. Pain radiated through my head and I struggled to focus on Declan, watching as his head dropped, his attention pulled to his phone. He glanced left, then back down at his cell, continuing to move forward.

The truck rumbled closer, rattling over a pothole, and I willed Declan to look up, to stop moving, to see the danger. His fingers moved over the phone's slick screen and he moved another step forward.

I imagined his new suit ruined, appendages jerking, those sexy glasses cracking, body SPLATTING. Another lightning bolt of pain ricocheted through my temple.

I dropped my bag and dug my hand in, the penis popping out like one of those snakes in a can. A big, swollen, flesh-colored snake. I grabbed it and swung it through the air. "HEY!" I screeched. "PURPLE PEOPLE EATERS!" I could have yelled his name, but I was trying to stay under the radar.

The people in my immediate bubble took a few steps back, giving me a wide berth. A girl wearing yoga pants and a sports bra lifted her phone and took a photo of me. I squatted down as low as my skinny jeans would allow and then sprung towards the sky, tossing the penis into the air. I snuck a look at Declan, who had glanced over his shoulder and was now turning back to the street, his head shaking. The pain in my head lessened, and I let out a sigh of relief at the garbage truck, which was now safely past, no gorgeous architect under its wheels.

A dude with rolled up pant legs and an EAT VEGAN shirt stopped in front of me. "You need help."

I snorted as the penis fluttered down and slumped on the sidewalk beside us. "I'm good." I glanced back at Declan, but he was gone, across the street and into his building, the huge skyscraper sucking him in.

It was the second time I'd saved his life, and I still hadn't gotten a sniff of gratitude in return. But, that was fine.

I reached down and pulled at the penis's stopper, watching as the nude appendage deflated with a loud sputter, its purpose fulfilled.

Letting out a sigh, I glanced up the building's face, and wondered where he was inside of it.

It didn't matter. I knew where to find him next.

2

Declan leaned against the glass wall of his office, his eyes on the street below, where his stalker moved through the crowds, a pool float of some sort under her arm. She was disrupting the flow of traffic, suits skirting around her, her bright pink sweater standing out in the crowd. She came to a stop next to the corner trashcan and tried to stuff the item into the swinging door. It wouldn't fit and she pulled it out, shaking out the design and attempting to feed it length-wise. He squinted, trying to see the item. Yep. He'd questioned the brief glimpse he'd gotten of her in the crowd, chanting her nonsense, but it was, in fact, a penis. Behind her, a man tried to help, reaching over to open the can. Any hopes she would turn her fixations on him ended as she held up a hand in a clear STAY AWAY FROM ME gesture. *What was this girl's deal?*

"Dec?"

He turned away from the view.

Nate held open the door to his office, his brow raised. "You coming?"

"Yeah." He followed his partner out into the lobby, attempting to focus on their upcoming meeting. The client was coming in from New

York City to review their proposal for a sprawling business complex. They were one of three firms up for the job and needed this one. The market crash hadn't been good for business, especially for a new company still trying to find its legs and market share.

Purple People Eaters? Is that what she'd said?

"You got the presentation?" Nate asked.

"Yeah." Nate pulled open the door of the conference room, and Declan got a glimpse of the client. Benta Aldrete. A thirty-year-old tech exec who had already verbally roasted Nate over their initial proposal. This was their second meeting with her, and the callback had increased their optimism. He reached in his pocket and withdrew the flash drive, confident about their design.

"We designed the second floor as an open workspace—one where your remote employees could work when they are in town, but also where you could meet with clients, or in small teams." Nate turned away from the screen and flashed a smile at the woman. It was a lost cause. Nate had turned on the charm at every opportunity and gotten absolutely nowhere with the exotic beauty.

"A flex space," Declan added, zooming in on the area.

"Right." Nate nodded. "This would solve the need for workspaces without having to chop up the floorplan. And the private rooms here..." he pointed to the edge of the plan. "And here—that would still give you small places for quiet or privacy if..."

What Declan couldn't figure out was what had brought this stalker into his life. The Purple People Eater episode hadn't been her first crazy moment. There'd also been the outburst at Chipotle, and at Trader Joe's. And those had been the *major* events. Just as alarming were the minor sightings. Her hidden behind big sunglasses and mixed in among the wives at his softball game. Her ducking in between cars in the Target parking lot. Reports from the reception desk of a blonde's repeated attempts to get up to his office.

"...the structure of the complex." Nate finished, glancing at

Declan. He nodded and tried to find their place in the presentation. Nate waited for him to pick up the reins, and then continued on. Declan straightened in his seat and vowed to focus.

How did this woman *pay* for things? She seemed available, twenty-four hours a day, to stalk him. Didn't she work? Hell, he could have sworn he saw her in the airport in West Virginia, a glimpse of her platinum-blonde hair swinging out of view just before he grabbed his suitcase from the baggage claim carousel.

Nate flipped to the next slide, showing the building's elevation, the tech complex modern and airy, full of glass and color—everything the client had wanted. They should have a good shot at the contract, especially given their design pricing, which was well below industry average.

He pushed back from the table and stood, coming to stand next to Nate, their heights almost identical. Nate's last girlfriend had dubbed them the two Archihotties—an unoriginal nickname she'd driven into the ground. Thank God that had ended, but the nickname had stuck, popping into his head whenever he joined Nate.

Declan pointed to the proposed courtyard, in the middle of the U-shaped structure. "You'd wanted an area for employees to eat lunch or work outside. The beauty of this courtyard is in its hidden shade. There are retractable screens built into these overhangs. If weather hits or the sun is too bright?" He nodded to Nate and the screen changed, a video playing, showing the extensions at work. Benta smiled, her first positive response, and Declan felt relief flood his chest.

He and Nate would get the account.

And he would figure out a way to lose his stalker.

3

"It's just that you're so *normal* in every other way." Ansley peered at me over the lid of her coffee.

I snorted. "I am normal."

"You used to be normal," she countered. "But ever since this all began, you've turned *completely* abnormal. Pretty certifiable. I was talking to Roger yesterday—"

"About me?" I interrupted. "Oh God. Please don't."

"He's a professional." She set down her foam cup and gave me the serious look, the one she normally reserved for deep conversations about funeral preparations or civil unrest in Nicaragua. "And he's one of the only people I know who wouldn't haul you off to a crazy bin."

"Dr. E hasn't hauled me off to a crazy bin."

"Which, quite honestly, amazes me. He was a total dick with me."

I eyed the cupcake on her plate. "Are you going to eat that? I think the one they gave me was undersized."

She pulled the glittery confection closer to her. "Anyway, Roger thinks this is an attempt to distract yourself from Mom's death."

It was an opinion shared by Dr. Eaton, though I wasn't going to give Roger *that* victory. I huffed out a breath, uninterested in either psychologist's opinion. "This isn't about Mom. And I don't expect you to understand."

Ansley continued staring me down as if I was torturing small puppies in my spare time.

"I'm not doing anything wrong." I folded the napkin in front of me in half, then thirds. "I'm keeping him safe. That's it."

"Find a different hobby," she urged. "Something that isn't going to get you thrown in jail."

My watch chimed, the timer going off. I pushed to my feet and silenced it. "Got to go."

She stayed in place, watching as I collected our trash. "Really? Where are you heading?"

I ignored the question, downing the rest of my milk in one loud suck of the straw.

"*Autumn,*" she said loudly. "Where are you going?"

I balled up the napkin and tossed it in the trash, my steps quickening. If I was going to get to Declan's office before he left for work, I needed to hurry.

The traffic wasn't cooperating. I tapped my fingers against the steering wheel and forced myself to go through my daily meditations, concentrating on anything BUT the traffic which, according to the law of attraction, would magically cause the traffic to clear up, since I wasn't thinking about it. Only, given my course of mental acrobatics, I *was* thinking about it. I sternly schooled my thoughts back to my list of affirmations.

I will find a 'real' job.

I repeated the phrase several times, envisioning the perfect job—one full of happy, friendly co-workers, doing something ... my mind always faltered on the *what* that was occurring. There was a reason I had two degrees and a resume filled with entry-level jobs. Nothing seemed to stick.

At the moment, my days were being filled with scrapbooking. I had one exceedingly happy client who paid me in slightly burnt apple crisps and information. Granted, scrapbooking was a complete waste of my education, but it was infinitely more enjoyable then any of my 'real jobs' had been.

I eyed the right-hand lane and put on my blinker, creeping up a little in hopes that the pick-up truck to my right would let me in. He didn't. I sighed and returned to my list.

I am grateful for my current position in life.

I took a moment, sending rays of thankfulness into the universe. It was the easiest of all of my mantras. I had so much to be thankful for. *Money*. After twenty-eight years of scraping loose change out of the couch cushions, and struggling under the staggering weight of my student debt, I was now rich. Well... I would be rich. As soon as the dates turned over on my thirtieth birthday and my trust was released. Assuming, of course, I could maintain my sanity in Dr. E's and the Leon County Court's eyes. In the meantime, I had a generous allowance that my cupcake and scrapbooking addictions barely touched.

I am grateful that I am healthy.

Oh, my freaking popsicle stick, if this traffic didn't MOVE I was going to miss him altogether. I shouldn't have met Ansley for lunch. I was playing with fire that my sister would be able to have a succinct conversation that didn't involve a detour down lectureville. And Roger wasn't any help. Go figure she married a psychologist. If she'd married the hot guy from the appliance store? I'd have a new washing machine and a lot less 'helpful' advice.

I eyed the navigation system on my car and debated about cutting across on Orange Ave. Declan was probably packing up right now. Rolling up plans and stuffing them under his elbow, though apparently that was a movie architect thing and not a real architect thing, because the most I'd seen him carry into his office was a giant bag of subs from the Capital Deli.

My phone rang, Ansley's face filling up the screen. I hit the ignore button and enjoyed a moment of peace, then a second call came through. I sighed and answered it. "What?"

"Tell me you aren't going to his office."

"I'm not going to his office."

"Bullshit. I'm behind you. You've got no other reason to be heading up Blairstone right now."

I cursed and craned my neck, looking into my rearview mirror and seeing my sister's minivan a half dozen cars back. "How did you get out of the restaurant so quickly?"

"He's going to file a restraining order against you."

I pulled open the center console and rooted around, moving tampons, Altoids, a dog-eared paperback and nail clippers out of the way, sighing with relief when I saw the bottle of Excedrin at the bottom of the pile. "He can't file a restraining order against me. I've never even talked to the man."

That wasn't *exactly* true. Six months ago, when all of this started, I tapped his shoulder in line at Publix and asked if he had a piece of gum. He'd glanced around slowly, shook his head, and pointed to an enormous display of brightly covered wrappers to our right. Then he'd taken a large step forward, crowding the woman ahead of him, who'd sniffed a little but then smiled.

Everyone smiled at him. It was annoyingly difficult to protect a man who attracts people from every direction. What if one of them was a stalker? A killer? A vengeful ex-girlfriend who wanted to cut off his ears and store them in a jar in her kitchen cabinet?

"He can still file a restraining order against you. And I don't have to tell you what that might do to your trust evaluation."

"I haven't done anything to him," I pointed out, twisting off the lid to a bottled water and popping two Excedrins in my mouth.

"Except be creepy. Super duper creepy."

"I'm not creepy. I'm... watchful." I don't bring up my fear—that something terrible is going to happen to Declan if I don't protect him. Whenever I mention words like 'premonition' or 'guardian angel' she turns super weird on me. I can't exactly blame her. It does sound absolutely psychotic, if you aren't in my shoes, straddled with fears of an architect's death, and struggling with the piercing onsets of doom I feel.

The truth is, something was going to happen to Declan Moss. Something terrible. Something deadly. Something I could stop.

The traffic ahead of me cleared, like a sign from God that I was right, this was meant to be, and I better hurry, dammit. I pressed the gas a little too aggressively and almost plowed into a Jeep.

"I'm following you," Ansley announced, like that would sway me from anything.

"Suit yourself." I waved the water bottle in the air in a nonchalant way I hoped was visible four cars back. "I'm sure Caleb doesn't need to be picked up from the babysitter."

"I'm booking you an appointment with Roger. Next Tuesday. He has an opening at three."

"I'm not talking to Roger. Dr. Eaton's got me covered. One shrink is enough for me. And if I did go—which I'm not—I'd have to tell him you've been thinking about John Diaggolo's penis."

She sputtered out a string of broken sentences. "I haven't—I don't —I told you that six years ago."

"And God, I still remember how beautiful you said it was. Veiny, right? Like a Coke can, I think that was the analogy you used. It scarred me, envisioning it. Envisioning it corrupting my sweet older sister. Maybe I *do* need to talk to someone about it. Thank God he has an opening. I really need to work through the entire thing in my—"

"Just STOP." She swore under her breath. "Fine. Jesus! I swear to God, I'm never drinking around you again."

I smiled. "I love you."

"You don't. You hate me, and you're proving it by heading downtown in this traffic."

I watched as she changed lanes, heading for her turn, and I lifted a hand in a wave. "Give Caleb a hug for me."

She growled into the phone, ended the call, and I swigged the last bit of the water.

Where was I? Oh yes.

I am grateful for my sister and all that she brings to my life.

4

This man was giving me a headache. I rubbed my temples and coaxed the stubborn muscles to unclench my brain.

Oblivious to my discomfort, Dr. E kept talking. "Let's talk about your mother." The shrink linked his fingers and examined me in the bored manner of someone halfway into a really long Wednesday. He probably kept someone in his garage, chained up by their ankles, and —instead of cutting them up in tiny bits like a normal psychopath—peppered them with questions about their childhood motivations for drawing stick families. At least my crazy was bright and obvious, and celebrated in glorious fashion. His breed—that of manipulation and observation—came with a giant price tag and the ability to yank my trust away.

And that's really why I was here. Not to talk about my mother, or my obsession with Declan Moss (though he loves to talk about both) but because my competency has to be verified before I receive my trust. And Johnson, Platt, and Falk—the pencil pushing pricks that control it—won't loosen those purse strings until this fart-knocker signs off on my sanity. I've got five more quarterly sessions to suffer through, though my enjoyment levels have increased dramatically since he added a bowl of Tootsie Rolls to the center of his coffee table.

I sighed, examining the strap of my purse, and waited him out.

Dr. Eaton hated silence. I realized this on our second appointment. His MO was to sit mute and wait for me to expel verbal vomit, but if I did the same thing? His pen started tapping and he'd eventually break by repeating my name, then moving on to another question.

"Autumn?" Dr. Eaton cleared his throat. Step 1, complete.

I stretched out my toes and examined my nail polish, freshly applied during last night's Forensic Files marathon. The color was called Pumpkin Carousel and it was the coolest thing I'd ever seen, a black jelly base with orange, green, purple and teal holographic glitters throughout it. Also, if I shifted my toes upward in the right light, you could see a gold glittery sheen that shifted green. Dr. Eaton seemed unimpressed by their kaleidoscope of activity, his pen tapping with homicidal insistence upon the page. I decided to put him out of his misery.

"I don't want to talk about my mom." She was one of his favorite subjects. Like so many, he was fascinated by a woman who sat on a small fortune while eating discount cereal and duct-taping the soles of ten-year-old shoes. To him, she was a case study. To me, she was an open sore, his questions only making the pain worse.

"Okay." He set down the pen. "Are you still following Declan Moss?"

Ugh. His second favorite topic. I slumped against the heavy velvet chair, propping my foot up on the ottoman. "Sometimes." A slight under-exaggeration.

He leaned forward and peered down at something on his desk. "Huh. That's interesting to hear. Your latest credit card statement raises some questions, Autumn."

"Oh?" I adopted my best bored expression, while frantically trying to remember last month's purchases. Another stipulation of my trust is that I have to turn in my receipts each month, proving I'm not being irresponsible with my current allotment, before I get the motherlode.

Which is ridiculous, but I'm not about to argue with how I receive my unexpected inheritance.

"I counted, and there are fifteen transactions at Jasmine Cafe." He glanced at me. "Isn't that directly across from Mr. Moss's building?"

"Is it?" I frowned. "Huh. They have a hot tea there I love. It's…" I mimicked the sort of shudder Ansley made when she described sex with Roger. "Ah-mazing." I made a mental note to start using cash.

"Right…" he drawled. His pen circled something on the page. "And I also see a deposit for Premier Fitness Club." He pushed his glasses up higher on his nose. "I don't suppose Declan Moss is a member there?"

I sputtered out a scoff and raised my hands in my best impression of bewilderment. "How would *I* know?"

"Ms. Jones." He set down the page. "Let me make myself clear, since you seem intent on these ridiculous attempts to hide your extra-curricular activities concerning Mr. Moss. I don't think it's entirely harmful, your fascination with him. In fact, I think it might even be healthy for you."

"You do?" This was a surprise. In fact, I'd have laid down odds that he wore a sparkly red banana hammock and swung around a pole as a part-time gig before I'd put down money on him supporting *anything* regarding me and Declan Moss.

"You were not able to save your mother's life, and you feel justifiable guilt over not being there to protect her. If you are transferring this perceived 'defeat'"—he made little quote marks around the word —"to Mr. Moss by protecting him and keeping him from harm, then it gives you a way to overcome your fears. This is a situation you are in control of, one you can manage." He gave me a solemn look, and if I didn't want to smack him for pouring gasoline on my stack of guilt kindling, I'd hug him for encouraging my Declan obsession. "I think you should explore how you feel when you are watching Mr. Moss. And if it gives you a sense of peace, continue it."

He leaned forward and his voice dropped. "But be aware that he is a human being. We are fragile, unpredictable creatures. It's entirely possible that something might happen to him—something you can't prevent and may not be present for. And if it did, I fear that any healing you are experiencing will be destroyed or will damage your psyche even more. If you plan on taking this burden on, you need to be aware of the risks involved. For his well-being, but also ... for your own."

"So, I need to keep him safe," I clarified.

"If that's how you'd like to interpret it. Yes." He nodded soberly, as if this was a huge revelation and well worth the three hundred dollars this session was costing my trust.

Keep Declan Moss safe. Well... duh.

5

Beneath the table, Margaret O'Keefe's foot brushed against Declan's shin and she blushed. "Sorry."

"It's fine." He shifted in his seat. "Common issue with long legs. I'm probably crowding you."

"No!" She shook her head. "It's fine."

Silence fell, and he was out of practice with this. He should have taken Nate up on his offer to double date. The man was a chatterbox. Now, without his conversation starters and jokes, the silence grew, suffocating him.

"So..." she picked up her drink, spinning the ice around in it with her straw. "Your profile said you were an architect?"

He nodded. "I worked at one of the big firms for a few years, then started a practice with my roommate from college. We focus mostly on commercial projects."

God, this was dreary. He tried to remember what her job was. Something in engineering, but an odd specialty. "Where'd you go to school?"

She smiled. "Here at Florida State. I got my degree there and stayed. This isn't exactly Silicon Valley, but I stay busy enough to pay the mortgage."

Tech Engineering. That was what her profile had said. He tried to find a subject centered on that and failed. "I'm sorry." He grimaced. "It's been a long time since I've been on a date. I'm a little out of practice."

She laughed, and she had a nice laugh—the sort that caused her whole face to light up. "It's fine. Honestly? This is the fifth date I've had this month. I'd much rather be in your situation."

He winced. "Ouch. Are you that picky or were they that bad?"

She held up her hands. "I think it's that I'm that bad. Five dates and only one follow up call."

He leaned forward. "Impossible. You're..." *Sweet. Smart. Attractive.* Too bad they had no spark of chemistry.

She raised a brow. "Intimidating. That's been the common consensus."

She wasn't intimidating, not compared to Benta Aldrete, who he and Nate had spent all day with. That woman was a force of nature. Compared to her, Margaret seemed like a pleasant change of pace. Still, he nodded to validate her hypothesis. "A beautiful and intelligent woman is intimidating to a lot of men."

She watched him closely. "But not you?" There was a hint of desperation in her voice and it was most likely *that* which had scared off other men. Even the question made him feel uncomfortable, as if he was being forced into a second date before they ordered appetizers.

He shook his head. "I'm not intimidated."

She gave a tentative smile. "Good."

This was bad. He was leading her on, couldn't decipher his own feelings to save his life, and they had barely sat down. He shouldn't be dating. It was too soon after his breakup with Nicola. He was like a lost bunny, caught in a trap with chickens, headed to slaughter.

Margaret's eyes caught on something behind him. "Oh my God..." she murmured. "You won't believe the woman that just walked in."

His back stiffened. Of course his stalker was here. He'd picked the restaurant specifically in hopes the swanky address and valet parking would keep her at bay. He'd sat with his back to the door, had taken a roundabout route from home and had all but sprinted into the restaurant in hopes of avoiding her. Everything for nothing. She was here and would probably do something absolutely ridiculous. He forced the stress out of his voice and picked up his water glass in the most casual manner he could manage. "Really?"

She leaned forward and shot him a mischievous look. "Don't look, but she's got the most enormous breasts you've ever seen."

His shoulders relaxed. Not that he'd examined his stalker's breasts, but from a side glance, they'd appeared perfectly normal sized. Nice, if you liked small breasts, which he always had. Which was why what had happened with Nicola had been so jarring. It—

"Hello, Declan."

He lifted his head and almost dropped the glass of water. "Nicola."

His ex stood beside their table, one hip cocked, her skintight dress barely containing the basketball-sized breasts she had purchased shortly before their break-up. According to her new bras, which he'd peeked at while she was in the shower, they were double Es. Double Es that looked like triple Fs on her tiny frame. He tried to look around them and to her face, a difficult feat given his seated position, her close proximity, and the four-inch heels she wore.

"Hi." His date smiled wryly up at Nicola. "I'm Margaret."

"Nice to meet you," Nicola cooed. That was another thing she'd adopted. After her breasts had come an entirely new wardrobe, giant new eyelashes, blonde hair and a raspy voice that giggled and fawned.

She leaned on the table, facing Declan, her elbows jutting into the sides of her breasts and pushing the giant balloons together. "You haven't been returning my calls."

His eyes met Margaret's and she tilted her head at him as if to say *Really, Declan? Why haven't you returned her calls?*

He smiled tightly. "Nicola, this isn't really the place or time to be having this conversation."

She huffed out a sigh, her eyelids drooping, and trailed a long red fingernail along the back of his hand. "We can't exactly *have* a conversation if you won't answer the phone."

"Margaret, I'm sorry." He pushed back his seat and gave her a grim nod as he rose. "Could you give me one moment?"

She spread her hands as if to give him all the time in the world. Pressing a firm hand on Nicola's back, he ushered her toward the front of the restaurant.

"You can't be doing this," he gritted out.

"Excuse me!" Nicola planted her heels into the carpet, yelling loud enough to cause the closest tables to look over in alarm. Declan stepped back and raised his hands in surrender.

"You know," she hissed. "I'm here on a DATE." She nodded to the right, and Declan didn't turn, feeling sorry for whatever poor bastard was witnessing this. "You're *embarrassing* me." She attempted to cross her arms over her chest but struggled, the massive appendages too large to allow a successful linkage of forearms. It was shocking, given the physics of her new anatomy, that she was able to stay upright.

He rolled his eyes. "Good. Go to your date and I'll go to mine." He turned and stopped when her hand grabbed at his bicep, her nails digging into his shirt.

"You know," she said softly, and in the look that flashed over her features for the briefest of moments... he saw the girl he once fell for. "I loved you."

"And then you changed." He pulled away. "Go back to your date, Nic." It was amazing. At one point, the thought of her dating someone else would have crushed him. Now, he only wanted her to move on and stay out of his life.

She stood there for a moment, a limp shell, her breasts even more ridiculous without the bravado behind them. Then, like a peacock lifting its feathers, she pulled herself back together and turned away, her hair tossed, stride strong, breasts re-extended.

He waited, watching as she rounded the hostess stand and slid into a chair across from a guy with a gold watch on his wrist and a bolo tie. Maybe this was the infamous douchebag she had cheated on him with. Was he the one who had paid for all of her surgeries? He wasn't sure whether to wish the guy luck or knock out his teeth.

Letting out a hard breath, he headed back to his table. Go figure, his first date in the six months since they'd broken up, and she was here. What were those odds? Was he just snakebit in attracting crazy women? Thankfully, his table with Margaret was on the other side of the restaurant, though he didn't see how he'd focus on the rest of the meal, knowing Nicola was in the same room.

Taking a seat across from his date, he picked up his napkin and smoothed it down over his lap. "Sorry about that."

She raised her eyebrows over the rim of her water glass. "Interesting girl you got there. Is that your normal type?"

The thought of trying to explain Nicola, and her evolution through the last six months of their relationship, was exhausting. He struggled to relax his features into a rueful smile. "Not quite. Though she had been, at one time. When I met Nicola, she had a much more ... natural ... look." A sunny smile, slightly crooked nose, a bit of an overbite. She'd had purple dreads when he'd met her, sweaty and slightly drunk, in a crowded concert in Panama City Beach.

She'd been so much fun. Relaxed. Carefree. She hadn't cared about the balance in his bank account, or worried over what people thought of her, or the condition of her manicure.

The changes had been gradual. Subtle. He'd barely noticed the changes until he woke up one morning, looking at a woman with a white bandage covering half her face. It was funny how it took the first *physical* transformation of her to really take note of her emotional transformations. Over the three years of their relationship, she had completely changed. The fun, lighthearted hippie was gone, replaced with someone hyper-focused on her social status, Instagram followers, and Declan's future earning potential.

"My ex always wanted me to have plastic surgery." Margaret tapped at the end of her nose. "You know. This beak."

"I think you're perfect as you are." He opened the menu and struggled to find a new topic.

Yeah. It was *definitely* too early to be dating again.

6

I sat in the middle of my living room, legs spread wide, latex gloves and fuzzy socks on, and picked through Declan Moss's trash. It was pretty good trash, much better than last week's. He recycled, which allowed me to skip the gross kitchen stuff and stick with the recycling bin, which yielded his receipts, mail, boxes, and a lot of odds and ends.

I didn't think you're supposed to recycle Q-Tips, but he did. And he used A LOT of Q-Tips. Thank God his ears are clean. I'm not sure I could take gunky yellow tips without gagging up my dinner.

I flipped another Q-Tip toward the trash and flipped through his mail. He wasn't a coupon cutter, which was a win for me, because he missed out on a 40% off Panera coupon. I set it to the side, along with a BOGO deal from a crafts store that carried my scrapbooking paper. Reaching over to scratch Mr. Oinks' stomach, I scanned over a Home Depot receipt, a cable bill, a letter from his homeowners association (dues are going up) and a credit card offer. Finishing, I leaned back on my hands and stared at the mess before me.

I waited.

Sometimes, when I watched Declan, or when I thought of him, everything went bonkers in my head. There were times when it was painful and obvious, like when that garbage truck was careening toward him. Other times, it was just a faint dizziness and some dots at the edge of my vision. But best I could tell, it's how my sixth sense alerted me that something was wrong in Declanville.

I closed my eyes. Inhaled deeply. Tried to feel any sense of impending doom.

Nothing. For once, my head was clear, headache and pain-free.

I let out a puff of air, then picked up his credit card statement and reviewed the charges. I was halfway down the list, taking special note of his Taco Bell addiction, when my phone rang.

I scooted across the floor on my butt and grabbed it off the table just in time. "Yo."

"Please don't answer the phone like that."

"Yo, Sexy Bitches Anonymous. How can I help you?"

My sister sighed. "He's home."

I perked up, half-rising enough to see the clock. 8:42. "That seems early." Beside me, stretched out between a row of Declan's beer cans and a pyramid of empty toilet paper rolls, Mr. Oinks bellowed out a sigh of agreement.

"Yes, I thought so, too."

I grinned at the interested tone in my sister's voice. "Admit it, you *like* doing my dirty work."

She snorted, and I heard water start to run in the background. "I'm not doing your dirty work. I'm washing dishes and happened to see him drive by. I'm just trying to save you a trip all the way out here."

"Ahh...." I pulled a shoebox apart at the seams, flattening it down so it would take up less space in the bag. "That was kind of you."

"I don't know what you're going to do if we ever move. Or if he moves. Or if I find something better to do than stare out my kitchen window at the guy across the street."

"At least he's nice to look at." I picked up a television manual, still in the plastic wrap, surprised that he threw it away. What if his remote needed reprogramming? Or he couldn't figure out the different presets? I set it to the side.

"Yeah," Ansley said grudgingly. "If you like the whole six-pack and strapping-build sort of look."

"Which you don't."

"God, no. Have you seen Roger's stomach? It's perfect for a pillow. I couldn't lay my head on a washboard and be comfortable. No one would want that."

"Right." I spotted a loose thread on my fuzzy sock and pulled on it. It grew longer and I paused, patting it back into place with a hope that it would magically retract. It didn't. I frowned.

"Who comes home from a date at eight-thirty?" The sound of water stopped as I imagined Ansley reaching for the dish towel next to the sink and drying her hands. "She must have been a dud."

"I should have gone," I said sadly, looking at the wasted evening, stretched out in neatly organized stacks of light cardboard, bottles and Q-Tips. "Maybe something exciting happened."

"Oh yeah," Ansley said sarcastically. "You could have sat next to them. Joined in the conversation. That would have gone well."

"I could have been discreet."

"You know what you *really* should have done?" Her voice rose in a manner that foreshadowed exactly what she was about to say.

"Gone on my own date?" I guessed.

"Yes. That's exactly what you should have done. Roger has a client who'd be perfect for you. He even believes in aliens!"

"I'm not an alien, Ansley, I'm a guardian angel."

"Oh, my GAWD, you're my little sister. You're not a guardian angel. Trust me, I'd know."

"Don't you think it's coincidental that you live right across the street from him?" Okay, so maybe not *right* across the street, but three doors down and catty-corner was pretty dang close.

"It's not coincidental considering that that's how you found him."

"He's not a lost kitten. I didn't find him, I..." I frowned, trying to find the right words to describe the cosmic event that happened the first time I saw Declan Moss.

It had been so hot. The sharp, burning pain in my head ... I'd thought it was the summer humidity. My vision blurred, and I'd blamed it on the tears. I'd ignored it until the moment that I couldn't, until the moment that pain had shrieked through my head like the scream of a fire engine.

And in that moment, Declan Moss had almost died.

7

The date hadn't been that bad. Declan mused over the night as he pulled into the garage and turned off the engine. Margaret had been sweet. She'd had a dry sense of humor that had been entertaining. And once they'd discovered a mutual love of country music, conversation had flowed in a more natural rhythm. He pressed the garage opener and listened to the hum of the door closing. And Margaret was an attractive woman, with all of the things he would look for in a mate. Kinda sexy too, in her own way.

Declan opened the truck door. So, why had he taken her straight home? And when she had hovered by the front door and invited him in, why hadn't he accepted? Had it been Nicola?

He got out of the car, trying to erase the memory of Nic's eyes, that vulnerable look she had given him. Four or five months ago, he wouldn't have been able to resist that look. He would have folded her into his arms and squeezed her tight, kissed the top of her head, and told her he was sorry.

But... for what? She had been the one who had changed everything. The woman that he once loved ... he couldn't even find her anymore. The more surgeries, the more she disappeared. Then she had quit her job and became a Hooter's waitress. A few weeks later, she'd had a phone full of strangers' phone numbers and started skipping date nights in favor of hanging out with her new friends.

Three and a half years together, and all of it for nothing. There was no reason for him to apologize to her. And nothing worth mourning over. Nothing to waste another moment thinking about.

He stepped into the house and flipped the hall switch, the dim light illuminating the rows of baseball caps. He hung his keys on the hook and wandered into the kitchen, letting out a breath as he surveyed the quiet space. He could have brought Margaret here. She could be settling in at the island while he poured her a drink. She would have moved closer, and they would have kissed. He could have lifted her onto the counter, run his hands up her shirt, then carried her into the bedroom.

She had wanted him. He had seen the heat in her eyes, hadn't missed the linger of her touch when he'd hugged her goodnight. He may have been out of the dating world for some time, but he could recognize when a woman was interested. And it wasn't like he didn't need some sexual release. God, it had been six months since Nicola. Six months, and he hadn't had so much as a kiss. His body was aching for a woman, yet he dropped her off with a friendly smile and drove away.

He was an idiot. An idiot who let Nicola fuck up his game and get into his head. He grabbed a bottle of beer from the fridge and twisted off the top. Tossing the cap in the trash, he headed for the living room.

His new TV sucked. He stared at a sports replay, the football field more yellow than green. Picking up the remote, he struggled through the complicated menu options.

It wasn't just Nicola and Margaret. His life seemed to be cursed when it came to women. Take this blonde girl, screaming nonsense on the street yesterday and lurking behind corners and menus every time he seemed to turn around.

He reached for his beer and accidentally dropped the remote, the menu changing, the words now all in Chinese. *Fuck*. He reached down, grabbing the slim control and tried to move through the menus and find the language dropdown. At least his stalker hadn't shown up at dinner. As well as Margaret had handled Nic, adding a second crazy person to their date might have been too much drama for her to handle.

He growled in frustration as the screen filled with foreign characters. Pushing to his feet, he tried to remember where he'd put the flat screen's manual. When he'd opened the big box, it had been with Nate's help, the two of them working together to mount the giant television on the wall. He remembered stomping on the box to flatten it, then tossing it into the back of his truck and taking it to the dumpster. But the manual… he grimaced, fairly certain he threw the thing away.

Draining the last of his beer, he walked out the front door and headed to the trash cans at the curb. Close call. A few days later and they would have been taken. Pulling the heavy green recycle bin toward him, he opened the lid and reached in, pulling out the top bag. Setting it down on the concrete drive, he bent over and worked the tie open. He smiled, grateful for his mother's strict rules on trash separation. Without her, this manual would have been covered in a mess of leftover Chinese takeout and soda. Now, it would be cleanly discarded alongside paper towel rolls and mail. He got the bag open and reached in, digging through the items. He paused, confused.

Hesitatingly, he pulled out a tampon box, and then a squashed bottle of strawberry tea. *This wasn't his trash*. He straightened and looked back in the recycle can, paying closer attention to the contents. Hadn't there been more bags than this? Normally he had at least three or four, the bin almost full. Now, there was just one other bag, which he reached in and withdrew. Opening it up, he saw more unfamiliar items. Water bottles, dozens of them. Cans of energy drinks flattened by one of those tools that some people had mounted on the wall.

It didn't make any sense. Why would someone take his trash and leave their own? It'd be one thing if someone had tossed their trash on top of his, maybe because their own bin was full. But to *exchange* his trash for theirs? He dug deeper into the first bag, coming across a women's magazine and a stack of mail. He flipped through it. It was all opened, mostly junk and all addressed to the same person. Autumn Jones. The address was on Frolicking Lane, the zip code one from the south part of town. He stared at the name. *Autumn Jones.*

Was she the one who had swapped out his trash? If so, why?

He dug deeper, finding a few crumpled receipts and then… a flattened cardboard box that spelled everything out in giant bubble letters on the glossy display.

Novelty Inflatable Penis: Great for bachelorette parties!

He had a brief glimpse of the blonde, her purse at her feet, swinging that giant dong around like it was a flare on a deserted island. Her shoes springing off the ground as she jumped in the air with it, the shaft extended to the sky and screamed PURPLE PEOPLE EATER at the top of her lungs.

Dropping the box, he picked the stack of junk mail back up, his eyes focused in on what he was holding.

The name and address of his stalker.

"So, *this* is her?" Nate held up the postcard, his finger pinned to the address. "You're sure about this?'

"One hundred percent." He nodded to the penis's box as proof. "Plus, it's the only thing that makes sense. Who else would take my trash?"

"A better question…" Nate countered. "Who would steal your stuff and leave a dozen pieces of evidence with their name and address on it? Do you really think she's that stupid?"

It was a thought that had also crossed his mind, the evidence pile too incriminating, once he'd gone through it all. Receipts from Jasmine's Café. An online order form for high-range binoculars. Even a recent ad they'd placed in a local magazine, doodles along the edge. Maybe he should be glad there wasn't duct tape wrappers and chloroform receipts.

He sighed and met Nate's inquisitive glance. "I don't know what to think. Maybe she's framing this Autumn Jones girl. But why?"

His best friend stood in the middle of his living room, his arms crossed, and considered the situation. "Yeah. You're right. It makes no sense." Nate scratched the back of his head and winced, then seemed to think better of what he was about to say. "I have to admit..."

Silence stretched.

"What?" Declan prompted. 'You have to admit what?"

"Nothing." Nate turned abruptly, pointing to the kitchen. "You got beer?"

Declan followed him. "What?"

"Fine." Nate grabbed a beer and twisted off the cap. "Bridget thinks you're making up the stalker."

"I'm—what?" He reached out and shut the fridge door. "How does Bridget even *know* about her?"

"You know my sister." Nate lifted the Budweiser and took a long sip. "She's nosy. Talks her fucking head off and pulls information out of me like I'm on trial for something. I had to get her off my disastrous love life, so I told her about yours." He flashed an unapologetic smile at Declan.

"I wouldn't call this psycho bitch my love life."

"Well, it was more exciting than the kindergarten-level of interaction you've had with women." He tossed the cap toward the trash. "I swear, my dog gets more action than you do, and he's neutered."

Declan raked a hand through his hair. "Let's get back to Bridget. She thinks I *made up* a stalker?" He spread his arms in the air. "Why the hell would I do that?"

"Ahh...." Nate swung one leg over the arm of the couch and fell back into it. "I think she thinks you're emotionally crippled and feeling rejected and inventing a rabid fan as a means of satisfying your inner need to feel loved and desired."

"You *think?*" Declan stared down at the man, who shrugged in response. "That's a pretty detailed hypothesis."

"What can I say?" Nate grinned. "I'm a good listener." He sat up on the couch. "Plus, you got to admit, you're the only one who's *ever* seen this girl."

"The lobby receptionist saw her," Declan pointed out.

"Tiffany has met a blonde chick who's trying to get up to our floor." He smirked. "Come on, bro. We both know the chances of that being for you versus me, and it is so minisculely low it's embarrassing."

"So, I'm inventing her? Are you fucking kidding me?" He surveyed the bag of trash, which he'd carried inside, the contents neatly stacked along the coffee table. "And this is what—trash I *stole* from someone to support this ridiculous story that I've fabricated?"

"Nah." Nate shook his head. "I think someone really did steal your trash." He gingerly picked up the cardboard box. "And apparently... the girl needs some dick in her life."

"How kind of you to believe me."

"So, hypothetically speaking, if you *do* have this girl who is stalking you..." He picked the card back up and looked at the address. "It's possible this is her."

Declan looked to the ceiling and resisted the urge to wrap his hands around the man's throat. "I'm not making up anything."

"Okay..." Nate flipped the postcard toward him, the square slicing through the space and hitting Declan on the chest. He captured it and looked down, focusing on the typed address. It didn't seem like a psychopath's location. It sounded like the sort of place with cute suburban homes and kids jumping around on trampolines.

"So?" Nate prompted. "What are you going to do with it?"

"I don't know." He thumbed one corner of the steam cleaning discount offer. "That's why I called you."

"Ah. The voice of reason. Thinker of brilliant thoughts. Deviser of schemes—"

"Drinker of beers and clogger of toilets," Declan interrupted.

"Don't give yourself too much credit. Ever since Carter got married, you're the best friend I've got. The choices were slim."

"Ouch." Nate winced, tilting back and finishing off his beer. "That's harsh." He fell silent and Declan looked back down at the piece of paper, rereading the name and address.

Autumn Jones
444 Frolicking Lane
Tallahassee, Florida 32311

"Hey."

Declan looked over to find Nate's phone out, his attention on the screen.

"Bridget says to look her up online."

Autumn Jones's Facebook profile was private, and it was one of the few things they found. She wasn't on Linkedin, and no company site listed her as an employee. She was, shockingly enough, listed in the phone book, and they found her home in the tax rolls—a two-bedroom in a nice neighborhood in the southern part of town. A records search came up empty, so she'd paid cash for the house four months ago, which was interesting. Where had that money come from? Nate speculated stripping, combined with an aggressive investment strategy. Declan thought a large ransom payout was more likely.

Bridget had called about an hour into the search, wanting to know everything and promising donuts and coffee if they would give her the girl's name.

Nate had perked up at the idea of food. Declan had flatly refused, and their research had hit a dead end at the Facebook page, which offered a profile photo and nothing else.

The profile photo was of the woman, and it was definitely her. Same long blonde hair. A sunburnt nose. She was scrunching up her face in the photo, her cheek being licked by a pig. No joke. A freaking *pig* was licking her face.

"She doesn't look crazy," Nate remarked. Declan flipped past a Seinfeld episode, the channel descriptions still in Chinese, and ignored the comment. She had chosen, out of every possible photo in her life, to represent herself with a pig. A pig that was *licking* her. It was the definition of crazy.

"She's actually pretty cute."

"Great," Declan drawled. "*You* find out who she is. Maybe she could be your next trainwreck of a relationship. A psychotic trash thief seems right up your alley."

"As much as I appreciate your crazy cast-off, I've got my hands full." Nate opened the door to the fridge.

"As long as they aren't full of Benta Aldrete," Declan muttered. The Brazilian had finally signed off on their contract before catching a plane back to New York, with threats to return in another month for site visits. Their new project was made more complicated by the fact that she was negotiating between three different parcels, each which would require different building footprints. She wanted to see their sketches for each parcel, which would help her decide which location to move forward with.

It was a gigantic waste of money on her end but would give them some much-needed income. Assuming, of course, that Nate didn't fuck everything up for them.

"I'm telling you, she's perfect." Nate shut the fridge, two beers in hand.

"You need to stay away from her, at least until this project is over. Six months, okay? Then you can go up to New York and go nuts on her."

"You're acting like I will fuck this up. Women love me. You know this."

It was annoyingly true. He won hearts as often as he broke them, smoothing every parting with a slick smile and flash of that dimple. He was, as Declan had experienced himself, impossible to stay mad at.

And the women kept coming back for more, even after he'd broken their hearts.

"Benta isn't most women," he reminded him. "You screw her over and she'll cut your balls off and deliver them to our office in a glass jar. Assuming she doesn't put it on her mantle instead." He found a late-night talk show and stopped, waving off the beer that Nate offered him.

Nate winced, one hand moving in front of his crotch. "Dude. Why would you say something like that? They can *hear* you. Besides, I'm not screwing her over. I can barely get a reaction out of her."

"I thought you just said that women loved you."

"Fine. Most women." He settled into the other end of the couch, setting the extra beer on the end table. Declan passed him a coaster. "She's just proving a little harder to crack."

"Well, *stop* cracking. We need this job."

"What we *need* is to figure out what we're going to do about Autumn Jones." He pointed to the laptop, still open on the coffee table. "I think you should invite her to be your friend."

Declan snorted. "Right."

"Come on..." Nate drawled. "Just hit the button. See what happens."

"I'm not hitting the button." Invite her to be his friend? The woman already had boundary issues. She was going through his household trash for shit's sake. Why the fuck would he ask her to be his friend on Facebook? Talk about inviting trouble.

Nate chuckled as he lifted his beer. "Come on. If you're not going to let me pursue the love of my life, let me live vicariously through you."

Declan shook his head. "The only thing less likely than Benta Aldrete being your soulmate is me inviting this crazy lunatic to be my Facebook friend. In fact..." He rose. "I'm going to bed." He closed the laptop, killing the image of Autumn Jones and that ridiculous pig. He stretched back and sighed with satisfaction as the bones in his back popped.

"Come on! It's not even eleven. You're like my fucking grandpa.

It's a Friday night. If you aren't going to invite hot pig girl to be your friend, at least go out with me."

Declan shook his head and headed down the hall for his bedroom. He glanced into the guest room that Nate once lived in, back when their lives revolved around parties, women and the occasional class. He almost missed having him as a roommate, the constant presence, restless energy, and soundtrack of eighties music and female guests. *Almost.*

"You're boring!" Nate called out from the living room, the insult bouncing across the worn wood floors.

He closed the door to his bedroom and rubbed his hands over his face. He needed a shower, something to cleanse away the feeling of being ... violated was too strong of a word, but there was still something invasive about knowing that she had been so close. He stepped to the window and adjusted the blinds, looking out on the driveway. His cans were back in place, lined up and lids closed, just as they were every night. Maybe he should start keeping them in the garage.

He scanned the dark road, the streetlights illuminating his neighbor's mailbox, a kid's bike lying beside it on the grass. Would she come back and return his trash? Did she do this every week? He eyed the driveway and considered putting a motion-activated light on the spot, maybe one that came with an alarm. That would serve her right, to sneak up to his cans and be assaulted by a whooping alarm and blaring spotlight.

Unfortunately, that would also wake up every person on their block, including that little old lady across the way, who made an excruciatingly painful trek to the mailbox each morning, her crooked body shuffling along the driveway. Twice, he'd offered to help, and both times, she'd glared at him and muttered something under her breath as she continued toward the box.

He closed the blinds and made his way to the bathroom, the sounds of the living room television faint and comforting. As much as he appreciated how peaceful life was without Nicola, there were the moments where the house felt empty.

Turning on the shower, he pulled his shirt over his head, the faint smell of his cologne dragging over his face. He'd gotten dressed up for his date, yet was going to bed with thoughts of a different woman entirely.

Autumn Jones. It felt odd, having her name. Her address. That photo. Despite the pig, she had been pretty. A different beauty than Margaret's angular features—or Nicola's surgically enhanced pout. This woman looked happy. Normal—which was terrifying in itself, and only reinforced his belief that Facebook was a false view of everyone's lives.

Fully undressed, he stepped into the shower and angled the spray toward himself. As his hand settled on his cock, he tried to picture Margaret, her eyes on him, her mouth soft, kissing him. Her hands trailing down his chest. Thoughts of Autumn Jones invaded his mind, pushing the image of Margaret aside. All he could picture was that selfie with the pig, and *that* was an erection killer.

He let out a groan and released his dick, reaching for the bar of soap and raking it across his chest. Maybe he should get a restraining order. Force this woman out of his life. Maybe he should move. Hell, this house was full of memories of Nicola anyway. It'd be nice to have a fresh start, away from all of them.

Closing his eyes, he put his head under the spray and tried to sort out the mess in his mind.

8

Mr. Oinks fell off the bed, a common occurrence, and one that created a strangled noise somewhere between a squawk and an oink. I leaned over the side of the bed, my hands swinging through the air, and found him, hooking both hands under his belly and hoisting him back onto the bed.

It wasn't a graceful act. Mr. Oinks used to be on the light end of a micro mini pig, which was to say that he was comfortably in the fifteen-pound arena. Now, he was inching up in size, and getting him up on the bed would soon require a firm stance, proper squat and a back brace.

"You're getting fat," I mumbled. He settled onto the bed and grunted, his nose rooting through my blankets until he found an edge and belly-wriggled his way underneath. He settled into place, his back hooves sticking out from the edge of the comforter, and I laughed, slipping my hand under and finding his ears, giving them a quick scratch.

I lay there for a long moment, the morning light beginning to trickle across my bedroom wall. Today, I had to swing by the craft store and I was taking Ansley's kids to the park. If Declan's house was vehicle-free, I'd return his trash before I picked up the girls. I reached over and grabbed my phone off the nightstand. From underneath the cover, I felt warm breath puff along my calf. I called out a warning to Mr. Oinks and moved my leg away.

That's the only problem with a pig. They think everything is food, and strawberry scented leg lotion? That's their crackpipe.

I had two texts from Ansley, both sent within the last hour.

> My baking attempt has turned into a clusterfuck. I've got a ruined pie for your pig if you want it.

I smiled and opened her second text.

> I cannot believe my life has turned into the sort of situation where I am sending texts like this. Why am I trying to cook pies? And WHY DO YOU HAVE A PIG?!

There was a series of emojis that combined barfing, eye rolls and lots of facepalming. I hit reply.

> I don't expect you to understand the finer things in life. You own a jetski for piglet's sake.

Her response came quick.

> Don't spit pig slang at me or I swear to God, I'll stop stocking the house with Sunkist.

I snorted in response, and I swear on Jesus, that wasn't intended to be a pun.

> ontday ebay tupidsay.. Ouyay ovelay unkistsay ootay.

I sent the pig-Latin then sat up in bed, kicking the covers loose and looking at Mr. Oinks. "You in the mood for pie?"

"You shouldn't have fed him pie." Two hours after Mr. Oinks' ingestion of Ansley's pie, the vet peered at me over his distended pig belly. This guy had really pretty eyes. Bright blue.

Mr. Oinks groaned, and my concern reared its head, pushing thoughts of the sexy vet off the table and into the trash pile. "I thought pigs liked pie. He likes... well, he likes everything." What I didn't say, but seems entirely noteworthy, is that I had a friend who visited Exuma and fed an entire island of pigs HOT DOGS, which they gobbled up with enthusiasm, and didn't seem at all unhealthy from it. And at the farm I'd purchased Mr. Oinks from, I'd watched them upend an entire trash can of slop that seemed to contain every food known to man, and hadn't received a single word of warning about pie. I'd shared pizza, subs, lasagna, scrambled eggs, and half of every one of my sister's culinary attempts with him, and he'd never so much as grunted in protest.

"It was the rhubarb." Dr. Diablo straightened, hanging his stethoscope around his neck. "It's extremely toxic to pigs."

Toxic didn't sound good. Mr. Oinks looked at me and I could feel his pain, not in the same magical guardian angel way, but in a horrible, I-am-a-terrible-parent and my-pig-blames-me-for-his-stomachache pain. I patted his side tenderly. "What could happen?"

"Well, right now he's having some oxalic acid poisoning. That's what's causing his muscles to twitch and his panting. Also, his heart is racing." He reached for my hand and placed it higher on his ribcage, holding it there. "Feel that?"

I could. Underneath my palm, Mr. Oinks' heart was jumping, a rapid bam-bam-bam-bam-bam. I moved closer, my fingers curving around his warm skin, and I could feel the edge of a hysteria attack pushing closer. *Toxic*. My alarm ramped up. "Could he—is he going to *die*?" I should have brought Ansley with me. She's better with stuff like this. When Roger's colon got blocked last spring, she was the one who spoke to the doctors, she was the one who received the terrifying news that surgery was immediate and life-savingly necessary. I was in charge of bringing us magazines, flipping the channel on the TV, and bitching at nurses for extra Jell-O. I can't... I can't lose Mr. Oinks.

With everything in my life, he's the only real thing that I have, the only thing that *depends* on me.

"I don't think he's going to die." He lifted his hand off mine. "It's good that you brought him in right away. Pumping his stomach was the most important thing, and now that that's done, we can get good fluids in him and get him back on his feet."

I don't think he's going to die. Not the most reassuring guy on the planet.

"If you can afford it, I'd like to keep him here overnight, possibly until Monday."

"I can afford it." I straightened. "Just..." I waved my hands in the air. "Stomach transplant, whatever. I just need him to be okay."

He laughed. "Just an overnight stay or two, and he should be good as new." He eyed me. "Just no more rhubarb."

I nodded, crossing myself. "None. Ever. I swear."

"And once we're through this, I'd like to sit down with you and discuss a better diet for him, assuming that you're interested in prolonging his life as long as possible."

"Yes!" I crouched beside the table and looked into Mr. Oinks eyes. They drooped slightly and I leaned forward, kissing him on the forehead. "I'll take notes and everything. Organic diet, low-carb, keto-happy, whatever."

Dr. Diablo smiled, stepping back and opening the door to the lobby. "Just make sure that Emily up front has all of your information. We'll give you a call in a few hours and let you know how he's doing."

"Okay." I leaned forward and wrapped my arms around Mr. Oinks, pulling him carefully into my chest. "I love you," I whispered. "Be good."

He didn't respond. Not that I expected a "Sure, Mom, see you later!" or anything, but his lack of movement, that heart still pounding in his chubby chest... I felt sick myself.

"I'll take good care of him." The vet smiled at me, and it was a nice one. His grin was a little crooked on one side, like that cocky kind where the guy knew that he was hot, and knew that you realized he was hot, and maybe, if you played your cards right, then he'd kiss you? That kind of smile. It'd been a while since I'd gotten that kind of smile.

I nodded, thanking him again, and headed for the door. As I passed him, my shoulder brushed against his coat and I felt, through the rhubarb fear and the guilt, what just might have been a spark.

9

"Get up." Declan reached down and poked at Nate's chest. He didn't react, and Declan straightened, moving through the living room and collecting empty beer bottles. "NATE," he repeated. Moving to the kitchen, he dumped the bottles in the recycle bin, grimacing at the reminder of Autumn Jones's trash theft. Picking up the can, he carried it into the living room, tossing more empty bottles in, each hitting the others with a loud crack of glass.

A loud curse came from the couch. "Could you be any louder?" Nate rolled over, pulling the cracked leather couch cushion across his face.

"It's noon." Declan tossed the final bottle in. "Get your lazy ass up."

"Shit." Nate moved the cushion off his head and squinted up at him. "How long have you been up?"

"A couple of hours." Long enough to hit the hardware store and grab a set of outdoor cameras. He'd pulled his ladder from the garage and mounted them at the corners of the house, both aimed at his trash cans. He'd also picked up a few window sensors and armed each ground-level window. If and when Autumn Jones came back, she'd have to fly in on a hoverboard through the chimney, or else he'd know it.

Nate slowly sat up and pressed on his forehead with the palm of one hand. "Shit, my head is *killing* me."

"Yeah." Declan looked down at the trash. "Best I can tell, you finished off another four beers after I went to bed."

"One of those fucking housewives shows came on. I needed the alcohol to cope."

Declan grinned. "Sure." Nate had likely binged on episodes until dawn then passed out. "You know, you can just change the channel. Or turn off the TV."

"Yeah, but then I would miss all the catfights." He stood up slowly, then carefully made his way to the kitchen. He opened the cabinet above the microwave and grabbed the bottle of Tylenol, popping it open and shaking out a handful of pills. "You already eat?"

"I was going to head over to MoMo's now. Figured you'd be hungry."

He grunted in agreement, grabbing a glass and filling it with water from the tap. "Hell yes."

Declan returned the Tylenol to the cabinet. "Let's take your Jeep. I want to keep a car in the drive, just in case." *In case she came back.* What a stupid thing to have to think about. Cameras. Keeping his blinds closed. Protecting his house. It was all probably overkill. But last night ... the more he'd thought about his missing trash, the more his feelings about her had changed. She went from being a harmless, almost entertaining annoyance, to something more ominous. Creepy.

He mused over the feeling as they drove, Nate's attention focused on checking out college girls and finding a parking spot near the popular pizza spot. Once they ordered at the counter and found a table, Declan broached the subject.

"Creepy?" Nate tilted his head at him. "Come on. You afraid of a girl?"

"She knows where I live. It's stepping over the line."

"And you have her address," he pointed out. "Look, of course, she knew your house. According to you, she follows you everywhere. You can't be surprised by this."

Nate had a point. Had he ever sat down and thought about it, Declan would have assumed that she'd had that information, just like she knew where he worked, the gym he used, and the sandwich place in Midtown he liked. But he'd never seen her near the house, and had lived under the pleasant delusion that she only stalked during business hours, and went away to her family or job or *whatever* during the rest of the time. He mentioned this and Nate squinted at him.

"So, you've *never* seen her at night?"

Declan considered the question. "I don't think so... Wait—our softball games. I've seen her there."

Nate frowned. "Why didn't you point her out?"

"It was only once. I didn't want to make a big deal of it." Also, he hadn't been positive it was her. It was hard to tell. The softball park was full of cute blondes in baseball caps, heads down or sunglasses on. And she was typically hiding behind something, her half-hearted attempts at subterfuge almost comical in nature.

"And you wondered why we thought she was imaginary."

Declan sighed. "Try not to be a giant douche about this. I need your honest opinion on whether or not she's going to hunt me down and kill me."

Nate barked out a laugh.

"Seriously." Declan leveled him with a stare. "Women do this. They obsess. They stalk. And when they don't get the guy, they kill."

Nate smirked. "We're talking about the same girl, right?" He leaned back in his seat and stretched out his legs, digging in his front pants pocket for his phone. "This chick." He tapped on the screen a few times, then turned it around to face Declan.

Autumn Jones's sunny smile was displayed, right next to the pig.

"Yeah, her," Declan growled.

"She's freaking adorable. She's..." he zoomed in on the photo. "Look. She's wearing a *candy* necklace. And she's with a pig. She's not killing you. I bet she doesn't even eat meat."

Declan pushed at the phone, shoving the image away. "It doesn't matter what she looks like. She's insane."

"I bet she tutors handicapped kids," Nate continued. "Volunteers for Meals on Wheels." He clapped his hands together. "She could even help your cause."

"What cause?"

Nate's grin widened. "The Get Declan Laid cause." He slapped the table hard enough that the table behind them turned around.

Declan sighed.

"Come on, man. It's been six months for you. *SIX MONTHS.*" He leaned forward. "I heard crazy girls are amazing in bed. Something about all that energy, that passion..." He closed his eyes in reverence.

"Please stop."

"I can't. It's a good thing I love you, because I would be all over her otherwise."

"So, you *don't* think she's going to kill me."

"Eh." He tilted his head from one side to the other as if weighing the probabilities. "Probably not."

"That's comforting."

Nate leaned forward, his face sobering. "I do have to tell you something though."

"What's that?" Declan asked dryly.

"I hadn't considered the possibility that she is violent. I mean, I didn't think she even existed, prior to you pulling her damn calling card out of the trash. And I think you're being a total pussy in terms of being scared of a woman. All that being said, you might want to keep your distance from her." He shrugged. "Just to be safe."

"What are you talking about? I *am* keeping my distance from her. I practically sprint in the opposite direction every time I see her."

"Yeah, but..." he tilted his head with a wince. "Sending her a Facebook friend request... it might have sent her the wrong message."

Declan shook his head. "I didn't send her a friend request."

"You did."

"No, I didn't."

"Well, technically *you* didn't." Nate turned his head, watching a girl walk by in yoga pants that showed every dimple in her ass.

"What does that fucking mean?"

Nate's attention returned to him. "It means I may have sent the request for you. After you went to bed."

Dread stabbed at Declan's gut, his breath shortening. "Shut the fuck up."

Nate leaned back, a wise move since he was a half second away from being punched in the middle of that pretty boy face. "I was drunk. It seemed like a good idea at the time."

"To invite the crazy stalker with no boundaries to be my Facebook friend?" Declan half rose in his chair, his voice rising.

"Chill." Nate raised his hands. "What's the worst that could happen?"

Declan stared at him and couldn't even formulate a reply.

10

"He invited you to be his friend?" Ansley stared at me over the top of Paige's head, her hands busy with a second French braid.

"Yep." I stared at my phone. "It's right here. *You have a friend invite from Declan Moss*." He has a cute Facebook photo. It's him in a suit, standing in front of the Reinhart Theatre, which he designed. He's all serious in the photo, as if he's far too busy counting corbels to smile.

Every other part of his profile is private, only available to friends. It's a good safety measure, one easily thwarted by me three months ago, when my fake profile of Olivia Sanchez was accepted by Nate, his business partner. It didn't take much to break into Nate's good graces —Olivia's big boobs and Seminole jersey got her right in, her friend request accepted within four minutes. Olivia then sent friend requests to Nate's sister and four of his female friends, all whom accepted and who—combined with 72 other complete strangers interested in Olivia's big boobs—gave her enough validity to seem like an acceptance possibility for Declan. I sent Olivia's friend request off with a prayer and celebrated with mimosas and a pedicure when it was accepted.

It had been a gigantic waste of effort. Declan's Facebook page was the most boring place on the internet. He posted about his opinions on sports and architecture—nothing that could help me save his life. No posts about allergies, or health conditions, or plans to try skydiving or eat fugu which, by the way, is twelve hundred times more deadly than cyanide if it isn't cooked *exactly* right.

And now, that super boring page is asking *me*—Autumn Jones—someone with absolutely zero friends in common and a no-cleavage photo—to be his friend.

"This is bad, right?" Ansley asked. "I mean, how does he know who you are?"

An excellent question. How had he found me? And why, once he did, would he ask me to be his *friend*?

I stared at the request for several minutes, weighing over my options. And then, before I had the chance to second-guess myself, I declined the request and then hit the next button that appeared.

BLOCK THIS PERSON

I let out a hard breath, the screen changing, Declan Moss's adorable scowl replaced by a picture of a poodle with lipstick on.

Ansley was right. This *was* bad.

11

"It's really not that big of a deal." Nate munched on a cinnamon-dipped breadstick, one he'd sweet-talked the cashier into on their way out.

Declan ignored Nate, his irritation at a nuclear level. It took a lot to piss him off. When they'd lost the Huntington Park deal due to Nate screwing Mrs. Huntington, he'd gotten over it. When Nate dropped their master set of property keys somewhere on Bourbon Street, he'd shrugged it off. When Nate picked a fight with two steroid-enhanced bikers, he'd joined in with a curse and a scowl. But now? Nate had opened a door with this nut job, a door that could jeopardize their business and Declan's safety. Hell, maybe even their friendship.

"Bridget says you can undo it. She said it takes two minutes."

That possibility was the only thing keeping him from yanking Nate out of the Jeep and swinging a punch. Nate turned into Bridget's complex and Declan reached for the door handle, grateful to see Bridget's bright yellow convertible parked in front of her townhouse.

Her front door was unlocked, music playing, and they walked through the house to find her on the back porch, sunglasses on, toes tapping to the beat, a paperback in hand. She looked up with a smile. "Hey, guys."

Declan shoved his phone forward without preamble. "Here. Fix it."

"Oh...kay." She swung her feet off the railing and stood, ignoring Declan's phone and grabbing her frosted glass. "Let's go inside and do it."

"Nate said you can fix it." Declan followed her closely, irritated when she went to the fridge and opened the door, pulling out a two-liter of soda and unscrewing the lid.

"Yep. I've done it before. Sent a friend request to that bitch next door. I had chatted with her down by the mailboxes, and she seemed pretty cool, you know. But then..." she lowered her voice as if she was about to share secrets of national security.

"I really don't care," Declan interrupted. "I need this fixed. Immediately. It is, literally, more important than your soda refill."

She blew out an irritated breath and set down the bottle. "Fine. I was going to tell a story involving three dicks and a blow-up doll, but whatever."

"Wait, what?" Nate stood up from the couch. "Is this the brunette? The one with the great ass?"

Bridget ignored him, flipping through screens on his phone. "What's this girl's name?"

"Autumn Jones."

"Shit." She mumbled. "I don't see her in your friend requests list. How long ago did you invite her?"

Declan turned his head, glaring at Nate.

"Ummm... like two in the morning? Maybe three?" Nate shrugged. "Something like that."

Declan closed his eyes, calculating the time that had passed. Almost twelve hours.

"But, we just saw it at lunch," Nate protested. "So, if she accepted it, she must have just done it."

"Shit," Declan rubbed his hands over his face. By now, she could have downloaded his entire friend list. Every photo, every post. Thank God he didn't put personal shit on there.

"Calm down." Bridget held up a finger. "She's not in your friend list. And I just scrolled through all of your notifications and she didn't accept your request. In fact..." She peered up at him. "I just searched for her, and unless she's a bright pink haired mother in Idaho, I think she blocked you."

"What?" Declan moved around the counter, getting to a place where he could see the screen. From the couch, Nate barked out a laugh.

"I'm serious." She reached for her own phone and pulled up Facebook, tapping and scrolling around the app. "Look." She turned her screen to him, Autumn's smile familiar, the same image as last night. "When I search for her, she comes right up. But when I do it from your account, nothing." She smirked at him. "Without a doubt, you're blocked. Creepy ass."

"I'm blocked?" He repeated. "That's bullshit. I'm not the creepy one. She's the stalker—"

"Ha. Bridget called you a creepy ass." Nate settled into the red couch, his feet kicking up and resting on a stack of magazines on Bridget's glass coffee table.

Declan felt his irritation return. "Right. Says the guy who invited her to be my friend." He turned back to Bridget. "So, what do I do? Can I block her back?"

She set down her phone and lifted the two-liter of soda back up, her attention returning to her drink. "I don't think you can block someone you can't view. Just..." she shrugged. "Leave her alone."

"Leave *her* alone?" This was fucking ridiculous. Nate was laughing at him, Bridget was acting as if he was the stalker and Autumn—the stealer of trash, watcher of lunches, screamer of ridiculous things in the middle of the street—she was blocking HIM. "I'd love to leave her alone. I'd love to never see her face again."

"Right." Bridget capped the bottle and set it back in the fridge. "Because you think she's stalking you."

He didn't even bother with a response. He grabbed his phone and pushed away from the counter. "I've got to get home. Nate?" He needed to be alone, away from his phone and Bridget and Nate's amusement with this entire situation. He needed to get in the gym, to sweat and push his body, to think about something else, anything else, other than her.

He shoved open the front door and jogged down the steps, moving toward the Jeep and wanting to kill someone.

12

My phone rang in my hand, startling me. I looked down, breathing a sigh of relief at the veterinarian's phone number. Twenty-four hours had passed since the rhubarb incident, but I still hadn't been cleared to pick up Mr. Oinks. "Hello?"

"Mrs. Jones, this is Adam Diablo, the veterinarian for Mr. Oinks."

"Yes. It's Miss. Not Mrs. I'm not married. Single, actually." Why was I telling him this? Mr. Oinks could be dying, his chest seizing, legs flopping, eyes wide, and I'm yammering on about my dating status like a crazy person.

"I understand. Ms. Jones, I just wanted to let you know that Mr. Oinks has made it through with flying colors. He's sleeping now. Lots of flatulence, but I believe you said that that was normal?"

I laughed. "Yes, it is. Can I come and get him?"

"He's ready, whenever you are."

I smiled. "Awesome. And thanks for having the nurses call me last night with updates. That was really kind." I caught the curious look that Ansley gave me and turned away, busying myself with reorganizing the cookbooks on her counter.

The vet spent a few minutes going over medicine I needed to pick up and Mr. Oinks' dietary restrictions for the next few days. I nodded, scribbling down a few notes in the margin of a piece of Ansley's junk mail. "Great. And again, thank you."

"No problem, Ms. Jones."

"It's Autumn. Please."

"Okay. I'll see you when you come in to pick him up."

I was smiling when I hung up the phone. Ansley watched me as she tied off the second braid. "Who was *that*?"

"The vet. He said Mr. Oinks is going to survive your terrible pie."

"Ah. Lots of giggling over my pie." She patted Paige on the back. "Go get your brother and tell him we're ready to go."

I sat down on the closest stool and watched as Paige tore by and up the stairs. "He *may* be slightly good-looking."

"Interesting." She raised a brow. "And I assume he finds you slightly good looking?"

I lifted both palms upward in a *duh* fashion. "Well, obviously."

She smiled, coming to sit beside me. "I'm sorry about the pie."

"You didn't know."

She sighed. "It's just ... you don't have anything in your life except for us and Mr. Oinks. If something had happened to him, I never would have forgiven myself." She reached out and grabbed my hand. "You know that I act like I don't like him, but I want you to know, if something ever happened to you, he would always have a place..." her voice broke and she sniffed, holding up a hand to stop me from talking. "He would *always* have a place at the local animal shelter. I already called and they said they take pigs, as long as he isn't over fifty pounds. So it's going to be really important for you to keep him under that weight."

I shoved her away. "Oh my gosh! Go jump off a bridge. I hate you."

She came up behind me and wrestled me into a hug. "You know I'm kidding." She pressed a kiss to my cheek. "But seriously, you are in danger of turning into an old lonely weird woman who stalks strangers. Be nice to this vet. Maybe he could be *the one*." She whispered the final words as if they were dusted in sparkly gold.

"I'm nice to everyone," I informed her, prying her hands off me. "Case in point, me taking your two demons to the park."

"We aren't demons." Paige bounced into the room. "We are *humans*."

"No!" Caleb interjected, following his big sister into the room. "I'm a ninja." He twirled and came to a stop, hands extended as if he was karate chopping someone.

"Yeah," I deadpanned. "Demons." I pocketed my phone and grabbed my purse. "Now, come on. Let's go let Mommy and Daddy have some happy time. After the park, we're going to pick up Mr. Oinks!"

The kids cheered and Ansley glared at me. "You're welcome," I mouthed.

She rolled her eyes and tossed me her keys. "Shut up and take the minivan."

13

On their way back into the neighborhood, he swore he saw her behind the wheel of a minivan, a child bouncing in the backseat. It wasn't her, of course. He knew that minivan, it was the cute mom from a few houses down, the one who overdid it each year with Christmas decorations and had a husband who looked like the type who irons his underwear.

"She's getting under your skin." Nate shifted gears, his to-go cup gripped in his left hand while he steered with his forearm. "You're seeing her everywhere."

It was true. It was getting hard to know when she was actually following him and when he was being paranoid. He'd scared the hell out of a woman in Target the other day, turning around and yelling at her to "go follow someone else" before he realized it wasn't her.

"I know the perfect thing to get your mind off it." Nate slowed, making the sharp turn into his driveway. Declan peered up at the security cameras, reassured when his phone hummed, a notification popping up. "Tinder."

MOTION DETECTED!

Press here to see the live video!

Declan pressed on the screen and watched as a clear image popped up, showing Nate getting out of the Jeep. Declan followed suit and caught up to his partner, holding out the phone. "Look."

The man examined it, then glanced up, waving at the camera. "Pretty cool. It capture anything while we were gone?"

"No." He shut down the feed and put the phone in his pocket, pulling out his keys and approaching the front door. It was stupid to feel disappointed that she hadn't returned. He should be happy. Maybe his Facebook invite hadn't been an entirely bad thing. Maybe it had scared her off.

"So, you in?"

"In for what?" He worked the key in the lock.

"Trying Tinder. To get your mind off Autumn."

It irritated him that they now knew her name, a new level of intimacy slapped on the relationship. "I'm not getting on Tinder."

"Come *on*." He followed Declan inside. "I found this chick on there last week who sucked my balls like that vacuum at the car place. And then she left. Straight walked out the door and got in her car. No cuddles, no talking, nothing."

"That sounds terrible."

"No, the ball sucking was good. Unexpectedly good." He settled into the couch as if he planned on staying there. "I was surprised too, because normally I'm not really into that—"

"Please stop talking." Declan hung his keys on the hook. "And go home."

His best friend had the audacity to look hurt. "What the fuck, dude?"

"I'm pissed off and visions of your balls getting sucked—believe it or not—isn't helping me."

"You know I only sent her that friend invite because I was drunk." Nate offered the explanation like it solved everything, like that action hadn't opened a possible line of communication with her, or ruined any advantage that Declan might have had, knowing her identity.

Declan rubbed his forehead. "I'll see you at the office tomorrow. I just need to work out and burn off some steam."

"Exactly." Nate didn't move from his spot on the couch. "Tinder. I'm telling you, it's magic."

"You act like you've never met me before. Do I seem like a fucking Tinder guy?"

"Every guy is a Tinder guy. *Trust* me." He set his cup on the coffee table and Declan automatically reached for a coaster, the replacement prompting a chuckle from Nate. "I should stay." Nate leaned forward. "What if psycho bitch comes tonight? You'll need backup."

"I won't need backup." Declan gestured to the door. "Get out of here."

"Fine." He stood. "But if you're not getting on Tinder, then call that woman from the other night. The one you went on a date with. You need some love in your life, man."

Talk about a hypocrite. Nate hadn't fallen in love since high school. Declan pushed him toward the door. "See you Monday."

"Call me if you need me."

He watched Nate leave, and mused over the suggestion to call Margaret. Moving back into the living room, he cleaned up Nate's mess and tossed his empty cup in the trash. He'd enjoyed her company and she'd handled the Nicola situation well. Plus, she was a beautiful woman. Successful. Had her shit together.

Nate was right. He did need some love in his life. Could she be the one to provide it? Or, to attend to the other need in his life, should he call her for a hook-up? His stomach turned at the idea, remembering her insecurity at dinner, her tentative inquiry whether he'd be taking her out again. She wasn't a woman just looking for sex, and it wouldn't be fair to call her unless he was serious about continuing a relationship with her.

Which… considering he could barely manage the effort to call her —wasn't a good sign. Hell, he'd gone through more hoops to get the latest UFC fight. He pulled out his phone and scrolled to her name. Stared at the number and tried to convince himself to press the *call* button.

One more date. A chance, away from Nicola, to see if he and Margaret had anything more than country songs in common.

He should give her a chance. Make the call. Test the waters. See how it went. Maybe it would turn into love, and this would be a funny story he'd one day tell their grandchildren. Or maybe sparks would fly, and they'd be ripping off each other's clothes with their teeth three hours from now.

He stared at her number, then brought his thumb forward and pressed the button underneath her name.

DELETE.

14

When I first saved Declan Moss's life, he never even saw me. He was running without a shirt on, his headphones in, muscular legs pumping. I was leaning against a tree, resting in its shade, when he jogged by, all abs and glistening sweat, like a commercial for deodorant. I watched him pass and my vision dotted, pain stabbing at my brain.

I didn't know what was happening. I staggered out into the middle of the road, my eyes pinching shut, my hands clasping at my head, my face, trying to pinpoint the pain. It wasn't the smartest place to be, especially not for a woman whose mother had just been hit by a car. But I wasn't thinking, my mind drowning in the overwhelming fear that something was happening, something was wrong. I stumbled after the jogger, holding out my hand and trying to flag him down. "Hey!" He would be able to help, could see if my eyes were normal, could tell me if there was a railroad spike poking out of my skull, or at least call someone for help. "HEY!" I screamed. My head pounded, alarm radiating through me. Something was *wrong* and I couldn't seem to pull my eyes off this guy long enough to figure it out.

I came to a stop, distracted by the jangle of the gate. Turning slowly, I saw the privacy fence behind me shake, a rough rattle of wood against wood, the dark metal latch clanging. I knew the yard. Paige was afraid of this house, made me lift her onto my shoulders whenever we walked by. She always thought the gate would break and the dog behind it—a giant Great Dane—would come out and eat her. I didn't blame her for being scared. Each time he clawed his way up the other side of the fence, he was all frothy gums and big teeth, snarling and ready to rip someone's head off. I joined her in the fear that he'd eventually make it over the side and tackle us, ripping Paige away from me and tearing at her delicate throat with his sharp incisors.

All reasons why I *shouldn't* have stepped closer to its gate. I shouldn't have reached for the latch. I *definitely* shouldn't have lifted it, freeing the catch. But I did. I shielded my body with the gate, and opened it, *letting the horrible dog out*.

The beast didn't hesitate, didn't pause, didn't notice or care about me. He charged through the opening, nails scraping against wood, paws kicking up leaves as he plowed forward, his body elongating, stretching, coiling and then unleashing. I watched his tail bob, his body move, and—for once—the demon was silent. Deadly. Bolting straight for the stranger, who jogged along, his back to the dog, his stride relaxed.

I had a sudden thought about my mom. Was this what it had been like for her? Had she had any warning in the moment before she'd died?

He was completely unprepared, unguarded and vulnerable when the dog's haunches gathered beneath him and he lunged. Declan had fallen, his hands swinging out, body twisting through the air. In my nightmares, I still heard the way he yelled, the snarl of the dog, the bunching of furry back muscles as he hunched over Declan's body. I should have run over and pulled off the dog, but instead I pinched my eyes shut and tried to block out the image of teeth biting into cheeks, ripping flesh, blood splattering. I spun away from the scene and tried to sort out *what* I had done.

What had I been thinking?

Why had I let loose a monster and endangered this stranger?

Was it the grief?

Had it twisted me into some awful, violent version of myself?

My thoughts were cut off by the screams, and I whirled around, unable to stop myself.

But the screams weren't coming from Declan. They came from a girl on the sidewalk, her face red, finger pointed skyward. I followed it and froze, staring at the plane that streaked across the tops of the house. It was too low and moving fast. Its engine roared, and I covered my ears, stepping back, watching in horror as its tail clipped the top of a brick home like Ansley's, its chimney crumbling, roof splitting. Smoke billowed and the girl ran toward me, looking back toward the plane, which slammed into the ground with the force of an earthquake, the impact jolting the ground beneath my feet. A Toyota SUV crumpled behind the nose of it, twin propellers on the wings scraping across the asphalt, and a wave of pebbles and debris peppered toward me.

I backed up, lifting my arms, ducking at the terrible screech of metal against metal, then everything stopped. A long moment of silence, eerie in its stillness. I lowered my hands and watched as the dog sprinted past me, his tail pinned tight to his butt. I looked past him, smoke pluming from the closest propeller and filling the air. Through it, I saw the runner stand, his hands brushing across his shoulder, his head turning to the plane. Had he been twenty yards further down the street, the plane would have killed him. He stood there for a long moment, his hands lifting to the top of his head and then, with no warning at all, the plane burst into flames.

I stumbled backward, my ankle turning, limbs tangling, and when I fell, the impact turned everything to black.

"You have a *date*?" Five days later, Ansley's daughter stood in my bedroom, teetering on a pair of my lime green heels, and frowned at me as if struggling with an addition problem.

I eyed her and wondered at the statistical probability of a broken neck on thick carpet and from a height of four feet. "I know. I am *also* shocked." I buttoned the top clasp of my dress and stepped back, looking critically at my reflection.

I should have gone shopping. I had assumed that the outfit I wore on my last date—a bright blue jumper—would work for this one. Only I couldn't find the blue jumper anywhere, and I had the faint recollection of dropping it off for dry cleaning but no memory of ever picking it up. I called the dry cleaner who can't seem to fuck her husband without having a ticket number, and gave up that hunt shortly before a string of filthy expletives got me blacklisted from Washy Klean for life.

I groaned.

"What?" Ansley wandered around the corner and pointed at her daughter, who was carefully attempting a forward step. "Paige, take those off before you kill yourself."

I caught Ansley's eyes in the mirror. "I look like a potato."

She smiled. "Yeah. Total potato."

"Who *makes* a dress like this?" The first issue was its color, a wishy-washy canvas brown. The design was worsened by the small black dots that scattered across it. When you added in the buttons—light tan bumps that looked like warts and ran from the knee-length hem to the bottom of my neck—and you had one giant potato, with my head sticking out of the top. The worse—or best—part of the design was the way the dress came in at the waist and suctioned-cupped itself to my ass. On the upside, my ass was my best feature. Unfortunately, it made the entire ensemble even more ridiculous.

"I think the better question is, who *buys* a dress like this?" Ansley flipped over the tag, which hung from one sleeve. "Damn, you are cheap."

"It was on sale," I defended. At the time, I had been pleased with the purchase. Somehow, the potato sack had looked cool and funky in the dressing room, its seventy percent off sticker too good to be true. I sighed. They should have paid ME to take this thing away. I bet, if I donated this to the Salvation Army, they'd frown at me and say *oh. Thank you, but noooo thank you.*

Ansley looked at her watch. "What time is he picking you up?"

"In about twenty minutes." I sighed. "Maybe a *belt* would make this better. Something to break up the brown?"

She shook her head. "Just go with your usual. Skinny jeans and a shirt."

"I literally have nothing clean." I eyed her T-shirt, desperate enough to snatch it off her.

The doorbell rang and Paige shrieked at the sound, her body pitching forward, arms windmilling. I dove to catch her and got a tiny elbow square in my left eye.

"Ouch." I heard the thunderous sounds of Mr. Oinks barreling down the hall. I rolled onto my back.

Paige climbed atop me and patted my cheeks, concern filling her eyes. "Is that him?" she whispered.

"Jeez, I hope not." I turned my head, Ansley gone, and attempted to roll onto one side and to my feet. The hem of the potato dress pinned my knees together and kept me on my side, my floppy movement causing Paige to kick off my heels and dash out of the bedroom.

"Aunt Auttie is PARALYZED!"

"Oh my God," I wheezed, rolling over further, until I was face down on the carpet. I should have gone with the steam cleaning special. I'd gotten the postcard last week, weighed the decision for less time than I spend at a fast food counter, then chucked it into the trash. Now, my cheek was digging into tan nape that smelled suspiciously like Mr. Oinks' farts. I tried to work my knees up, my elbows digging into the carpet. "I'm not paralyzed!" I called out.

I got my knees underneath me and pushed up on my forearms around the time that my bedroom door swung fully open, Ansley and Adam sharing the doorway. Between them, Paige squeezed through. Her face lit up, my sister started laughing, and Adam glanced away to save me the embarrassment of being a doggie style potato.

"Adam's early," my sister said unnecessarily. "And it looks like you aren't paralyzed. Medical crisis averted." She patted Adam on the arm. "Maybe… give us a few minutes?"

"Absolutely." He paused, catching my eye. "Hey Autumn."

"Hi." I waved.

"You look really pretty."

Behind him, Ansley swooned and Paige made the gagging motion, both of which caused my awkward smile to widen into a real one. "Thanks."

He disappeared down the hall and I let out a sigh. Ansley straightened out of her swoon and laughed.

I held out my hand and gestured for her to help me up. "*Why* did you let him back here?"

"Umm... because Paige told me you were paralyzed? He's a doctor. I thought he could help."

"He's a vet. And that's such bullshit."

"Okay, so I didn't want to stand there and make small talk while you changed outfits nine times." She hoisted me to my feet and brushed off the front of my outfit. "Now he's seen your outfit, you're stuck with it. Plus, he thinks you're pretty." She leaned forward and kissed me on the cheek. "Grab some shoes and go."

I groaned, catching sight of myself in the mirror. The dress hadn't gotten any cuter during my faceplant. I pulled a pair of flats out of the bottom of the closet and sat on the edge of the bed.

"Oh...no." She shook her head. "Heels. Something tall and sexy enough to distract him from thoughts of mashed potatoes and gravy."

I mumbled something snarky and tossed the flats away, reemerging from the closet with a pair of nude stilettos high enough to make my soles cry. "There. Happy?"

"I'll be happy when you give Paige and Caleb cousins."

"Ha!" I hopped on one foot as I pulled the first pump on. She extended an arm and I held on to it, managing the second heel without falling over. Avoiding the mirror, I breezed out the bedroom door without allowing myself another moan over the outfit.

Confidence, according to our mother, was all a woman needed. I rounded the corner and Adam looked up from his spot on the couch, one of my magazines open on his lap.

"Ready?" He smiled, and I suddenly didn't feel like I was wearing a potato.

I felt beautiful.

15

Even though pigs have four toes on each foot, they only walk on their front two. That was a fun fact I learned while having a romantic date with Adam. It was interesting, and also explained why Mr. Oinks always looked as if he was tiptoeing places.

Here was another interesting fact: Adam wasn't over his ex-girlfriend. He started talking about her when the valet took his car (she worked one summer as a valet), and revisited her during the appetizer (funny story about shrimp...) and again in the wait for the entrée. When I gently questioned if he still had feelings for her, he apologized all over the creamed corn and then promptly confessed his undying love for her. We spent dessert discussing ways for him to win her back. I flipped over my napkin, pulled out a pen, and we had the workings of a game plan by the time he signed the check. The first step was for him to run, lickety-split, to her house and confess his love. Right away, without wasting valuable time taking Autumn back home. I stayed strong, all big smiles and encouraging hand motions, until the moment he got into his car and drove away.

Then, the pity party began. The restaurant's bar was dead, so I wandered a few doors down, to the sports bar on the corner, and found an empty stool at the bar. With a martini in hand, I bemoaned my steadfast dedication to singledom. I should have had *some* sort of serious relationship by now. I was twenty-eight. In the olden days, I'd have grandchildren by now. Instead, I'd wasted all of my youthful vigor on relationships that were shorter than my ovulation cycle. Lots of kissing. A few dry hump sessions. Some struggling attempts at oral pleasure and three really forgetful intercourses.

I found a couple of aspirins in the pocket of my purse and washed them down with the remainder of my drink. I set down the glass and attempted to lick some sugar off my cheek.

"Want another?" The bartender, a chick with piercing blue eyes and steroid-enhanced shoulders, grabbed my glass and raised her eyebrows at me. I nodded. Someone bumped into my stool and I scooted closer to the bar, the place filling up. I glanced down at my dress, feeling self-conscious, the vegetable couture out of place in this setting. A heavily tatted guy squeezed up to the bar next to me, resting his massive forearms on the bar, and flashed me a smile that probably had its own mugshot. "Hey."

I managed a smile and unlocked my phone. I should call Ansley and ask her to pick me up before it got too late. The bartender slid another bright yellow drink toward me and I picked it up, taking a big sip. I tried Ansley, didn't get an answer, then texted her.

I need a ride. I'm downtown. Call me.

The tatted-up stranger moved closer and I avoided eye contact, gluing my eyes to the television above the bar. Sitting at the bar had been a bad idea. So had running Adam off. Rethinking it, he hadn't needed to go to his ex-girlfriend's *right* away. It was Friday night for pickles sake! I bet she was on her own hot date, clueless of the fact that she had a heartbreakingly lovely man abandoning other women and pining for her.

"I've got a place around the corner." The man's voice was gruff, and he moved into my personal space, the proximity bringing an aroma of French fries and smoke. Unfortunately, French fries are a bit of a weakness for me, and I found myself leaning in for another sniff, almost as if I was interested.

I forced myself to straighten on the stool and busied myself with another sip of my cocktail. "Thank you, but I'm not interested," I said, in a rather prim fashion that would have made Miss Manners clap her hands with joy.

"Aw, come on. A little thing like you, all alone in here?" His hand settled on my lower back. "You look like you need a man to protect you."

I choked back a laugh, thinking through the many ways to die. A public bar, stocked with bouncers and witnesses, was one of the safest places a person could be. Assuming you didn't get trampled in a panicked crowd, captured in a freak fire that sealed the doors shut, or involved in a bar brawl, the chances of death were similar to that of a local library. My biggest danger would come when I left the place, which would sure as heck not be with him. "Nah, I'm good."

He leaned forward, going in as if for a kiss, and I jerked away when the bristle of his beard brushed against my cheek. "Excuse me!" I shoved my hand against his sternum and raised my voice loud enough to be heard by every bar-hopper in a ten-foot radius. "Go away!"

His face darkened, a scowl forming, and just like that, my over-friendly ex-con turned into a pissed-off drunk.

16

"Okay, where is she?" Nate raised his voice as they entered the sports bar, the noise from the crowd a sharp contrast from the quiet street.

Declan looked over the crowd, trying to see Nicola's platinum-blonde hair. He glanced down at his phone. She had started texting him fifteen minutes ago, when they were over at the Ale House, enjoying a bucket of beer and wings. Unlike her normal texts, which were a wide range of begging him for sex, or bitching at him for breaking up with her, this string had been different.

> Are you busy?
> I'm at Bullwinkle's, and there's a guy here that won't leave me alone.
> I lost my purse at Poor Paul's and don't have money for cab fare.

He'd responded, and let her know they were on their way. Paying their tab, they'd headed straight over, battling the downtown crowd to rescue her, a plight that Nate had bitched about the entire time. Declan sent her a text.

We're here. Where are you?

"I swear, it's like you don't *want* to get laid. Those girls at Ale House were ripe for the picking."

"They were idiots." Declan squeezed past a group of coeds, and scanned the high tops by the window. No Nicola.

"They were drunk college girls. Do you know the next time we'll have a shot at eighteen-year-old pussy?" Nate dropped his voice on the last word and flashed a smile at the closest woman in apology.

"Umm... now?" Declan nodded to a group of girls at a six-top. "Go for it."

Nate gripped his shoulder, pulling him closer as they moved toward the bar. "All I'm asking is for you to act interested. Smile. You're like going out with that guy from the Addams Family... the creepy quiet one."

"They're all creepy and quiet."

"And... none of them are getting laid. Point made."

His phone buzzed and Declan glanced back down, a text from Nicola popping up.

I found a ride. Sowry.

She had attached four emojis of varying emotions, from teary to laughing out loud. *Wow*. He held out the phone and let Nate read it. His gaze bounced from the phone's screen to Declan. "Seriously?" They rounded the corner, moving past a spirited argument on the Jaguars defense strategy and Declan's arm shot out, stopping Nate. "Wait."

His eyes settled on the tiny girl and the big man. That familiar blonde hair. Her finger was jabbing up into his chest. His stance was intimidating and advancing forward. The bartender shouted at them.

A crowd was forming. Uneasy looks were darting between the onlookers.

Nate cursed. "Holy shit. Is that—"

Declan ignored the question and stepped forward, shouldering past a drunk jersey.

"You think you can just—" The blonde's words cut off when the tatted-up asshole reached forward and grabbed her hair. Declan's hand shot out, wrapping around the man's wrist and he squeezed, catching the guy's attention. Nate's fist connected with the man's nose, the crack audible, the grip on Autumn's hair released. She turned her head, saw Declan, and froze.

Her Facebook photo didn't do her justice, and there was nothing like a damsel in distress to light every masculine bone in his body on fire. Maybe it was the three beers that he'd just had, the adrenaline rush from the confrontation, or the frustration over Nicola's flakiness. Whatever the reason, in this moment, they didn't feel like enemies. She looked beautiful, he felt protective, and the urge to yank her away from this guy and carry her out of this bar was overwhelming.

The stunned look dropped from her face, and with her next words, the crazy came back out to play. "Do you *know* how many people die in bar fights every year!" It wasn't a question, it was a scream of accusation, the sort his mother would level at him when she found his football uniform on the floor of the bathroom, or her embroidered hand towels covered in grease.

Something plowed into the back of his leg and he fell into her, their bodies colliding with the edge of the bar. He held her up and looked over his shoulder, watching as the guy ducked a punch from Nate, then staggered upright, blood dripping from his nose.

"We have to get you out of here!" She held her head as if she was in pain, yelling the words in his ear and he fought to remind himself that she was the enemy. It was a struggle when the heat of her body was flush against him, her soft curves taking his mind in a hundred directions. Her hair tickled against his neck and when she leaned in to yell at him, he wanted to tighten his hand on the small of her back and pull her closer—

He dragged his mind back, and attempted to respond to her words, which were ludicrous in themselves. *They had to get him out of here?* She was the one in danger. There was a loud crash as Nate took the man back to the ground. He followed the action, jerking his foot back when the guy's tattooed hand clenched around his ankle, his face twisted in anger.

"The slut's not worth it," he spat out.

"Let's GO!" Autumn screamed in Declan's ear, twisting away from him and stepping over the biker. Lifting one impossibly high-heeled shoe, she stomped on the man's thigh, causing him to wheeze in pain, and the surrounding crowd to cheer in approval. She held out her hand for Declan's, her face pinched and worried. "HURRY!"

It was as if she thought the place was going to explode, a time bomb winding down, each second precious. She frantically waved her hand at him and he took it, letting her pull him through the crowd, out the revolving door and finally, into the quiet night.

"I had it under control." Autumn Jones knotted her arms across her chest and glared at him. "You shouldn't have come over. It was too dangerous." She turned, rubbing at her forehead with a wince, and he took a moment to get a better look at her. Shapely legs. A killer ass. She was wearing a potato sack of a top that completely hid her upper body, but he remembered the curves she'd pressed against him.

He looked away.

"Aren't you *worried* about your friend?"

He chuckled. "Nah. Nate can take care of himself. He grew up in a boxing gym. This is his opportunity to show off to all of the ladies." He glanced back at the bar, the foggy windows hiding whatever was happening inside.

She stepped forward with a purpose and came to a stop just in front of him. He watched with interest as she peered up at him critically. She reached for his face and he held his breath, surprised when her fingers gently gripped his jaw, moving his head to the left, and then the right, examining every inch of his face. When she finally looked at him, her eye contact direct and unemotional, he felt something in his chest flip.

"How are you feeling?"

Confused. Conflicted. Like I should be dragging you down to the police station, but I'd rather take you to my bed. He wet his lips. "Fine."

"You didn't hit your head? He didn't inject you with anything? You feel normal?" Her hands moved to his ears, pinching across the edges of them as if testing for lumps, then patted down his neck, her thumbs brushing over his lymph nodes. It shouldn't have been erotic, but his dick was confused. "Huh?" She looked at him pointedly, and he struggled to follow her questions.

"*Inject* me with anything? No. Why would he inject me with anything?"

She removed her hands and he resisted the urge to step closer to her. Fuck, Nate was right. It *had* been too long since he'd been with a woman. That was the only explanation for why he wasn't running in the other direction from this girl. What had Nate compared him to? A creepy, quiet ghoul. He delivered his best charming smile to combat the image.

She glared at him. "You *have* to be more careful."

She was weird. Adorably so. And gorgeous. Nate had been right. How had Declan never noticed that? Then again, he'd never been so close to her before, had never interacted with her, or seen the cute little way her face scrunched up when she was perturbed.

A car drove by, rap music thumping, and she glanced at the street, then pushed him farther from the curb, shoving him back until his shoulders hit the brick building. The aggression was hot and he let her maneuver him, his hands gently settling on her hips. It was the perfect blend of ingredients for a kiss, and he dropped his head, seeking out her lips.

"What are you *doing*?" She swatted away his hands. "Oh my God, is it this dress? First that guy, and now you?" She leaned forward, sniffing the air. "Are you drunk?"

"A little?" The comparison to that tattooed asshole was alarming, and he leaned against the wall, critically re-examining his actions. "I'm sorry. I read you wrong. I thought—" *I thought that since you've stalked me for the last six months, that you had some sort of a crush on me. Apparently, you're just fucking crazy.* He swallowed the intended words and let the sentence hang.

She didn't let it go. "You thought... What?"

Fuck it. "You've been stalking me. I assumed you had a romantic fixation on me. So, I thought you'd *like* it if I kissed you." It had sounded much better in his head. Less cocky and more debonair.

"Oh my God..." She flexed her hands, like little T-Rex claws, her eyes pinched shut, and he had a pretty good idea that she was envisioning his balls in those hands, a visualization that made him shift uncomfortably. "You..." Her eyes opened. "You're..." She looked away, visibly stumped.

"I'm... right?" He guessed.

"No." She shook her head violently, her blonde hair swinging. "But I *do* understand how you might have been confused over the occasional times you *may* have seen me before."

"The *occasional* times I *may* have seen you before..." He shook his head. "Wow. That's an interesting way to put it."

She fell silent, and he waited for her to offer an explanation, something other than her romantic obsession with him, which, apparently, didn't exist.

"Okay," she countered. "I admit, I follow you around."

"Uh, yeah. I know. Everyone within five blocks of my office knows. There are photos of you at the security desk of our building."

She blew out an irritated breath. "I just... worry about you."

Worry about him? This was interesting. He readjusted his stance against the building. "In what way?"

She looked away, and it was the first glimpse of her vulnerability. A vulnerability that made him even more interested in whatever it was she was about to say. She sighed. "You're going to think I'm crazy."

"I hate to break it to you, but that boat sailed a long time ago." He smiled to soften the blow and she caught the gesture, her own lips turning ruefully up at the corners.

She laughed and clamped her hand over her mouth to stop the sound. "Oh my God," she moaned. "You do. You think I'm crazy." She pivoted, coming to stand beside him, and leaned back against the brick, mirroring his position. "It's okay. My sister thinks I'm crazy too."

"Because…?"

She groaned, dropping her head in her hands. "Do you remember —" she stopped. "Of course you remember." She turned to meet his eyes, and she really *was* beautiful. Someone like Nate would have found her too small. He liked curvy women as tall as he was. But for Declan, she was perfect. Soft and beautiful. Delicate yet strong. Feminine. Irresistible.

And … crazy, he reminded himself. Batshit crazy.

"You know the night of the crash? The plane crash?"

He nodded, unsurprised that she was aware of it. It had been all over the news, their neighborhood swarmed by national news vans, crime scene tape and gawkers. It'd been weeks before you could even drive down Lake Drive without going through a three-ring circus of coverage.

"I was there that day. My sister lives in your neighborhood, and we were holding a Celebration of Life for my mom." She tilted her head back, her gaze on the night sky, and he could sense the pain radiating off her, still raw and unhealed. "I had a headache and went for a walk, just to get away from everyone. And then I saw you." She turned her head to meet his gaze. "And I *felt* something. Not like hearts and romance," she hurried to finish as if my confusion needed instant remedying. "It was more like this *alarm* inside my head. It was so intense that I thought I was having a panic attack. With the grief and the stress over my mom…" The door to the bar opened, a group spilling out, and Declan stiffened, praying Nate wasn't among them. They turned left, stumbling away, and she watched them go, then returned her attention to him. "But the feeling, the alarm, it seemed tied to *you* somehow."

He turned to face her, readjusting his position against the brick, and tucked his hands in the pockets of his jeans to keep himself from reaching for her. He tried to follow her disjointed explanation of events. "I don't get it. What does this internal alarm have to do with anything? You think you knew the plane was going to crash?"

"Sort of." She frowned. "I… it was more that something was going to happen to *you*. The plane crash just happened to be *what* was going to happen to you."

"But I was fine."

"You were fine because that dog attacked you." She clearly enunciated the words as if they meant something. "The dog that *I* let out."

She looked at him expectantly, as if she'd just revealed something big and he should be easily connecting these dots.

He stayed silent, working through them, and then sort of figured out what she was saying. "So, you let out the dog. Because you thought something was going to happen to me. And you're saying that, if you hadn't let out the dog, that the plane would have hit me?"

"Yes."

"And what does *that* have to do with you stalking me?"

She sighed, and he felt a combination of stupidity and arousal, which made a lethal combination.

17

He didn't get it. Go figure that I was tasked with protecting some eye candy who turned out to be dumb as a bag of rocks. I cleared my throat, frustrated by his blank stare. "LOOK." I clapped my hands in the air between us, a trick I'd seen Ansley use to get Paige and Caleb's attention. He blinked, which I took as a good sign. "I'm your guardian angel, okay? I let out the dog, he stopped you from moving forward and into the plane's trajectory." I moved two fingers along an imaginary path and used my other hand as the plane, letting it swoop down and … I made the explosion sound with my mouth and did a complicated sparkly hand motion that Caleb would have understood perfectly. Declan squinted at me.

"Got it?" I raised my eyebrows.

"You think you're my guardian angel?" he asked slowly.

"Yep." I nodded, irritated that it was such a ridiculous title. I swear, if it had a title like "Protector of Life", it'd be taken seriously. It was around this point in the story where I lost Ansley. Granted, her response was a little different. She had started shaking with laughter before making a fake call to a mental institution, but I preferred that to *this*, his silent appraisal, which gave me absolutely no clue of what he was thinking.

"Huh." He pushed off the wall and stood, and I had the distinct impression that he was about to turn and madly sprint away, his hands jack-knifing, slick sole shoes peppering along the asphalt. "So... you've been following me around to let out more dogs?"

"In a hypothetical sense. I don't expect any more planes to crash down on you, but I *do* think you are coming in contact with danger, and I think I can anticipate and hopefully stop something bad from occurring to you." Maybe he wasn't about to run. Maybe he understood what I was saying and wouldn't think I was crazy. Maybe this would be a successful interchange between two adults without words like 'psychopath' or 'crazy lady' being thrown into the mix.

"And how's protecting me been working out for you?" The corner of his mouth twitched and he definitely wasn't running. He seemed amused by the idea, which I could work with. Amused people didn't call the police. Amused people could be protected. He raised one brow as if it had been a serious question, and I considered the inquiry.

"Not great," I admitted. "I—"

"Shit, there you are." His friend approached from the left, his hand rubbing over the back of his head.

Declan watched him approach. "Where'd you come from?"

Nate gestured behind him. "They made me leave out the back. I walked around the block and back up front." He looked over at me. "Ahhh. Autumn Jones. We finally meet. I'm Nate."

So, the Facebook invite hypothesis was true. Declan had known my name. And so, apparently, did his inner circle. *Great*.

Nate extended a hand with a grin. "You know, you're quite the local celebrity. I've got a sister who's dying to meet you."

"Nate," Declan warned.

Nate's smile widened. "What? She does." His hair was mussed, the top button of his shirt undone, but I couldn't see any damage, though there was a smear of blood across the front of his blue shirt. He followed my gaze and shrugged. "All his, none of mine."

"Awesome," Declan drawled. "We were so worried."

"Oh, I'm sorry." Nate stepped back, his head ricocheting from Declan to me. "Did I… interrupt something? Were you two having a *moment?*"

"No!" I interrupted hotly. Jeez, this guy was the king of awkwardness.

"Where's the other guy?" Declan asked, and I snapped to attention, realizing the imminent danger. We shouldn't be standing here. That guy could leave the bar at any moment and storm over, a broken beer bottle or makeshift shiv in hand. I started to feel hot, and wasn't sure if it was a sign of trouble or just pure embarrassment.

Nate shrugged, and with such a reckless best friend, I didn't know how Declan had lived this long. "The manager has him. The guy pulled a knife, so they're calling the police." He waved away the news, and I felt faint. *A knife.* I thought of the man's hand closing around Declan's ankle, the fury in his eyes. He could have been reaching for his knife right then. He could have stabbed Declan's leg, hit a major artery, and it would have been all my fault.

"Cute outfit." Nate tilted his head at me. "You going to a costume party or something?"

I wanted to sink into a puddle and ooze through the sewer grate. He didn't intend the question to be mean, and that made it even worse. Here I was, in this ridiculous dress, provoking a man with a knife into a bar fight, and bringing *Declan* into it. I put him in danger. *Me.* And all in heels that I could barely walk, much less protect anyone, in.

I felt a surge of emotional hysteria coming on and stepped back before it hit. "It was nice to meet you both." I managed the words without beginning to cry, a Herculean feat, and turned to walk away. Declan called my name, and I increased my pace, digging in my purse, searching for my phone.

"Autumn!"

Tears began to burn the edges of my eyes, and I skittered along the sidewalk, cursing the unfleeability of my heels. He jogged up beside me, cutting me off, and I stopped, my head down, eye contact avoided as I frantically rummaged through my purse. Why in God's name did I have so much inside it? Who needed ten tampons? Or a spare package of tissues? Ohhh! Tissues. I pulled the little package open, then thought better of it, preferring to hide my tears behind a casual brush of my hand.

Declan moved directly in front of me, blocking my path, and I abandoned the search for my phone and zipped up my bag, adjusting the strap higher on my shoulder. He repeated my name and I blew out a breath. "What?" I snapped.

"Look at me."

Yeah, that wasn't going to happen. I snorted and moved left to skirt around him. He matched the motion. I moved right and he did the same. I growled in frustration and made a mental note to burn these shoes when I got home because oh my *piglet*, my toes were killing me. A woman shouldn't have to deal with losing a wonderful date, public groping, a brush with danger, ridicule, a potato dress *and* painful shoes, all in the same night.

He stepped closer and I caught a hint of his cologne as I inhaled. Damn, he smelled good. In the bar, it had been mixed with grease and beer and strangers but out here, the night crisp and empty, the surrounding scents muted, I was hit with the full force of it. His hands settled on my shoulders, pulling me a little closer, and he leaned down and whispered in my ear. "Thank you."

It was so unexpected that I lifted my head, risking a glance up, and when his eyes met mine I wanted to sink into them and never come up for air. *He was so beautiful*. It was the wrong moment to be around a man like that. I was too weak, too fractured. I needed my bed and my pillow and the gentle sounds of Mr. Oinks' snores. *I should run*. Turn and take off, before I did something stupid. He was *thanking* me? I thought of Mom, all alone, stumbling out onto that street without anyone there to protect her. I *will* protect him. *I need him to be safe*. I couldn't handle the gentle comfort of his touch, the kindness in his voice, this tender look he was giving me. I reached forward, clutching the front of his shirt and then, unable to stop myself—he was so freaking everything—kissed him.

I kissed him like I had never kissed anyone before. My lips were rough. Needy. I tightened my grip on his shirt and rose up on my toes, bringing us closer, my tongue begging, his mouth opening, deepening, taking. His hands found my waist and pulled me tight to him. My hands clawed up, past his collar, skating over his strong jaw, those perfect ears and stealing into his hair, my nails raking into his scalp, my fingers pulling at his hair while my mouth fought over his and poured out every emotion that was pumping through my heart.

Fear.

Need.

Loneliness.

Want.

I felt a sob well in the back of my throat and I pushed away from him, my eyes flooding with tears. "I'm sorry," I choked out, my words barely audible. Reaching down, I yanked at the straps of my heels, freeing one painful foot, then the other. I abandoned the pumps and turned, ignoring Declan and sprinting down the sidewalk, past the closed restaurants and open bars, running until my bare feet burned and my chest ached from the exertion.

Thank you. Two words, and I'd be damned if they'd broken every latch around my heart.

18

Declan sat in the passenger seat of Nate's Jeep and watched as passing streetlights illuminated spots of the city. A homeless man, curled up on a bench. A chain of newspaper stands outside a closed convenience store. He should have chased her. She had been all alone. Downtown, despite the city's improved initiatives and efforts at revitalization, wasn't a safe place for a single woman. What if someone attacked her? Took her somewhere? What if she stopped at another bar and got drunk? He thought of that tattooed prick and his hand tightened reflexively into a fist. Maybe this one would be a smooth talker in a suit. Someone who'd feed her drinks and listen to her woes. Run his hands up her thigh and under the tight hem of that dress. Lean in and offer to take her home.

That was how women died. And he'd let it happen. He'd let her run off without shoes, down that filthy street, and hadn't chased her. What the *fuck* had he been thinking?

"She's like Cinderella, man." Nate chuckled from his place behind the wheel.

Declan glanced down at the heels in his lap, understanding the analogy. He picked up one of the tan pumps, turning it over in his hands. It was scuffed, and he remembered her attempt to kick it off.

"So, what now? We show up at her house and stick that on every one of her stepsisters' feet?"

"Your knowledge of the story is impressive."

"I blame it all on Bridget. She watched that damn thing on repeat. You want to hear the mouse song? I know every word." Nate rubbed the back of his neck and looked over at him. "Stop moping."

Declan didn't respond, his thumb running over the heel's smooth sole. He studied the dash's clock, trying to calculate how much time had passed since he'd last seen her. Thirty minutes? Forty-five? He'd had Nate circle downtown, checking every block for her. Lots of drunk blondes, but no Autumn. No curves of temptation, no mouth that... his stomach tightened at the memory of her kiss. Fuck, she knew how to kiss. Her tongue, her reckless passion...

"She'll be fine," Nate insisted. "Crazy takes good care of crazy."

"She's not crazy." It was the dumbest statement he'd ever made. Because clearly, she was nuts. No one who thought they had an ordained calling to protect a stranger would be considered sane. Especially someone who took it to the extreme she did. *Batshit crazy*, that was the term he and Nate had used so many times, back when they'd thought her fascination with him had been a romantic one. Now that he understood the motivation behind the stalking, he hated to use such a cruel term. She was ... misguided, he decided. Adorably delusional.

Thanking her had been an act that came out of left field. Still, it seemed as if something should be said for her dogged efforts, all which seemed to be centered around a selfless plight to keep him safe.

Nate made the turn into Declan's neighborhood and he watched the dark homes pass, the families inside asleep. Crazy that one of them belonged to her sister. He smiled at the thought that she had been so close. How often had he come in contact with her and not known it?

"What's so funny?"

Declan shook his head. "Nothing. I'm just thinking over everything."

Nate pulled into his driveway and shifted into park. "I've got to admit, you're freaking me out. This situation isn't funny. It's alarming. And you've suddenly gotten stars in your eyes over this girl. Don't forget everything she's put you through."

"Says the guy who wanted me to be her Facebook friend. Plus, she hasn't really put me through much." So, she had followed him around. Had fucked with his trash. Occasionally thrown a public spectacle. It had been entertaining. Flattering. It had definitely gotten his mind off Nicola, which had been a blessing in itself.

"Wow...." Nate chuckled. "That's a hundred-and-eighty-degree turn in thinking." He reached for the door handle and Declan stopped him.

"You should head home. I have something I need to do."

Nate winced. "Come on, man. I can't have you wandering around downtown looking for her. What if a stranger offers you candy? It's not safe."

"I'm not going downtown. Just head home. I'll see you tomorrow." Declan stepped out of the Jeep, and Nate shrugged.

"I'll never understand you, Dec."

He smiled. "Be safe. And go put ice on that hand."

Nate scoffed and revved the engine in response. Declan lifted his hand in a wave and walked up to the house, pulling out his cell when it buzzed.

MOTION DETECTED! Press here to see the live video!

He glanced up at the cameras, remembering the anxiety he'd felt when he'd mounted them. The annoyance and stress that he'd had, all over some missing newspapers and empty bottles. Why had he cared so much?

He should have just approached her the first time he noticed her following him. Introduced himself and realized, at that point, what a harmless and adorable woman she was. He could have saved them both a lot of headache and stresses over the last six months.

Stepping inside, he flipped the switch and looked at his house with new eyes. The couch, a carryover from college, sagged in the middle, the worn leather perfect for weekend football and early nights, but ugly as hell. The walls were bare, Nicola taking the artwork with her when she'd left. The walls were taupe, a result of one long weekend with Nate and Bridget, covering up the pale blue color Nicola had obsessed over. At least the place was clean. He had been well trained by his father, who believed military precision should carry through every aspect of life, the easiest aspect done with a broom and dustpan. Had Autumn come home with him, she would have found fresh sheets on the bed, the edges tucked at diagonal angles, the toilet clean, shower scrubbed down this morning right before he stepped out of it.

It only took a second to find the postcard, still waiting in the middle of his kitchen counter. Autumn Jones. 444 Frolicking Lane.

He grabbed his keys and headed for the garage.

Her house was straight out of a Southern Living magazine. A white picket fence. Craftsman-style home with a wide front porch, the square columns wrapped in jasmine, a swing on one end. A gable roof with dark blue staggered shake siding. Her porch lights were off, and he climbed the front steps quietly, her heels in hand. He put his ear to the door and listened for any sounds from inside. Nothing.

He hesitated, warring between leaving the heels on the front mat or ringing the bell. It was past midnight. Too late to be waking anyone up, if she had a roommate. He placed the shoes on the front mat and stepped back, examining them. Moving to the truck, he opened the glove box and looked for a piece of paper, settling on the back of a receipt. Uncapping a pen, he attempted a note.

Thought you might want these back— Declan

He crumpled it up and flipped through more glove box junk, finding an expired printout of his insurance. The page was bigger, giving him more room. He started over.

I'm worried about you. Call me when you get home.

That was great. Just the sort of thing a mother would write. He grimaced at the poor choice of comparison, then scratched through the line. Tossing the paper and pen on the bench seat of his truck, he quietly shut the door and wandered back to the porch. Leaning against one of the columns, he decided to wait.

Nate was probably right. She could take care of herself. Call a cab. Get home safely. But, just to be sure… he'd wait as long as it took.

She had been worried about him. He'd seen the depth of her concern in her eyes when she had examined him, her pinched features relaxing the more she had patted him over. How long had it been since someone had given him that feeling? That amount of care? He was lying to himself if he said it hadn't felt good. Just being in her presence… that had given him a feeling he hadn't had in a long time, if ever.

So, he'd return the favor. Worry about her and wait to make sure that she made it home safely. And it had absolutely nothing to do with wanting another kiss.

19

I knew better than to take off down a dark street while drunk. Public intoxication was one of the easiest ways to die, with potentially embarrassing repercussions. Take Elisa Lam, a delightful Canadian gal who got drunk and drowned in a large water tank on the roof of a Los Angeles hotel. Her dead body floated in that tank for over two weeks before it was found. Want to know how they finally found her? Guests were complaining about the *taste* of the water. Yeah. Think about *that* next time you rinse your mouth out at the Marriott.

So, no hotel rooftops or swimming for me! Nope, I was taking the much more likely rape-and-be-killed route, walking along the edge of downtown and rummaging in my bag for my phone. I found it and breathed a sigh of relief, pulling up my text to Ansley, now an hour old and still unread. Go figure. I pulled up a car app and scheduled a ride, leaning against a light pole and scanning my surroundings for any potential threats.

God, I knew how to screw things up. If Declan Moss didn't think I was crazy before, he certainly did now. Between the bar fight, the tears, subsequent kiss, then my dramatic kick-off-my-heels escape...

Oh, plus my confession that I'm responsible for his safety. That golden nugget would have been the sparkly cherry on top of my Certifiably Crazy cupcake. I should have just run with his belief that I was following him around for romantic reasons. I could have played like I had a crush. Hung onto his words with big doe eyes. Fawned instead of pushing him away.

It would have been fun to pretend that I was in love with him. Especially since he hadn't seemed entirely averse to the idea. In fact, if I had to guess, I think he sort of *liked* the idea of me lusting after him.

I glanced both ways down the street, no lurking strangers (or my ride) in sight. I slid my back down the pole and sat on the curb, taking a moment to examine the bottom of my feet. They were filthy. I had a cut on my left sole and a valet ticket stuck to my right. I peeled off the ticket and apologized to my feet, promising them a long pedicure tomorrow, at that place with the ravenous little fish that would eat away all the dead skin.

Declan had actually been really nice about the whole thing. Distractingly so. I think he'd been drinking also. Alcohol would have explained the way he'd acted around me. I shivered a little at the memory of his hands, which had been *very* friendly. It had been a long time since I'd been touched like that. *Looked* at like that. And all that had contributed to the kiss. A woman starved for affection couldn't be expected to act rationally. Add in three drinks and an unexpected gesture of appreciation and I'm surprised I didn't strip down in the middle of the street and ask to have his babies. I sighed. He'd make pretty babies.

A minivan with a duct-taped front bumper slowed to a stop next to me, the hot pink logo glowing at me. I heaved to my feet and pulled open the back door. The woman behind the wheel nodded at me. "Just crawl over the carseat."

I followed her instructions, finding a spot by the window on a cloth backseat that smelled slightly of baby wipes. She pulled away, turning up the volume on the radio. "I'm in the middle of an audiobook," she called out. "Sorry."

"That's fine." I pulled the seatbelt across my shoulder and settled into the seat. Finding my phone, I confirmed the pickup, then texted Ansley.

Nevermind. Found ride. Thank God I didn't die.

I added a wide-eyed emoji for emphasis, then a gif of a psychopathic clown with a knife, stabbing the air.

Loud moaning caught my attention and I lifted my head, tuning in to the audiobook, which was diving into what appeared to be a *very* explicit sex scene between Joel the plumber and Bethany the lonely divorcee. The male voice spoke, deep and rough, his voice cracking as he urged the woman to open her legs wider and take his—I flushed, sinking deeper in my seat and resisted the urge to plug my ears with my finger.

A detailed accounting began, so raw and unfiltered that I felt I was *there,* in bed with the couple, watching the man's thick erection myself. I pulled at the neck of my dress and pinned my knees together, willing the woman to drive faster and get me home already.

"Ummm...." I said tentatively. "Could you—"

"Shhh!" the woman said excitedly, her hands gripping the wheel, shoulders hunched forward, as if she was about to crawl into the speakers and join in. "It's getting to the good part!"

Getting to the good part? Oh no. Talk about sustained erotic torture. I bet this is what Sergey Tuganov's two women felt like. The twenty-eight-year-old mechanic bet them $4300 that he could have nonstop sex with them for twelve hours. TWELVE HOURS. And he did. Got his $4300 in winnings, which was *such* a specifically random number, then had a heart attack and died. Doctors deduced his heart attack was due to the entire bottle of Viagra that he popped just before his twelve-hour session.

I can do this, I decided. If they could last twelve hours, I could surely last the ten minutes or so that this painfully sexual ride would entail. I closed my eyes and tried to concentrate on something other than the sordid description of her pleasure, which really did sound quite enviable. I tried to remember if I ever plugged in and recharged my vibrator. I hoped so. There was nothing worse than approaching the peak only to have it sputter to a stop.

My phone, which had been cradled between my thighs, started to ring, a sound paired with a delightful vibration that only added to my torture. I groaned and picked up the phone. "What?"

"Jeez. Just making sure you had made it home. I just woke up to pee and saw your texts." She hesitated, the pause coming at a terrible moment, the woman beginning to cry out the announcement of her orgasm. "Ummm… where *are* you?"

"In a Lyft, sitting next to a car seat and in the middle of some finger-banging. It's a long story. I'll tell you about it tomorrow."

She was silent, and I wondered how many explicit details of the man's cunnilingus were audible through the phone. "Riiiight. I'm going to let you get back to that."

"Thanks," I said flatly. "Such a dear."

She laughed, then hung up the phone. I closed my eyes and, for the next four minutes, tried to block out the image of Joel the Plumber's thick, pulsating member. It was hard. Literally *and* figuratively speaking.

The ravenous sex scene ended just as the minivan rolled to a stop at the end of my cul-de-sac. "Whew!" The driver said. "Good timing, right?"

I didn't respond. I couldn't. I had a blinding need to get inside, strip naked, and satisfy every craving that Bethany and Joel had just unleashed. I squirmed my way over the car seat, tossed her a tip, and practically shimmied my way across the lawn and up the front steps. I had my hand in my purse, swiping around for the keys, when a dark shape moved off my swing and toward me.

"AHHHHHH!" I threw my purse over my shoulder at the intruder, the forward lunge causing me to step on a bear trap of some sort, one that pierced the bottom of my foot and caused me to squeal in pain. I grunted, hopping on my other foot as I attempted to move away without falling down the front stairs. This was why I should have gotten a dog. Something fierce, that would have been snarling at the window, warning me of an intruder. Chances were, Mr. Oinks had fallen asleep on my office couch, watching The Weather Channel, stuffed on last night's leftover meatloaf and an extra helping of butter bread.

"Careful!" The man loomed closer, and I caught his profile in the faint moonlight. *Declan*.

I stopped hopping toward safety and made it to the rocking chair behind me, collapsing into it, my injured foot in hand. "Are you trying to *maim* me?" I asked, watching as he bent down and picked up the trap, bringing it closer to me. As my eyes adjusted, I saw that it was one of my heels from earlier, which he seemed to have placed on the welcome mat, which was a *dumb* idea on all accounts.

"I'm sorry." He carefully set the stiletto down and leaned against the porch rail across from my chair. "Here, let me see."

Giving this man my filthy foot was probably not the best idea. I tightened my hold on it. "It's fine."

"Just...." He reached forward and gently pried the appendage loose. "Let me see it." He carefully pulled on my ankle, bringing my foot to him.

I almost mewed at the feel of his hands on me, the injured flesh all but rolling over and showing him its belly. "It's dirty," I protested.

"I can see that." He bent over, peering down at it. "I'm worried you got cut by the spikes on the strap. It's going to get infected with how filthy your feet are."

He was right. Death by infection was a strong probability. I might as well plan my funeral arrangements now.

I attempted to pull my foot back. "I'll get it inside and wash it. Thank you for bringing them to me. You didn't have to do that. Also, lurking in the dark shadows and scaring the bejesus out of me." I gestured to the other end of the porch. "That was also not necessary."

He grinned. "Noted." Letting go of my ankle, he stood. "Let me make it up to you." He held out his hand. "Declan Moss, part-time EMT. Let me clean and examine that cut."

I didn't move. "You aren't an EMT."

"I'm practically an EMT," he countered.

"No," I countered. "Two first aid classes freshman year don't count for shit."

His grin widened. "It was three. And… do I want to know how you know about that?"

"You failed the third," I reminded him. "And I have a lot of spare time and excellent snooping skills." The first aid classes had given me a momentary sense of peace in his wellbeing, the recess in worry short-lived in duration.

"That's so creepy." He didn't look creeped out. He looked… well, I didn't know this look. It wasn't one I'd seen very often. *Intrigued*? Is that what that cocky grin was communicating?

He reached down and pulled me up to my feet. "If you've done this much research, then you know I'm trustworthy enough to take care of you."

"But…" I protested, my hands scrambling for his neck as he bent down and scooped me up. "Wait, what are you doing?"

"Carrying you inside. You can't track all of this shit through your house." He looked concerned, and I couldn't believe he was carrying me with such ease. I wasn't exactly a porterhouse, but I was a well-rounded girl. He should have grunted a little when lifting me up. The muscles in his neck should be flexing from the weight. Ansley's husband once put me on his shoulders during a chicken fight, and he flushed tomato red, his knees wobbling under the strain.

But Declan was smiling down at me, and close enough to kiss. That realization made me remember my embarrassing pillage of his mouth and I looked away, distracting myself with looking for my purse. I spotted it on its side near the column, half its contents spilling out, including a maxi pad big enough to act as a Titanic life raft. I forced my features to remain calm. "The keys are in my purse."

He kept me in his arms, one under my knees, the other supporting my back, and did a squat, his hand awkwardly shuffling through the brown tote.

I groaned. "Let me." I reached over, my elbow almost taking out his cheek, and grabbed my purse, bringing it to my chest and rummaging through it like a raccoon going through trash. I found my keys and sorted through them, finding the one covered in a sunflower print and holding it up. "Here. Please don't kill me. And if you do, take my body with you. I have serious fears of my pig eating me."

His grinned dropped. "That's morbid."

"It's a side effect of nervousness. Trust me, I get a lot worse." One side effect of constantly stressing over a man's untimely death—my walking encyclopedia of macabre possibilities.

"I'm not going to kill you." He worked the key into the lock and turned it, pushing open the door with his foot.

"Light switch is on the left." I reached over, dropping my purse on the entrance table and returned my hands to their proper place around his neck. It was pretty romantic, him bringing me over the threshold. If I was in a wedding dress and he loved me, this would be the conclusion of every dream I'd ever had. Of course, I wasn't in a wedding dress. I was in a *potato,* so we could stab that fantasy in the eye and move on.

He swung the door shut, the impact loud. From down the hall, I heard a crashing sound—Mr. Oinks falling off the couch—then the click of his hooves as he nosed his way out the door and down the hall toward us, grunting with excitement. Fun fact: pigs have horrible vision. He was almost on top of us before he realized that I was suspended in Declan's arms, a turn of events that had him scrambling backward, an alarmed squeal coming out.

"Oh God," Declan said. "The pig *lives* with you?"

"Of course he does," I said indignantly. Leaning forward, I cooed at Mr. Oinks. "It's okay, buddy. Everything's just fine." I straightened. "Just ignore him. You can put me down, you know. My floors have seen worse. They can handle it."

"Nah." His hands tightened. "Where's the bathroom?"

I considered the possibility of him cleaning my foot in the powder room and dismissed it. "Down the hall to the left. The double doors."

My bedroom wasn't prepared for entrance. The bed was unmade, the television still on, my discarded outfits slung over every surface. He breezed through without comment, nudging open the bathroom door with his knee and bringing me into the master bath. Mr. Oinks followed, grunting in pleasure when Declan carefully set me on the edge of the garden tub. His tail wiggled and I leaned down, scratching his ears. "Good boy."

Declan rolled up his sleeves and turned the bathtub's handles, his forearms flexing from the motion. Water spewed out of the faucet and he reached out, testing the temperature. I was reminded suddenly of Joel, the plumber, and how he'd dragged his wet fingers across Bethany's lips. A whimper involuntarily slipped out. He glanced over, his brows knitting in question, and I coughed. "Sorry. I just bumped the cut."

He nodded, all business, completely unaware of the arousalfest that was doing jumping jacks in my panties. Pulling me closer to the edge of the tub, he knelt and lifted up my left foot.

"I can do this," I blushed. "I mean, thank you, but you don't have to—"

"I want to," he interrupted me. "It's the least I can do for a woman who took the trouble to dig up my college transcript." He glanced over at me and grinned, and my libido really couldn't handle this image. His strong build, kneeling before me. Those capable hands on my foot. His hair still tousled from our kiss, those perfect teeth exposed as he grinned. He had a few days of scruff on his face, and that, paired with the tan skin and the white button-up, was the most delicious thing I'd ever seen. No wonder the universe needed me to protect him. Men like this had to be preserved, be kept safe, had to grow up and father a dozen more mini-Declans to preserve—

"Are you okay?" He peered at me. "You're starting to pant. Are you feeling faint?"

Oh, God. I'm panting. I've become Bethany. "Uh… maybe?"

"Did you eat anything today?" He abandoned my feet and moved closer, his hand sliding up my calf, and thank *God* for my failed date with Adam and the shave job I had tackled as a result.

"I ate a lot today." It came out as a whisper, and I really hoped it was my imagination working overtime, and that my voice didn't really sound all husky and full of need. Mr. Oinks farted, one of his really loud and wet ones, and the horrified look on Declan's face ... I burst out laughing.

"Please tell me that isn't going to smell," he stage-whispered the plea, as if Mr. Oinks might hear and get his feelings hurt.

I smiled. "Sometimes it does. Do you mind putting him out in the hall?"

He rose to his feet, carefully releasing my feet, and I put them under the water, watching the dirt bleed off. I turned my head, watching as he awkwardly herded Mr. Oinks through the door, his hands shooing at the air, his legs moving side to side as if he was a soccer player guarding a goal.

When he returned, closing the door behind him, he had a triumphant look on his face. "One farting pig removed." He sniffed the air, his hands on his hips, and grinned. "And... no smell."

I raised my hand for a high five. "Team No Fart."

He hesitated, then met my palm in the air, his hand closing around mine.

20

He'd never seen such a sexy woman. Every part of her. Her adorable motions. The unexpectedly awkward things she said. Even her lightheadedness was sexy. It gave her eyes this wild need, her breath coming harder, her hands beginning to tighten on the hem of her dress.

He returned to the floor, kneeling on the tile and picking up a half-used bar of lavender soap, using it to suds up his hands. Her feet were in the water and he pulled one free, carefully working across the dips and arches of her feet, moving his fingers in mini circles, his forehead tightening in concentration as he removed the dirt while trying to steer clear of her injuries. She actually had several cuts, micro-skins likely caused by running on the sidewalk. She inhaled a few times as he worked, and he glanced over in concern. Each time, she waved off his worry, but she wasn't looking well. Her mouth was slightly open, and she seemed to have trouble breathing, one hand moving to grip the edge of the tub, her knuckles turning white.

It shouldn't have been a sexual moment, but it felt like it was. Her pain indicators sounded so fucking erotic that he had to shift his position as he moved to the second foot, turning away from her in an attempt to hide his arousal. God, the way she was squirming. He tightened his hold on her foot and brushed his knuckles across her sole, softly, and then deeper, massaging the tight muscles there. "Stay still."

There was a thud and he looked over to see her head dropped back against the wall, her eyes closed, one hand fisting at the front of her dress. The tight hem of it had risen higher, exposing more of her thighs, thighs he wanted to spread open, plant kisses up along the length of them, and settle his mouth between, exploring and tasting her, getting his fill of—*Jesus*. He swore under his breath and refocused on her feet, willing his dick to soften, willing her to stop doing *everything* she was doing. Her toenails were painted a tangerine pink and he moved her foot under the water's flow, watching as the soap dribbled off them. Her feet looked so delicate in his hands, and he'd never had a foot fetish before, but maybe this was how it started. He cleared his throat. "I think we should get you on the bed."

"What?" She panted out the question, and if he didn't know any better, he'd say she was aroused. All hazy eyes and flushed cheeks. He stood and bent over her, taking the opportunity to lift her into his arms, though there was no reason she couldn't stand.

"I can walk," she mumbled, her hands fisting in his shirt. One of his buttons fell undone and she flushed.

"I don't want you to slip." He paused at the bedroom door, studying her closely. "Are you sure you're feeling okay?"

"I'm fine." She wet her lips and was absolutely stunning. "Maybe I *should* get on the bed."

"Yeah. That way I could treat the bottom of your feet."

"Right." She wet her lips again, her soft pink tongue darting out and he struggled not to lean forward and kiss them.

He should move into the bedroom. He could be done in ten minutes and headed home. There was no reason for him still to be standing in the doorway of her bathroom, holding her in his arms. She looked up at him. She had pretty eyes. He hadn't realized that earlier. Blue, with little brown flecks in them. And she was wearing eyeshadow, pale gold eyeshadow with some of her mascara dotting it. He reached up and brushed some loose strands of her hair off her forehead. "You are a *very* beautiful woman," he said softly.

Her hands tightened on his shirt. "Declan?"

"Yes?" he asked gruffly.

"Please kiss me."

It was the wrong thing to say to a man on the edge and he kicked at the door, getting it fully open and launching her onto the bed. His mouth found hers, his hands feverishly pulling at the fabric of her dress as he toed off his shoes. He broke away from their kiss to look down at her dress, his fingers struggling with the buttons. She shook her head, her own hands pulling at his shirt, dragging it over his head. "Just rip it."

He gripped the cloth and yanked, the sound of the tear adding to the passion of the moment. As he met her mouth he slid his hand inside the open dress, greedy at the forbidden access, his hand roughly traveling up the curves of her bra and pulling the lace down, her breast popping free.

He paused, watching as his hand reverently passed over the nipple, soft and pink, the tip of it pebbling under his touch, her back arching into his hand, offering it up to him and greedy for more. She was so exposed, so trusting, and so, so beautiful. He needed everything, all at once. To push inside of her, to taste her, to bring her pleasure, to hear her cry. He wanted to rush but take his time. Take but give her pleasure. Savor yet inhale her need. He brought his mouth down to her breast, his grip biting into her, pulling her tighter, his control barely in place as he worshipped the skin with his tongue. She groaned, thrashing underneath him, her hands raking through his hair, his name a cry from her lips. She clawed at her dress, trying to work it over her shoulders and cursed when she got stuck with it over one arm. "Scissors," she panted. "Top drawer."

He pulled off, taking the moment to peel off his socks and yank his belt open. He opened the drawer, a set of yellow shears next to a paperback novel and a single blue condom wrapper. He pulled his attention away from the condom and picked up the scissors.

"Cut it off," she begged, pulling the fabric away from her. "Hurry."

He opened the shears and hesitated. "We could probably get it off you if you—" She snatched the scissors with an animal growl and proceeded to hack through the material like a madwoman. He grinned, her raw need clear in this unrestrained moment. She was so beautifully artless and sexy. *God, I want her.* Then her dress fell away, the lavender lace panties exposed, and he stopped thinking about anything.

He swore, pushing his jeans to the floor and climbing on top of her. Her skin was flushed, the matching bra half off, and he pulled the other strap down, baring both breasts to him, and feasting on the view.

"Please," she begged, her hands reaching for him. "You have no idea how much I need this."

He had a bit of an idea. There was a good chance, if she touched him right now, that he'd finish before she pulled him out of his underwear. He dragged his fingers down her body and along the seam of her panties, inching under the lace, exploring her, her greedy body pushing into his touch. She was so wet, so warm. He pushed two fingers in and she gripped him tightly, the feel of her incredible, and he closed his eyes at the sensation. Her hips moved, grinding against him, and he almost came undone.

"More," she grunted, clawing at his chest as she pulled on the top of his underwear and caught his dick when it popped free.

She was a sexual beast. Unafraid. Unashamed. She was so different than any other woman he'd ever been with. So open. He moved his fingers quicker and hissed when she tightened her grip on him. She pulsed her hips up, meeting his hand, and stared up at him, mouth falling open, body tightening. The feel of her on his fingers ... it was heaven. How would that feel around his cock? He swore at the thought, watching her face change. She was close to coming, and he could see every bit of her climb, saw the flush as it hit her skin, felt the tightening of her body, the grip of her hand, the tremble of those perfect thighs. When she broke, it was the most erotic thing he'd ever seen in his life, a full-body bloom of pleasure, unfiltered and unrestrained. She rode it, owned it, her body tightening and flexing in perfect sensual waves around his fingers. His cock flexed in her hand, jealous of the sensation. She came down, going limp and her eyes dragged open, finding his.

"Get the condom," she groaned. "I need you, now."

21

His cock was beautiful. I watched him slide on the condom, the latex tightly stretched over the head, and almost asked him to take it off. I had this raw, animal need to have him take me bare, to experience the feeling of our skin against skin. But I didn't. I closed my mouth, and watched him climb onto the bed, that cock bobbing up between his thighs, and coming closer to me.

"I want to ride it." I don't know who spoke, but it couldn't have been me, because I don't even know how to ride a man. My inexperience shrieked in alarm as I pulled him down to the bed, gripped him in my hand (so hard) and straddled his hips.

I went slowly, his girth more than I was prepared for, and I hissed out a breath as I lowered myself down on him, my eyes closing at the delicious sensation of him impaling me.

"Open your eyes." His voice was guttural and dominant and his hands bit into my waist, his hips lifting in short thrusts, a subtle hint as to what he wanted.

I opened my eyes and rocked forward, my hands on his chest, squeezing at the muscle as I instinctively rocked up and down his shaft. His eyes darkened, his hands gripping my hips, and I must be doing something right because *holy hell* his eyes were smoldering with arousal.

"Fuck, you feel incredible." He held my gaze and I increased my pace, my breasts beginning to jiggle, his eyes drawn to them. I watched as his mouth dropped open a little, his eyes glazing over and he slid his hands up my side and forward, cupping my breasts and squeezing them, eyes pinching shut as he let out a guttural groan. "God damn, woman."

I released every self-conscious thought and focused on my own pleasure, dropping forward and pumping my hips over his stiff dick, shameless in my use of him, my orgasm coming, vibrating up my thighs and exploding, the pleasure causing me to falter, my rhythm off. I…

His hands closed on my ass and he brought me to his chest, taking over the action, matching my prior strokes with a perfect precision that grabbed my orgasm and carried it forward, stretching it out, the pleasure shuddering through every inch of me before wringing me dry.

We rolled, and I was on my back, looking up at him, his hand braced on the bed behind me, his muscular chest rising and falling before me, my body slick and sensitive around his cock. I raked my nails down his chest and along his abs, grabbing at his ass and encouraging him to go *deeper harder faster* in a voice I didn't even recognize as my own.

He moaned my name as he came, his eyes devouring mine, his orgasm hard and furious, as he thrust deeper, his breath coming faster, his eyes pinching shut as he gave one last shuddering grunt inside of me.

He fell beside me, the mattress squeaking, and blew out a hard breath. "Holy fuck, Autumn."

I didn't say anything. I didn't know what *to* say.

He rolled onto his side and sat up, heading into the bathroom. I lay there, the television still playing quietly in the background and tried to process my feelings.

I didn't even know sex could be like that. That combustive. That fulfilling. We hadn't felt like strangers. Where had been the awkwardness? The insecurities? In their place, there had only been this overwhelming wave of pleasure and sexuality and synergy. And now, in the moments afterward, I felt drunk on a heady mix of pleasure and emotion.

"Damn." He returned from the bathroom and crawled onto the bed, propping himself up above me. "That was insane." He gently tucked my hair behind my ear and kissed me with a tenderness that threatened to break my walls. "You're addicting, you know that?"

I managed a strangled half-laugh, watching as he rolled onto his back.

"Come here," he said gruffly, his hands prying me off the bed and pulling me against his chest. I let him roll me into his arms, my head comfortably against his shoulder, and frantically sorted through my feelings.

Happy? Check

Post-orgasmic bliss? Check

Concerned? Check, check, check, check ... check

Becoming friends with Declan Moss could only help my ability to protect him. But sleeping with him and developing feelings for him... that was a new ball of yarn. I wasn't sure it was feasible to protect him properly if I had romantic feelings for him. I certainly hadn't been looking out for any dangers in the last twenty minutes.

What had just happened was a mistake. I *had* to stay vigilant and focus on his safety.

Danger was lurking, and soon, my alarm bells would ring again. I could feel it coming. Building. Waiting to pounce.

I waited until Declan fell asleep, then carefully slid out of bed and snuck out of the room.

Mr. Oinks sighed, one hoof waving in the air as I rubbed his tummy. I stretched out my legs, my body deliciously worn out. I closed my eyes and inhaled deeply. *I slept with Declan Moss.* If I had a guardian angel advisor, she was no doubt up in heaven, screaming at me with a giant megaphone and finding a thunderbolt to smite me with.

The bad news was, I'd been completely at fault in all of this. Sure, I'd started off right. Outside of the sports bar, when he'd bent down to kiss me, his eyes full of smolders and sweetness, I'd pushed him away. Ranted and raved and successfully changed the subject until, ten minutes later, when I lost all sense and took a hard right-turn into Hoochieville. I blamed a combination of alcohol, abstinence, and that damn audiobook. What normal, slightly drunk, sexually deprived woman would be able to resist Declan Moss with bedroom eyes, shirt sleeves rolled up, massaging her feet?

No woman. NONE. I leaned back against the back porch post and absentmindedly scratched Mr. Oinks, his contented grunts adding to the chorus of frogs from my koi pond. I let my gaze wander over my yard's azalea-lined border, the faint smell of my orange trees in the air. I worked hard on this yard. Prior to Mom's passing, I'd rented one bedroom of it from Mr. Clevepepper, a sixty-three-year-old piano teacher. This yard had been a giant mess of weeds and grass tall enough to hit my knees. I cleared the bulk of it with a machete, unearthing two water moccasins before I invested in a pair of snake boots, the thick leather boots suffocating my poor feet as I hauled away the cuttings. Mr. Clevepepper's ancient lawnmower had bad gas, and it'd taken the help of the two high school boys to get it running. Mr. Clevepepper had watched me struggle from the air-conditioned comfort of the living room, grunting in disapproval when I would come in, sweaty and covered in dust, his eyes critically watching to make sure that I removed my boots before stepping off the front mat.

I teared up briefly at the memory of Mom seeing this yard for the first time, after all of my hard work. She'd hugged me and nodded in approval, then told me the hibiscus by the fence would never survive. I smiled. She'd been right. They'd wilted and died with the first cold snap, despite my ragged attempts to keep them warm.

A few months after she passed, I got approval from the trust to buy this house. Mr. C hadn't hesitated, picking out a Villages condo before the ink had dried on the contract, his heavy oak furniture loaded in a

U-Haul and rattling down the driveway without a backward glance. He didn't even let his students know. For two weeks after he left, I'd answered the doorbell to expectant clients, their sheet music in hand, confusion clouding their features when I told them Mr. Clevepepper didn't live here anymore. The first kid I told stood there for a long moment as he absorbed the news, then he literally threw the sheet music in the air and jumped up, his tiny fists punching the air, whooping with glee as he all but cartwheeled down the front steps to tell his mother, his lined pages left behind, littering my freshly-painted porch.

My second visitor took the news much more somberly, her face falling, liver-spotted hands plucking at the expensive string of pearls around her neck. "He just *left*?" she cried, her voice wobbling on the question. "Without saying goodbye?" I'd hugged her, unsure of what else to do, and had to hold my breath at the heavy scent of her perfume. Mr. Clevepepper, sneaky man, seemed to have broken a heart in his hasty exit.

I was properly concerned. The history books are full of untimely deaths, caused by broken hearts. Sometimes it's a heart attack or body shutdown. But there are more interesting side effects of separation. Take Kurt Godel, who would only eat food that had been cooked by his wife. When she was unexpectedly hospitalized for an extended period of time, he *starved* to death.

Ms. Clutch-Her-Pearls didn't die. I made sure to get her phone number and connected her with a younger, much more handsome, new piano teacher. We had lunch a few weeks later where she met a baby Mr. Oinks and lectured me on the dangers of sugar on my body. She was unhappy with her new instructor and planning a move to the Villages. She had already found Mr. Clevepepper on "the Facebook" and had a seduction plan in place that involved a pair of hot pink spandex pants and some fuzzy heels.

I was happy for her and hopeful of her plan, though I couldn't imagine anyone intentionally choosing to spend the rest of her life with a man who read National Geographic with his morning oatmeal. But c'est la vie. Everyone should find their person. Ideally, Declan's soulmate would be an emergency room doctor who enjoyed hanging out in padded rooms with a bland diet of non-chokeable, hypoallergenic food. I could be their gardener and nanny, hovering on the edge of their perfect life and popping in whenever my spidey sense went haywire.

I mused over a few other corrections I could make to my schedule and his, now that my subterfuge was no longer necessary. Access to his calendar, that was a must. And any travel arrangements, I'd need to know those in advance. I glanced at my watch, the only piece of my outfit he hadn't torn off, and wondered if I should wake him back up. I got to my feet, holding open the door for Mr. Oinks, before shutting and locking it behind us, then tiptoed down the hall, stopping by the mail hutch to grab a pen and notepad. Easing open the door, I crawled on top of the bed and peered down at him.

God, he was pretty. He'd thrown off most of the blanket, leaving his upper body exposed. He was on his back, one arm curled up under the pillow, his bicep impressively displayed. He had a tattoo on the underside of the muscle and I leaned forward, struggling to read the cursive. *Even angels fall.* I frowned, the tattoo a little morbid, especially given my self-proclaimed angel designation. I moved on from it, taking another moment to savor the look of his strong chest, notched abs, the peaceful angles of his handsome face. *He was safe.* Maybe waking him up was a bad idea. I sat back on my heels and reconsidered the thought. He had a nick on the edge of his jaw that I'd never been close enough to notice—a scar where no hair grew. Such thick eyelashes. God, a mascara company needed to hire him for ads. I'd use half a tube of Maybelline and come away with spider lashes before I ever achieved that.

There was a loud scratch at the bedpost and I looked down to see Mr. Oinks, his corkscrewed tail wagging, looking up at me. I shushed him, and the time for ogling was over. Not that it hadn't been justified. The chances of this bed ever having such a perfect male specimen again was embarrassingly low. Like ... Heidi Montag coming back into social relevance, low. Cleveland Browns winning the Super Bowl, low. Me sticking to my Weight Watchers points goal, low. Mr. Oinks scratched again and I refocused on the task, reaching forward and softly pushing a finger into Declan's chest. Wow. High-five to his workout regime. I slid the finger lower and tried again, this time in the first ridge of abs. He stirred, and I let my other hand play, drumming over the slack six-pack before nudging him. "Declan," I whispered. He grunted and I climbed higher on the bed, straddling his hips and leaning over him. I can't believe I had *sex* with him. And not just sex. *Filthy* sex. I made sounds I didn't know I had. He … I sighed, pushing away the swoony feelings that came into play with how sweet and tender he had been. I gently shook him by the shoulders. "Declan."

He opened his eyes, and blinked, focusing on my face. His free hand moved, sliding up my bare leg and gripping my thigh.

I ignored how much I enjoyed the connection and gently pushed it off. "I'm going to need access to your calendar. Will you tell your assistant?"

He blinked and seemed confused. "Okay."

"And travel arrangements."

"Okay." His voice was thick and he pulled his hand free from underneath his head and tugged me down, my weight awkwardly falling on his chest.

I struggled not to react, my arms slack at my side. I forced my mind off how deliciously warm his skin was and concentrated on my to-do list. He smelled amazing, a cocktail of scents I'd never experienced before. So, *this* is what romance novels were always trying to describe. His breathing started to deepen and I clamped down my focus before I lost him to sleep. "And your full medical records."

"Sure." His fingers ran up my back and I'd pay a thousand dollars for someone to do *that* every night. "You smell really good, Autumn Jones."

I searched widely for anything else I might need, since he seemed to be in such a giving mood. "Would you be open to a bodyguard? Someone non-obtrusive."

"Sure." He bent his head forward and inhaled deeply. I think he was *smelling* my hair. Had he meant it? *Did* I smell really good? I attempted my own secretive sniff, but came up with nothing but him.

Maybe he was smelling himself and confused. Though, now that I thought about it, I'm not certain we can smell ourselves. No, scratch that—after an afternoon in the yard, I had *definitely* smelled myself before. It's our own breath, I think that's what we can't smell.

"Relax." He nuzzled my neck, his fingertips continuing their lazy journey across my back. "You're all stiff."

I forced my muscles to slacken, aided by the dramatic sigh of Mr. Oinks as he gave up on getting into bed and flopped onto the floor, his hooves skittering into place.

I hadn't fallen asleep next to a man in years. The last attempt had been with a twenty-two-year-old barista who had eaten potato chips next to me while thumbing through channels. He'd half-heartedly offered me some of my own chips before shushing me, so he could hear the television. Mr. Oinks had liked him. He'd joined us in bed and licked the bag clean, finding several crumbs in the sheets and smacking his gums with excitement. I had told the guy that I didn't eat in bed, and didn't want to give Mr. Oinks any ideas, to which he had stared at me, before informing me that *Mr. Oinks was a pig*. As if the giant nostrils and fat pink belly didn't give it away. I had kicked him out a few minutes later, slamming the door dramatically and swearing on a stack of Cosmos that I was done with men forever.

But this wasn't all that bad. It was pretty great, actually. I rested my head on his chest and closed my eyes. Maybe, for a few minutes, I could forget about all of the latent dangers, ignore my responsibilities, and just enjoy the moment.

From the floor, Mr. Oinks grunted in approval.

22

Declan woke up alone, the sun streaming through half-closed blinds and painting lines across the opposite wall. Lifting his head, he listened, the faint sound of voices coming from somewhere else in the house. He looked around for his phone and winced at the time. Almost nine-fifteen. Late. Then again, he hadn't had that sort of workout in a while. He grinned and swung his legs over the side of the bed and stood, finding his jeans in the corner of the room and pulling them on. His shirt was twisted in the sheets. He unbuttoned it and pulled the first sleeve on as he walked down the hall, following the voices.

The hall opened to a living room, one he vaguely remembered passing through last night. What he hadn't noticed then was the dining room alcove, situated on the far end of the room. The space was now filled with Autumn and three men in suits. He came to a stop, wary at the sight of the strangers, who all hulked over Autumn. She flitted between their intimidating builds, a clipboard in hand, and didn't hesitate at the sight of him. "Oh good, you're awake!" She beamed, and he couldn't help matching her smile. She was so gorgeous, especially like this—barefoot in a thin white T-shirt and faded jeans, her hair loose and wild, eyes bright and excited. She whirled to one side and pointed to the first suit. "This is—" she consulted her clipboard—"Mark. And Cooper." Her pen swung to the third man. "And France. I've already spoken to each of them, but thought you might want to do mini-interviews before we made a decision? Or, several decisions?"

He'd missed something. He slowly pulled his arm through the second sleeve and tried to piece together the clues. Big strangers. That he was interviewing. For him and Autumn to make a decision. Or several decisions. He worked his hand through the cuff and didn't miss the brief moment when Autumn's eyes dropped to his abs. He tightened them and appreciated the flush that hit her cheeks. God, she'd been so fucking sexy last night. So expressive. So responsive. She'd come alive under his touch, demanding pleasure while delivering it, her body bucking under his, her legs wrapping around him, hands traveling all over him. He met her eyes and grinned, fighting the urge to lift her over his shoulder and carry her back in the bedroom right now, random strangers with unknown purposes be damned.

She put a fist on her hip and raised her eyebrows. "Well?" Judging by the all-business look on her face, she wasn't as blown away from last night's memories as he was. If he did heft her over his shoulder, she'd most likely knee him in the balls.

"Could I talk to you for a moment?" He stepped back and tilted his head toward the porch. "Alone?"

"Sure." She tossed her clipboard on the table and moved through the living room and out the front door, holding it for him. "But you should button up that shirt before you give my neighbors a heart attack."

He shut the door behind them and glanced through its window, checking on the three men, who were all still in place. He turned to Autumn. "I seem to be missing something. *Who* are these guys?"

"Potential bodyguards." She delivered the statement as if it was perfectly reasonable.

"For you? Is this because of the guy from last night?" That wasn't a bad idea. She'd had a traumatic experience and needed to know that she was safe. It was overkill, but if it helped her to... She shook her head, interrupting his chain of thought.

"No. For you. You agreed on a bodyguard."

"No, I didn't."

"Uh... yeah, you did. In bed. Right after you told me that I could have access to your calendar and travel schedule."

He shook his head. "No. I didn't say any of those things."

She huffed out an irritated breath. "Yessss, you *did*. You can't change your mind now. I already signed a contract with the security firm."

"You WHAT?"

There was a cheerful honk from behind them, and he turned to see a minivan pull in next to his truck, the passenger door opening. A miniature blonde body tore around the front of the van and sprinted across the lawn and onto the porch, her arms outstretched. "Auttieeeeee!"

Autumn bent down to pick up the child, who started talking the moment her feet left the ground. "Mommy let me drive in the neighborhood. I steered and everything."

"Oh really?" Autumn rubbed her nose against the child, and his heart skipped a beat at the sight. The child looked like it could be her own, and he shifted uncomfortably at the rapid right turn his brain took at the vision. It must be the sex, clouding his brain and sending his thoughts into left field.

Speaking of which.... He angled left, trying to get in Autumn's line of vision. "What do you mean, you signed a contract?" He couldn't afford bodyguards, and had definitely not agreed to one, much less three.

"Hello." An older version of Autumn stopped on the bottom step, a toddler in hand, and looked up at him. It was the cute mom from his neighborhood, the one married to the pencil pusher. And oh... the pieces clicked into place. Autumn had mentioned a sister, who lived by him. This was her? Sister and cute mom were one and the same? Maybe she hadn't been checking him out when he'd run by. Maybe she had been taking notes and reporting back to Autumn. His self-esteem slumped off to lick its wounds.

The woman peered at him. "You don't look like Adam."

And... who was Adam? He had never experienced jealousy with Nicola, but it suddenly barreled into this situation, ears pricked and guns holstered.

"Adam's in love with his ex-girlfriend," Autumn tossed over her shoulder as she put down the blonde child. "This is Declan. I mean, I know you know who he is, but it feels like we are crazy people if we act like you know who he is."

"Right." The woman's grin widened as she met Declan's eyes. "Because, obviously, we aren't crazy."

"I'm Paige!" The young girl stepped forward, somberly sticking out her hand while sporting a one-tooth-missing grin.

He bent at the waist and shook her hand. She let go and skipped past him, yanking open the front door and swooping into the house. He glanced at the boy, who hid behind his mother's leg.

"This is Caleb," the woman offered. "And I'm Ansley, Autumn's sister." Hypothesis confirmed, though his confusion was still at nuclear levels.

"There are STRANGERS in your house!" Paige reappeared in the front door, alarm on her face. "Three STRANGERS!"

For shit's sake. This was a three-ring circus. Autumn waved her inside. "They're safe. Just ignore them and take Mr. Oinks outside. Help him find his ball. You too, Caleb."

The little boy sprinted past Declan as if he was the boogie man, leaving his mother standing on the step. Ansley folded her arms across her chest, a knowing expression tugging at her mouth as she glanced between him and Autumn. "So... this is an interesting course of events."

"Super interesting," Autumn agreed. "Turns out, Declan is absolutely cool with me protecting him, and we are ramping up security protocols to improve his safety." She turned on one foot, breezing past him and into the house, his attempt to catch her arm easily thwarted with a move that could have earned her a Heisman.

He followed her into the house, the screen door almost slapping him in the face. "We need to discuss this. I don't know *what* you're talking about, but there's no way any of these guys"—he nodded to the suits who were still in their place around the table—"are following me around."

Autumn stopped on her way to the kitchen and turned, peering up at him. "You said I could."

"I strongly disagree with that statement."

"You were a little sleepy." She shrugged. "But you did, you told me I could hire these guys, and now I have so...." She smiled sweetly up at him.

He narrowed his eyes, her eyelashes literally batting at him. "You can't do that. I can't"—he lowered his voice—"I can't afford them."

"Oh!" She waved a hand in the air. "I'm paying for them. Don't worry about *that*." She dismissed the costs of three armed guards as if she was covering his hamburger at a fast food joint.

He glanced at the security and stepped closer to her, resisting the urge to cup her waist and drag her against him. "I don't think you can protect someone against their will. If I don't want them following me, they can't follow me."

"Ah, but that statement flies directly in the face of her full-time job," Ansley butted in, her voice sing-songy as she waltzed past them and into the kitchen, pulling a gallon of milk out of the fridge.

"Look how quiet they are," Autumn pointed out. "It's like they aren't even here!"

Declan gritted his teeth. "I'm going to say it one more time, and then I'm going to walk out of here. I don't know what I told you last night, after whatever voodoo magic your body unleashed, but I'm not having a bodyguard. And I'm not sharing my schedule or notifying you of travel arrangements." He pointed to the trio of men. "If I see any of you anywhere near me, I'm calling the police."

He stepped back and Autumn's face fell in disappointment. "But..."

Before she had the chance to say another word, or bat those big eyes, or seduce his mind into signing over his entire life, he stormed out the front door and got into his truck, leaving all of the crazy behind.

23

I sent the gentlemen from Met Security on their way with a plate of brownies, mucho apologies, and a voided contract. They let me keep my deposit, which was a nice gesture, especially considering the early Saturday house call. Ansley didn't let me off the hook as easily.

"Voodoo Magic your body is unleashing? This I need to hear. Now, sit. Drink. Talk." She pushed a hot cup of coffee toward me and took the closest stool. From the backyard, Paige and Caleb tore back into the house, chased by Mr. Oinks. Ansley pointed to the living room without turning her head. "Watch cartoons," she called out.

"Nickelodeon?" Paige called out.

"Sure. Whatever."

"Easy. That's a slippery slope to a life of crime." I widened my eyes theatrically. Paige's ban of SpongeBob was completely unfounded, and a rule I broke with wild abandon every time I babysat her kids.

"Shut up and talk. Please tell me he made passionate love to you all night long." She clasped her hands in front of her as if in prayer.

"Yes." I lifted the coffee cup and took a tentative sip. It wasn't bad. Too much sugar, but I could deal with that.

"NO," she gasped, covering her mouth with one Alex & Ani-laden hand.

"YES," I whispered, hiding my grin behind another sip of the coffee. "But that's all over now."

"All over," she said slowly. "Why is it all over?"

"Well, you saw his dramatic exit, in which he threatened to call the cops." I listed the first hurdle off with my thumb, then moved on to my index finger. "Then the bigger issue, which is that I am *not* here to have wild and delicious sex with Declan Moss."

"You're not?"

"No. I'm here to *protect* him." It's like she doesn't understand what mortal danger is. A PLANE almost smote him. It took out a Toyota Highlander. There was a mailbox who never got to say goodbye to its family. Half a house that was pulverized in the explosion. Everyone was just tossing this humongous event aside as if it was a fender bender in the Publix shopping center.

"Oh, God." Ansley rolled her eyes. "Have you ever thought that this is the universe pushing you two together? Just ignore your ridiculous idea of premonitions and mortal dangers and embrace the fact that a real live man spent last night in your bed."

I groaned, wilting sideways on the stool. "And oh my God, it was so good. Ansley... he..." I tried to find the words to describe the event.

"Was talented?"

"Beyond talented. Could be a gigolo in his spare time."

She slid the coffee creamer in between us and looked down at it suggestively. "Would you say he's *built* like a gigolo also?" She ran her hand up the height of the jug in a way that made her meaning perfectly clear.

I knocked her hand off the container before she started jacking it off. "I don't want to ruin your day with a detailed description of how gorgeous his coffee creamer was. Just know that keeping him safe has become a lot *harder* to do." I pulled open the fridge and stuck the creamer on the shelf.

"Oh, a lady? That's what you are?" Ansley scoffed, giving an exaggerated nod. "Good to know. Alright, penis size aside, just tell me. Was it just sex or was there emotion in it?"

Of course, my sister would ask the one question I didn't want to ask myself. I scratched an itchy place on my scalp. "I don't think two strangers can have emotions between them."

"He's not a stranger to you," she pointed out. "You've known him, in some way shape or form, for ... what, three months now?"

"Six," I corrected her. "It was right after Mom." *Died.* I couldn't say it, but didn't need to. I straddled the stool and picked up my coffee.

"Right." Her voice softened. "So... six months. I've never asked you, because you're so damn business-like about the entire thing, but don't you think you've developed some feelings for him during that time?"

"No!" I pshawed the idea, blowing on the top of my coffee in an off-hand gesture that completely hid the windmill of thoughts that churned around my skull.

I hadn't developed feelings for Declan. Not when I saw him drop off a bagel every morning for the homeless woman who sleeps behind the downtown bus stop. Not when I saw him play basketball with Ansley's neighborhood kids. And not when I watched him laugh, his eyes crinkling, teeth showing, dimple popping. Or when he worked over lunch, his glasses on, pen scratching across a pad of paper, handsome brow furrowed.

I had not developed any feelings whatsoever for Declan Moss. And those non-existent feelings had definitely not deepened by having his eyes soften when they'd roamed over my body. My professional composure hadn't cracked when he'd whispered my name across my skin, his lips skimming, breath tickling. I hadn't fallen even a little bit when he'd been inside of me, his mouth on mine, the warm weight of his naked body above me.

"It's okay if you like him," Ansley said gently.

"I don't." I shook my head emphatically and she gave me a *look*, the sort of one she used to give me when I ate all the ice cream and then lied about it. But the truth was, it didn't matter if I liked Declan Moss. It was irrelevant. Declan Moss may have given me the best sex of my life, but I wasn't going to stack orgasms and tingly kisses on top of a man's safety and well-being. End of discussion. Goodbye, toe-curling ecstasy. Hello, binoculars and portable first aid kit.

"And he doesn't like you?" Ansley scooted her stool closer to the counter and pried open the foil on the plate of remaining brownies.

I ignored her question, moving back through Declan's last words, directed at the bodyguards. *"If I see any of you anywhere near me, I'm calling the police."* Maybe it *had* been a little too sudden of me, to call the security company and conduct interviews. I'd just gotten excited at the prospect of bringing in professionals, men with guns, advanced surveillance, and those cool little ear mics.

Ansley broke one chocolatey square in half, offering it to me. I dipped it into the coffee and took a small bite, trying to find a new angle to approach him with. Something to do sober, with my clothes on, all professional-like.

"Let's talk about damage control." Ansley tapped the counter in front of me to catch my attention.

"Okay." I pulled my hair into a high ponytail. "Damage control. How do I do that?"

"I think you should give him some time," Ansley suggested. "You've just freaked him out a little. I mean"—she gestured to the bare spot where the bodyguards had previously stood—"I don't know why you thought inviting three Dwayne Johnson lookalikes to a post-sex breakfast was a good idea, but I can go out on a limb and say that he probably thinks you're insane. Especially if you told him the reason you're following him."

I considered her advice. It was pretty solid. I could give him a few days. Let him cool off, then approach him with an organized proposal, the start of a negotiation, one where I'd wow him with my PowerPoint skills and he'd turn over full access to his life, or at least his calendar. And I could drop the idea of bodyguards for now. That request came from an ego inflated on post-coitus bliss, encouraged by his easy acceptance of my other requests. In hindsight, maybe I should have made sure he was fully awake.

"So, I should leave him alone." I tested the idea aloud. "For a few days."

"YES." She smiled, and she had dots of chocolate in her teeth. "Just forget about him for a little bit. Let him come back to you. Trust me, he will. And in the meantime, maybe you can find a new focus for your life. Something that doesn't involve this gorgeously virile man who you have absolutely no attraction for."

"I'm working on a scrapbook for Mrs. Robchek," I pointed out. "A new one."

"Awesome," she said dryly. "Anything else?"

I fell silent, my life pretty empty once you pulled out Mrs. Robchek's latest keepsake. My backyard had never looked more beautiful, the damn thing behaving perfectly with only an hour or two of work per week. I was considering ripping out the front planters just to give myself something to do. "Maybe I'll go back to—"

"You're not going back to school," she interrupted. "You've graduated from that damn school twice now. The only thing you're learning is how to throw money away on useless degrees."

I made a face at her, twisting in my seat to avoid the sight of the framed diplomas, hung neatly beside my fridge. My mind flitted back to Dr. E's recent suggestion that I start a business. I had wasted a lot of time thinking over what I might do, but short of starting a pig rescue farm, I was drawing a blank.

"And when's the last time that Mrs. Robchek paid you?" Her chocolate teeth situation was getting worse, but interrupting her to point it out would have been rude. Better to let her waltz off to Trader Joe's with a muddy smile, since she had so much nitpicking on her plate. I ran my hand over the granite island top and wondered if they were still running the special on mangoes. If they were, I'd have her pick me up some. A mango and strawberry salad sounded scrumptious.

"Huh?" She reached over and poked me.

"Mrs. Robchek's on a limited budget," I defended the poor old woman.

"Then she needs to stop ordering scrapbooks for her dog. There aren't that many events that need chronologizing in a dog's life. And speaking of which..." she glared at me. "I haven't even gotten a scrapbook for Caleb yet. And he's THREE."

"I'm working on Caleb's book," I promised. "It's going to be fabulous." Talk about demanding clients who didn't pay. At least Mrs. Robchek walked Mittens and Morkie past Declan's house three times a day and gave me updates. With that sort of intel, who needed timely payments?

She stood up and stretched, her body twisting left and right as she attempted to pop her back. "Don't forget, we're going to the fair next weekend."

I nodded, stealing the remainder of her brownies.

"There's still an open invitation for you to come. You can ride the Gravitron and barf on teenagers."

"As delightful as that sounds, I think I'll pass."

"Whatever." She shrugged, and lifted her bag over her shoulder. "I'm headed to get groceries. Want to come?"

I mused over the idea of staying, stretching out on the couch with Mr. Oinks and watching Squidward giving Spongebob the business. Instead, I pulled a paper towel off the roll and passed it to her. "Sure. And here. You've got brownie all over your teeth."

24

The day of the plane crash had started with a dick. One in full color and high resolution in the text messages of Nicola's phone. Declan had stared at the image, unable to comprehend what it meant. His eyes had slowly dragged up to the text that had preceded the image.

Still hungry? I got something for you...

The dick pic came from a sender named Brittany Gym, which was equally puzzling, until he realized that Brittany was a code name, and whoever had sent the photo had clearly screwed his girlfriend, and on multiple occasions. He scrolled back through the text history, his anger growing with each one. By the time he got to the earliest text, one three months old, he'd wanted to rip the phone in half and climb a hundred-story building, just to chuck it off the roof.

He'd resisted the urge to go through every one of her other text conversations and set down the phone, yanked on his Nikes, and gone for a run. He'd been on his third mile when the dog had taken him down. If Autumn Jones had been anywhere in the vicinity, he hadn't seen her. He hadn't been able to see anything but that damn penis, the pic taken in a restroom, khakis and dress shoes underneath it.

The image had disappeared from his mind when he'd been knocked on the ground, the dog exuberantly happy, his wet tongue swiping over every nook and cranny of Declan's face, his breath horrible, saliva-dripping, dirty paws firmly planted on his chest. Then, there had been the deafening noise of the engine. The rigid shudder of the impact. The heat from the fire.

Nicola had been waiting for him at the hospital, her face pinched in concern, that treacherous phone gripped against her chest, with no idea of what he'd seen. It wasn't until after the tests, his minor scrapes and burns patched up, that he had confronted her with the truth and ended things.

Now, he sat at his office and clicked past photos of the crash. Miraculously enough, the pilot had lived, along with his nine-year-old daughter, who he'd pulled free of the cockpit, despite his broken back. The plane had nosedived into an SUV, pushing the vehicle into a home, the left wing taking out the mid-century modern's dining and living room. He clicked forward, the newspaper's photos giving him a close-up view of the charred Highlander, the deep tracks in the lawn, the black scorch marks from the fire.

In all of the madness, he hadn't taken the time to think through what would have happened if the dog hadn't tackled him. If he had followed the path he had taken on his prior laps, he would have continued down the street until the dead end, then turned left and gone up the hill. Unfortunately, Autumn Jones was correct. Had he continued straight, and been twenty yards farther, he would have been directly in the path of the plane.

Or… he could have stopped to tie his shoe. Or stretched. Or decided to pull out his phone and end things with Nicola right there. There was no guarantee that fate wouldn't have intervened in a dozen other ways than that stupid dog.

On the nineteenth photo in the slideshow, he saw Autumn. On the edge of the frame, lying on the ground, a paramedic bent over her. She hadn't mentioned getting hurt, and he frowned, zooming in on the photo and trying to see her injury.

"Hey." Nate appeared in the doorway. "Lunch is here. And we have that call with Benta at two."

Declan nodded. "Give me a second." The next picture was an aerial shot of the crash, the plane dominating the shot, him and Autumn gone by the time the photo was taken. He frowned, remembering his own trajectory, then examined the aerial photo closer, zooming in on the dog's yard, the gate still open in the pic.

What had prompted Autumn to open the dog's gate? Why would someone do that? He knew that dog, had run by it a dozen times before. He had always thought it was dangerous, as—he assumed—she had as well. For a woman so obsessed with safety, the prudent thing would have been to lock the gate tighter, not let the damn thing out. They were both lucky it had been friendly and not the snarling attack dog it always appeared to be.

He found her sister's house on the map, the crash in between the dog's gate and her split-level ranch. He frowned. Had Autumn been on her way back, or on her way out? If she'd been on her way home... he ran his fingers along the path, her journey to release the dog one that would have taken her a few minutes.

Technically, if she hadn't detoured to release the Great Dane, she herself could have been passing by the Highlander, directly in the path of the plane.

She was so convinced that she had saved his life, but was it possible that letting out the dog had also saved hers?

Eleven hours of design work, and his back was screaming in protest. Declan leaned back, then threw the ball forward, watching as it hit the garage door and bounced back, ricocheting off the driveway and into his hand. He repeated the motion, shuffling left to catch the bounce. He thought of his dining room table, covered with their marked-up plans, and groaned. They had at least another two hours of work before they could call this a day. Still, despite the long hours and hellacious reworks, it was exciting work—fueled by Nate's exuberance for the project. Thanks to Bridget's sleuthing, they now knew the full scope of Benta Aldrete's purposes for the space—an erotic playground for her family's online sexual matchmaking enterprise. It had certainly amped up the entertainment factor in their sketches, as well as decimated any chances of Nate losing interest in their client. Still, Benta Aldrete had shown an incredible ability to resist his charms, a stonewall that was only encouraging the man.

They were both going through a rough streak. It'd been three days since he had fallen into Autumn Jones' bed and she hadn't so much as blinked in his direction. No glimpses of her at Starbucks, no blonde hair flashing through his peripheral vision… nothing.

"Just give up and call her." Nate tilted back in a lawn chair, a bright green Gatorade bottle in hand.

"Nah." Declan scooped down to catch a low bounce. He couldn't call her. She should be calling him. She owed him an apology. Blinded by a buzz and the impact of her beauty, he'd been pretty cool over her delusion of guardian angelship. That allowance hadn't given her free rein to plow over any boundaries and elbow her way into his personal space with three earpiece-wearing strangers. He shook his head. "She's too invasive for me."

"She's *been* crazy, man. You can't suddenly be surprised at that." Nate swatted at a wandering fly. "Let's discuss the bigger situation."

"Which is what?" Declan turned and tossed him the ball without warning, Nate dropping the bottle to catch it.

"That you didn't deliver the dick properly. Three days without her calling you?" He lifted one eyebrow. "That's a sign."

Declan held up his hand for the ball, shaking off the insult with a smile. Autumn Jones may be stubborn as hell when it came to apologizing, but there was no way that a disappointing night in bed was the cause for her silence. That bed had almost caught on fire from their chemistry. He tried to push away the memory of her body, curving and flexing beneath his, her soft moans and gasps… hell, his back still carried the marks of her nails. She'd been a sexual animal, which had been an unexpected surprise, one he hadn't been able to get out of his head. Distracted at the thought, he missed the ball when Nate threw it back.

"Brush it off," Nate called after him. "We can't all be blessed with raw sexual talent."

"Says the guy who can't close Benta Aldrete." The ball rolled under a bush, and Declan moved into the push-up position and reached out, swiping at it. "Not that I want you to," he called. As talented as Nate was at landing women, he was even more skilled at tossing them aside.

"Hey," Nate called out. "Don't talk shit about my future wife. We're a work in progress. And getting back to you, you need to sort it out ASAP. I'm not having you mope through this weekend."

Declan stood up, swinging his arm in the socket to loosen up the muscle. "What's this weekend?"

Nate glared at him. "Come on. My *birthday*. The hunting camp. Beer. Steaks. Skeet." He waited for Declan to respond, his face falling at the blank expression. "There's no way you forgot this."

"I didn't forget it," Declan lied, his mind riffling through all of the work he'd have to finish before they left. Normally, he'd enjoy a chance to get out in the woods and blow off some steam. But his mind was too twisted over Autumn and this project. Wasting a weekend on Nate's stories and shooting … sounded like hell.

Nate got that look in his eye, the one that typically preceded a terrible idea. "Maybe you could invite your girl. Flex your masculinity some. Impress her."

Your girl. He would wager a guess that Autumn wouldn't be in love with that moniker. He squinted at Nate. "You want Autumn, the 'crazy bitch' as you've referred to her, to come with us on your birthday weekend?"

"Look." Nate leaned forward. "You called her that too. I didn't know—we didn't know—that there were going to be sparks between you two."

He started to argue that fact, but Nate had already given him three days' worth of grief over the fact that he considered Declan to be *smitten*. That was the actual word he'd used—over-used—as he had tortured every detail of the night out of him. Well, not every detail. He was, despite all the evidence to the contrary, a gentleman.

He threw the ball toward the garage door, and mused over the idea of inviting Autumn to the camp. "It'd be awkward, the three of us."

"You're right." Nate was as transparent as glass as he 'pondered' their dilemma and then 'came up' with a solution. "I could convince Benta to stay over for the weekend. It could be fun."

"No," Declan said flatly, catching the ball and slinging it back with more aggression than necessary. "I'd like to actually keep this client until we finish and are paid."

"Dude. It's my *birthday*. I don't want to sit in the fucking woods and stare at you and your girlfriend all weekend."

This is how people died. He turned to Nate, ready to shove that Gatorade bottle down his throat, and stopped at the wide grin on his face. The issue was, he was impossible to be mad at. It was the most infuriating quality about the guy, yet the one that saved their asses more times than anything. He pointed at Nate and struggled to keep his own smile off his face. "Listen to me when I say that you cannot fuck up this Benta Aldrete situation. Do you understand?"

Nate spread his arms in a 'surrender' gesture. "Never planned on it."

Right. He never did. Declan turned back to the garage, swinging his arms and fighting against the knot of tension between his shoulder blades. Should he invite Autumn to the camp? It wasn't likely she'd come. With her silence, and complete absence from his life, she had likely moved on from him altogether, and found another charity project to shower with care and protective actions. Inviting her would be the worst thing to do right now, and would reopen the door to let the crazy back in.

Only… he kind of liked her crazy. He wasn't smitten. Nate was wrong about that, despite all of his knowing glances and *I've known you for fifteen years* bullshit. He wasn't smitten, but he did want more of her. Was she mental? Probably. But if someone was going to be off-her-rocker about one thing, this was a pretty good flaw. It was like being overly neat—an affliction Nicola had stamped on him more times than he could count. Or overly loyal.

So, what if she did truly believe that she was tasked with protecting him? So what? It was kind of nice to have someone so utterly devoted to maintaining your safety and well-being. The way she had examined him outside that bar, such concern in her features... it had been sweet. Warm. Touching. Assuming she hadn't moved on to someone else, it'd be nice to have that focus swung back in his direction.

But she'd never agree to go to the camp. It was too dangerous. Guns. Poison Ivy. Splinter possibilities everywhere. Some rare tick that caused sudden death.

He smiled at the thought, then realized the truth of the matter—the surefire way to get her to go would be because it was dangerous. If she really thought that she had some unique ability to ward off danger, she would feel obligated to go.

It was like holding a secret weapon. Would using it be evil? *Probably*. Manipulative? *Yes*. Was having her there worth it?

He rolled the tennis ball through his fingers and slowly warmed to the idea.

25

Out of every hobby imaginable, scrapbooking is one of the safest. The scissors are the most dangerous part of it. Get over-enthusiastic with your cutting, and you might nip off part of a finger. The glue is another danger zone, but you have to be intentionally reckless to sniff yourself to death.

I sat at the dining room table, dangerous glue bottle in hand, and carefully laid down a white line for the border, which I planned to highlight using a glittery silver rope. On the radio, Sam Cooke crooned. I really loved Sam Cooke, but talk about an unromantic way to die. Shot by a hotel manager after attempting to rape a girl. Or, if you believed the theories, set up by a prostitute, robbed, and *then* shot by a hotel manager. Either way, had the man been at home with his sweet little wife? He wouldn't have died. I pressed a heart to the construction paper, holding it in place while it dried.

I rolled my bare feet along Mr. Oinks' belly and listened to him snore.

It was very boring, not having Declan Moss to protect. My worry still ran through my head, but without knowing where he was, and what he was doing… I didn't have much to worry about. I felt hopeless, being so far away from him. I closed my eyes, a dull headache still lingering, despite the 800 mg of Ibuprofen I'd taken. What if my head went haywire right here? What would I do? I had no idea where Declan was. The best I could do would be to get in my car, head in the direction of his office, and likely die of an aneurysm on the way.

If Ansley were here, she'd tell me that I was an idiot. She'd point out, if I *did* have this hypothetical power of danger prediction, that it wasn't necessarily confined to Declan. Maybe I could protect anyone in sudden danger. Then again, I'd only gotten the piercing pain and nausea spells three times. Once, the day of the plane crash. And then three weeks ago, right before Declan stepped in front of that truck. And then a small episode at the bar, during the fight.

Three instances. All with Declan. My head still hurt just from the memory of it. I rubbed my forehead, nursing my current headache and wondered if there were lingering side effects of this condition.

Beside me, my phone sat, silent. I could call him. He'd left his business card on my bedside table, his cell phone circled in one of Paige's red magic markers. In a normal situation, I would have called him already. Thanked him for his return of my heels, and apologized for bringing the men over without having a middle-of-the-day, fully awake, conversation about it.

But… there was the slight issue of our sex. Lots and lots of thrusting. Kissing. Bodies rubbing. Moaning. I crossed my legs together to try and satisfy the ache of desire that bloomed at the memory. It wouldn't have been so bad if I hadn't been so…. I paused, half of the silver cord put into place, and tried to find the right adjective. Carnal? Ravenous? Jenna Jamesony? Let's face it. If I'd had a cowboy hat handy, I would have been whooping and waving that thing in the air, a bridle quickly fashioned out of my bra straps.

I'd been an embarrassment to guardian angels everywhere. How could I ever *attempt* to have a serious conversation with him about his personal safety when he knew what I *tasted* like? Oh God. I dropped my head down on the page without thinking, my forehead landing smack in the middle of a dab of glitter paint.

Even if I pushed the guardian angel stuff aside and just focused on bare womanhood, there was a precedent set. Mom hadn't taught me much, short of the atomic weight of Mercury, but she had ingrained a few rules in me from the time I could talk.

Chewing gum in public is tacky. She once elbowed me so hard that I fell over, to point out a Mercedes-driving blonde with a mouthful of Big Red. *Tacky* was a word she liked to use a lot. Miracle Whip was also tacky. And ripped jeans. And convertibles. And hoop earrings and scrunchies.

Always pass the salt with the pepper. I once skipped this rule at Sonny's BBQ, and mom *threw* the salt shaker at my wrist. It was a heavy glass one, the sort that pairs with a pepper grinder, and left a swollen black bruise for a week. That was around the time that Ansley and I started to realize Mom was a little off her rocker.

Women don't call men. Period. If there was an occasion where we needed to speak, they could figure that out and call us. Granted, this rule only applied during the courtship period and could be abandoned without thought once a relationship had progressed to commitment, but should be picked back up during times of fighting or punishable male behavior. But after a date? It was always the man's job to call a woman. On a holiday? Man's job. If your roof had caved in and you needed assistance from the hunky next-door neighbor? He had eyes. He could damn well figure out what a damsel in distress was.

Obviously salt shakers and chewing gum didn't apply here. But I had always agreed with her firm stance on not calling men. Of course, I was also approaching thirty and single, so it was entirely possible that said firm stance was kryptonite in today's female-empowered dating environment.

I lifted up my head and eyed the phone, willing it to ring. My phone number was listed. He had access to the Internet. Three seconds of searching, and he'd have it in hand.

I rubbed at my forehead, the glitter addition stubborn, and licked my finger to give it more oomph.

Maybe he was busy. Working away, designing someone's next office complex. I uncapped a bright purple marker and began to fill in the page's title. Maybe I should become an architect. How hard could that degree be? You're just *drawing* stuff. Adding eaves. Creating little squares and labeling them MASTER BEDROOM and KITCHEN. Tilting back my chair, I snuck a sniff of the grape-scented marker and envisioned it. I could work in his firm. Be an apprentice. Establish clear evacuation and emergency plans while keeping an eye on him.

The doorbell rang and Mr. Oinks slipped and skittered along the tile in an attempt to get to his feet. I caught a glimpse of his cute little hooves before he knocked my chair over and I slammed backward against the tile.

Ouch. I lay there for a moment, assessing my injuries. My head was saved, though the impact had kicked up my headache a notch. The high-backed chair had seriously dented my shoulder blades and my knee had knocked against the table, an impact that was still vibrating through me.

Mr. Oinks began to jump against the front door. The doorbell rang again and I groaned in response and attempted to roll to one side. "Just leave it, Don!" I called out, listening to Mr. Oinks work himself into a lather. "I don't need to sign it!"

I waited for the sound of my delivery driver's feet, heavy down the front steps, but there was only silence, followed by a strong knock against the wood. *Jeez Louise.* I dragged myself along the floor, untangling my damaged knee from the chair of death and struggled to my feet. Hobbling to the front door, I ignored Mr. Oinks' frantic grunts and twisted the handle, pulling the door open.

It wasn't my lovable delivery man, beaming and expecting a bottled water. It was Declan. He rested one hand on the doorjamb, had his phone out in the other, and looked up as I swung open the door. My hurt knee threatened to buckle, and it was completely due to the injury and not the fact that he was in a button-up and tie and delicious enough to eat with a spoon. I'd seen a suited Declan Moss before, but always from afar. Close up… I felt a little faint.

"Am… I… interrupting something?" He scanned me from head to toe and the corner of his mouth twitched into a grin.

"Actually, yes." I pulled down on the front of my Hulk Hogan shirt, and cursed myself for not wearing a bra. I also could have thrown on something other than these baggy sweatpants, which had a fresh blackberry jam stain from my breakfast. "I'm working."

His gaze lingered on my face, and I reached up to brush at the glitter spot in the middle of my forehead. "Any chance you'd like to get lunch? To discuss my safety, of course." He added the last sentence in grave undertones, and I was too flustered to tell if he was making a joke or being serious.

"Ummm... lunch?" I stalled. "Right now?"

He glanced at his watch. "I could wait in the truck if you need some time. I just need to get back to the office by two."

I drummed my fingers along the doorknob. Lunch sounded innocent enough. To discuss his safety. How could I refuse *that*? I glanced down at my t-shirt and sweats. "Sure. I just need five minutes."

He smiled, and he must have shaved this morning. It was odd, to see him without the light facial hair. "Sure. I can wait out here."

"Oh." I stepped back and gestured him in. "No. Come on in. Just..." I looked around. "Make yourself comfortable. You remember Mr. Oinks."

He bent down and gave him a scratch. "Hey bud."

"I'll go get dressed." I stepped back, doing a quick scan of the living room for anything embarrassing. My search came up clean and I skirted around Mr. Oinks and headed down the hall. "Five minutes!" I called out.

Who knew where I got five minutes from, considering I took that long just to floss. I warred between taking longer to look nice, and the risks that leaving an unattended man in my living room presented. I hesitated in the doorway of my room, then stripped, pulling on a pair of worn jeans, bra and a Wonder Woman tee. Grabbing a pair of yellow Converse and socks, I worked them on and listened for noises from the living room. Was that a cabinet door opening? I yanked at the final knot of my laces and breezed into the bathroom, coming to a sudden stop when I saw my reflection in the mirror.

Bright purple marker ran a jagged line across the tip of my nose and down my chin. It must have happened during the chair fall. The glitter on my forehead was almost unnoticeable compared to the thick doodle that covered half my face. I rushed to the sink, turning on the water and dousing a washcloth. "No....no!" I injected four pumps of hand soap into the terrycloth and leaned close to the mirror, scrubbing furiously at the crooked line. I breathed a sigh of relief as it faded, and sent grateful praise up to the angels at Crayola, for favoring washability over longevity.

At least fifteen minutes had passed before I made it back to the living room, half of my face red and tender from scrubbing. Declan sat on the floor, Mr. Oinks' head resting on his ankle, and held my fallen chair on his knees. A screwdriver and toolbox sat next to him. He looked up and smiled. "Looks like your chair quit on you."

I struggled not to swoon at the image and crouched beside him, running a hand over the pig's belly. "Did it break?"

"It was fixable." He held a staple gun in one hand and fired off a shot into a joint. "Almost good as new."

"You didn't have to..." I stammered, getting to my feet and helping him up. I watched as he slid the chair back into its proper place, then tested it with his hands. "Thank you."

"You might want to hide it if anyone with some heft to them comes over. I can't vouch for its stability." He dipped down to grab the screwdriver and staple box. "Here, I found these under the kitchen sink."

Thank God he hadn't opened the coat closet. Talk about risking death. I'd have found him under a pile of clutter, gasping for air. I took the items from him. "Again, thank you."

It wasn't fair. I couldn't be expected to resist feelings for a man who looked past my crazy behavior, fixed my chair, and was now crouching down and scratching Mr. Oinks on the head, the pig's eyes closed in bliss. I busied myself putting the items back, watching him out of my peripheral vision as he wandered into the living room. He stopped at a photo of Ansley, Mom and me, and tapped it. "This your Mom?"

"Yeah." I did a quick wash job of my hands and patted them dry with a kitchen towel. "She passed away about seven months ago. Two weeks before the plane crash."

"I'm sorry to hear that." He set down the frame. "Was it sudden?"

"As sudden as a distracted housewife in a Ford Explorer can be." I grimaced. "She'd started to have spells of dementia and had taken to wandering around. She was in the middle of the street…" I felt the familiar well in my throat, the one that normally came right before I burst into tears. I struggled to contain it. "and she got hit." The story never seemed to get easier to tell. Yet, for some reason, I wanted him to know.

His face tightened. "That's terrible."

"Yeah." He didn't know the worst of it, and I busied myself with kneeling down to retighten my shoelaces. "Especially…" I swallowed. "Especially because I was supposed to be home, watching her. I'd stopped for coffee, then the bookstore…" *and then I'd gotten the call.* It'd been a frantic one from Ansley, telling me to meet her at the hospital. I stood and turned away from him, grabbing my bag out of the closet. "Ready?"

He pulled me into his arms, a fierce, protective gesture that caught me off guard. Out of reflex, I resisted, then melted against his chest.

There was a long moment where we did nothing but stand, my arms wrapped around his waist, my head turned, ear pressed into the warm beat of his heart. I let out a sigh, feeling the sadness seep through me, and sniffed back a surge of emotion.

I hoped he wouldn't say anything, and he didn't, giving me time, my eyes closing, the clip of Mr. Oinks' toenails sounding as he tapped over to his bowl. I smiled at the loud sound of him slurping water, the liquid splashing, and pulled my head back, looking up at Declan. He ran his hand over my hair, and tilted forward, pressing a kiss onto my head.

"I lost my mom three years ago," he said gruffly. "It takes a long time. Don't feel pressured to rush it."

I nodded, unable to speak, and pulled away from him, digging in my purse for my key.

Declan reached for the door handle and looked down at Mr. Oinks, who wandered back from the water dish, his snout dripping along the tile, and wagged his tail in response. "Do you do anything with him?"

"Nope." I cleared my throat, the word coming out thick, and bent down to give Mr. Oinks a kiss on the top of the head. "He's a good boy." There wasn't a need to share all the times he hadn't been a good boy. Like when he got into the trash and dragged the Hefty bag all over the house, snacking on different items along the way. Or when he found the new bag of toilet paper and ripped twenty-four rolls into a gazillion tiny pieces.

I pulled the door behind us and locked it, taking a deep breath and refocusing my thoughts on what was about to happen. Lunch, just Declan Moss and me.

I couldn't let this opportunity pass. I didn't know what had prompted his visit, or this lunch invite, but this was my chance to smooth the waters, refocus our relationship off the smoking hot events of last weekend, and set a new precedent we could move forward with. All I had to do was stay level-headed, avoid swooning, and come across as un-crazy as possible.

One lunch. I could certainly manage those three things during that short timeframe. Checking the door, I turned away and hurried down the front steps after him.

26

I struggled with the chicken sub, the extra banana peppers slipping out of the side as I held it. A glob of ranch dressing dripped out of the end and hit my napkin. I sighed, and attacked the sandwich, managing a bite without everything falling out of it. Declan watched me, his eyes crinkling, and I reached for the napkin and carefully wiped my mouth, avoiding the drop of ranch. "So… anyway. That's why you shouldn't use a SlimJim. Not if you value your jugular vein."

His smile widened, and he could hurt a girl with that thing. Slice right through her chest plate and mortally nick her heart. "Let's talk about something less morbid."

"Okay…" I lifted my cup of Sprite and took a sip. "Like what?"

"Who's Adam?"

I swallowed the soda. "Mr. Oinks' vet. There was a major event lately, involving some rhubarb pie—which is toxic to pigs—and Adam saved his life."

"Really?" He seemed skeptical.

"Yeah, really."

"Just a whole heap of life savers. You guys sound like the perfect match."

It took me a minute to recognize his perturbed scowl as jealousy. It was cute on him, and absolutely unnecessary. "You don't have to be worried about Adam."

He leaned forward. "In what way?"

"I'm just saying, if you're jealous of Adam, you don't have to be. It was a failed date. First and last sort of thing."

"Huh." He took a bite of chip and chewed. "And you think I was jealous of him?"

It was a dangerous road to wander down, but I still took the bait. "Yeah." I studied him. "You were, right?" Maybe I had read him wrong. Maybe I'd been out of the dating game so long, I was reading flirtations where they didn't even exist.

"Possibly." He frowned. "Not that I like getting called out on it."

"Well, don't be jealous. I mean, in part because Adam's and my relationship is dead in the water, but more importantly, because you and I… this"—I gestured between the two of us—"can't happen." There. Boundary set. I would have patted myself on the back but I'm not that flexible.

He tilted his head at me. "I think it already did."

"Well… Something did," I allowed. *Lots of … somethings. Somethings I haven't been able to stop recreating, every time I close my eyes.* "But nothing else. Vagina is closed. Orgasms over." I made an X symbol with my hands and he laughed. "It's not funny," I insisted. "I'm serious."

"Okay," he allowed. "No sex. Fine. Truth be told, it was a little sudden for me, too."

Huh. He was saying I was a hoochie momma. Red-blooded slut tart. A Skankapotomus. I bristled a little at the comment, then had a second heart attack at his next words.

"So let's start over. This can be our new first date. Where are you from?"

Uh… nope. Uh-uh. No thank you, Mr. Sexiest Man I've ever met. I am not interested in a "new" first date from you, or any repeat of what happened last weekend.

I thought it all. I just didn't say any of it. Instead, I slowly chewed a chip, my brain stuck on the realization that Declan Moss knew little to nothing about me. While I could tell you almost every detail available through intensive background checks and snooping, his knowledge of me was... what? Glimpses of a woman screaming and waving a giant penis in the air? The dirty bottom of my downtown-trodden soles? Well... he did know a few of my more carnal details. The sound of my pleasure. How to kiss me into submission. The look on my face when I was about to...

I cleared my throat, a crumble stuck in an awkward place, and reached for my drink. "Yep. Born and raised here." He's from Los Angeles. I knew that, but guessed it would be odd of me to acknowledge it. I took the faux clueless path. "What about you?"

"LA." He grinned. "My career as a surfer didn't pan out."

"Smart move." I picked up another chip and bit it in half. "Anyone who tries to compete with Paul Brand is doomed for failure."

He raised his brows, impressed. "You're a surfing fan?"

I shrugged. "Not really. I worked in a surf shop in the mall during college. He was on all of the posters. And he looks realllly good in a bathing suit." I smiled, and it wasn't too much of a confession. Anyone with two eyes could see that his ass and abs were built for board shorts and nothing else.

"Maybe we could go to a competition sometime. They have some over in Daytona Beach." He nodded, as if he liked this idea, as if he and I would ever get into a car and travel the four hours east to attend a surfing competition.

I let out an awkward laugh. "You know... like a week ago, you were running from me like I had the plague."

"Perfectly justified response. I thought you were crazy." He took a beat, then amended the response. "Crazier."

"Thanks," I said dryly.

"Well, you did steal my trash," he pointed out.

My sandwich, which had been creeping its way back up to my mouth, stalled, my hands tightening on it, half of the contents giving up their fight and free-falling to the plate. *He knew about that?* I tried my best carefree snort of innocence, and came out sounding as if I had a buzzsaw stuck in my nostril. I composed myself and tried again. "I didn't steal your trash."

"Uh… yeah, you did. Left about thirty pieces of evidence behind with your name on it. I still got the tampon boxes and energy drink cans if you want them."

I grimaced. I knew I should have done a trash swap with Ansley but noooooo. She'd been all hoity-toity about that. As if Roger's psychology magazines and bottles of Pedialyte had a dedicated space allotment in her trash bins. I'd broached the idea with Mrs. Robchek, but apparently, her wild ways stopped with walking by Declan's house. Anything more and she wanted me to sign a confidentiality agreement with her. I'm not exactly sure what I was swearing confidentiality to, or what said agreement would protect her from, but the demand had caused me to give up on decoy trash and just cross my fingers that he never noticed the difference.

I made a mental note to remove "crossing my fingers" as a viable method of guarantee-ability.

He was waiting for a response, one brow raised, and I scrambled. "At least you know I'm not pregnant. I mean, with the tampon boxes. You wouldn't want a pregnant girl protecting you."

"I don't really want anyone protecting me," he said slowly.

"But, imagine," I babbled on. "If I was waddling along behind you, trying to catch your attention, but too heavy with child to move fast enough. And then BLAM!" I clapped my hands together to stimulate a pancaked Declan, and the woman at the table beside us jumped. I winced at her in apology, then continued. "You are a splat of guts and bone, under a semitruck, and I'm going into labor from the stress of it all."

"A semitruck? Am I wandering along the *highway*?" Declan bit his bottom lip and I swear on McDonalds, I think he was trying not to laugh. "Where exactly is this impromptu accident and labor delivery occurring?"

"It doesn't have to be a semi," I defended myself. "It could be a normal car." *Like the one that killed Mom.* I felt a sharp pain in my heart and looked down at the sad remains of my sandwich. "People get killed by cars all the time."

He reached out and grabbed my hand, threading his fingers through mine. "Hey."

I looked up at him and he smiled.

"You're right. I'm glad you're not pregnant."

I scoffed, grateful for the distraction. "Um... thanks? Me too." *I guess.*

We ate in silence for a while, and I foraged through the destroyed chicken sandwich and used my fork to stab up the remaining pieces. It was a peaceful silence, one I felt comfortable with, so I was surprised when I looked up to find him studying me, something on his mind. "What?"

"*Could* you be pregnant? I mean, if it wasn't for the tampons." He pulled at the neck of his tie, loosening it from his collar.

"What?" I sounded like that parrot, the one that Ansley bought during college, who we tried to teach a dozen phrases to, but stubbornly only squawked 'what' a gazillion times a day. It would have been humorous if he didn't love to scream it at the top of his tiny parrot lungs at four a.m.

"I mean..." He rubbed his palms down the top of his thighs, as if they were sweaty.

"You mean from the other night?" He's a grown man. An extremely intelligent one, based on the As that had covered every line of his college transcript. He has to understand condoms, their use, purpose, and the minuscule risks that were associated with them. "I mean, I guess. If you're feeling ninety-nine-point-nine percent unlucky."

"No. I mean, from someone else." He picked up the tabletop display and studied it. "Did you want some dessert?"

Oh... Understanding dawned. He wanted to know how often I panted my way across a man's body, and if I was doing my little orgasm act around anyone else. "I'm not really sure that's your business."

His eyes found mine. "You're right. We don't have to get dessert.

Or, I can look away if you want to secretly order it." His mouth twitched and I recognized the horribly weak attempt to redirect the conversation into a joke.

I didn't let it slide, choosing to capitalize on his discomfort. "I'll tell you about my sordid sexual past if you agree to get a bodyguard."

He frowned. "No. And you were right, it wasn't my business."

This put me in a bit of a pickle, since I was now curious about *his* sexual history, and taking the high and mighty road didn't seem nearly as fun. I scooped up a bit of mayo with a potato chip and crunched down on it. Actually, this was the responsible thing to do, right? Weren't you supposed to discuss sexual history with someone *before* you had sex with them? Here I was, the touter of all things safety, yet I had dragged him to my bed without finding out anything about his proclivities. Did he *have* proclivities? What exactly was a proclivity?

"You're frowning."

"I am?" I looked up, finding him watching me, an amused look on his face. "I was just wondering what a proclivity was. Do you know?"

"It's an inclination. A tendency to do something a particular way."

"Oh. So, it's not a sexual thing."

He laughed. "I think it could be an anything thing. Why?"

"No reason."

"Shit." He leaned forward, lowering his voice. "Okay, now I do want to know your sordid sexual history. Especially if it involves proclivities."

"And… you agree to the bodyguard if I tell you?"

He gave me a look, and it was a good one, the sort that was stern yet playful, and made me want to crawl over the diner's table and kiss it right off him. I schooled my own features into a scowl, forced my attraction back into oblivion, and sighed. "Fine. But only because I believe that sexual partners should share their history with each other. And we are—or rather, were—sexual partners."

"Are," he corrected.

"WERE." I huffed out my breath, then continued on before he had a chance to re-dispute the classification. "So, to answer your question, no—I couldn't be pregnant. Prior to our night together, the last one was…" I counted backward on my hand, then squinted, double-checking my memory. "Eight months ago."

"Who was that?"

I curled up my face. "This guy from a marketing class I was in. Entirely forgettable. And wore a condom," I added. "Every guy I've been with has worn a condom. Including you."

"Yes," he smirked. "I remember."

"So…" I glanced at his plate, which had been cleaned with quick efficiency, no stray fries in sight. "What about you?"

"Three girlfriends. The most recent relationship ended the day of the plane crash." He wiped his mouth, then balled up the napkin. "Nothing since then, except for…"

"Us." I flushed at the word, then hurried to move the conversation forward. "But you've gone on dates since then."

"A date. It didn't lead to anything."

"Why not?"

He shrugged. "Not sure. It just wasn't right." He folded his napkin in half and smoothed it down on the table. "Speaking of dating, I need to talk to you about something." He leaned forward, and my guard was instantly up.

"What?"

"This weekend, it's Nate's birthday." He gave me an apologetic look, and I tried to find the end of this conversational path.

"Yeah, so?"

"I was wondering, given the new parameters of our relationship—"

"Our non-relationship."

"Whatever." He shrugged off the rebuttal and forged onward. "I was wondering if you'd come with me. Just to keep an eye on things. It may be dangerous. Very hazard-filled. Lots of potential disasters."

My Guardian Angel side did a happy little dance along my cerebral cortex while my common sense called bullshit. "What's this danger-filled *thing*?"

He shot me an apologetic look. "It's a hunting trip."

"A hunting trip?" I stirred my empty Sprite with the straw, moving the ice around. "And you want me to go?"

"Sure." He nodded, then seemed to amend his response. "I'd like you to come."

I stared at him blankly, and tried to understand the swirl of emotions fighting for room in my chest. I hadn't done too well in this lunch. In terms of acting crazy, I had done quite well. But in keeping my arousal in check? Pretty lousy. In keeping the conversation strictly business and away from any sex, relationship, or personal conversations? I'd failed terribly.

Now he was proposing something that terrified me in about ten different ways. He was right in his assessment of a danger-filled event, but the entire thing reeked of a set-up. What was the real reason I was coming, because he was accepting my "protecting your life" thing a little too easily, compared to the reactions of everyone else I mentioned it to. Which left the dangerous possibility that he wanted me to come so he could attempt another seduction. What had he said about our night? Voodoo magic? I blushed at the compliment, one I was close to framing in giant neon letters above my bed. And if he was bringing me on a hunting trip to seduce me, or to get another chance at sex ... would I be able to resist?

"You seem to be giving this a lot of thought."

I stabbed the straw into the ice with a little more aggression than I had intended. "I am."

"Then let's scratch the hunting trip. You don't need to go."

My deep thought process did a sharp 180. What was I doing, overanalyzing this situation? If—one week ago—I'd known that Declan Moss was going on a hunting trip, and I'd been offered a front-row seat to the event, I'd have sold my left pinky for the ticket. I swallow. "I can go."

"No. Honestly, it's fine. We're hunting skeet. I couldn't get accidentally shot if I tried."

What a stupid statement. That's the entire thing about getting accidentally shot. No one was *trying*, or else it wouldn't be an accident.

"I can *go*." I straightened in my seat, my mind made up, and if he thought he was grabbing a gun and going anywhere without me, he was delusional. "There are just a few issues I need to sort out first."

I saved the issues until we got into the car, the process delayed by Declan's overkill cleanup of our table, one that included wiping down the surface and realigning every condiment bottle and salt shaker in the end cap. Once we were settled in and buckled, I brought up the first problem.

"Here's the first problem. I have a pig."

"I'm well aware of your pig." He drove with one hand, his arm stretched across the bench seat and resting on my headrest. We turned a sharp corner, and his fingers brushed at my neck.

"And I like animals."

"So, you don't want me to shoot anything."

"I don't want a gun anywhere *near* you." In the time it had taken him to sanitize our tabletop, I had googled firearm statistics, which had been one thing I hadn't even known to worry about. "Did you know that eight-two people died last year in hunting accidents?"

"I was not aware of that." He brushed his fingers across the back of my neck and I swatted at his hand. "But, no pigs are in danger. It's a skeet trip."

"You're still shooting skeet," I pointed out. "I don't like the idea of you shooting anything." I had never seen a skeet, but they sounded adorable. "I'm not going to be able to sleep at night with a dozen skeet deaths hanging over my head."

"You're joking." He shot me a look, half his mouth lifting in a wry smile, which fell when he saw my blank look. "You're serious."

"Of course, I'm serious!" I threw my hands in the air.

"Have you ever *seen* a skeet?"

I fought the urge to Google one. "Yes."

"You have?"

"YES," I snapped.

"And you don't want me to shoot one…" he said slowly. "Why?"

"They're adorable," I said sullenly.

"Fine." He looked to the left, out his window, his face hidden from me. "I won't shoot one."

"Promise?"

He looked back at me. "I swear. But you should come with me, just to make sure."

He didn't need to twist my arm. The moment I heard the invitation, I mentally printed a map, ordered bright orange fluorescent vests, and malaria-fight-worthy bug spray. Still, I went through a big production of reluctance just to seal the deal. "A few more things. Will we have separate bedrooms?"

"Sure."

"And, it's just one night?"

"Yep."

Separate bedrooms. One night. My odds of escaping with my sexual composure intact rose. "Can I bring Mr. Oinks?"

"Hell no."

I scrunched up my face, then let out a long and dramatic sigh. "Fine. But this is definitely not a date. Work trip only."

"Not a date," he repeated solemnly. "Work trip only." Then he smiled and it was a good thing I was a stone-cold pro. Because this man? He was deadly.

27

"I don't like this." Roger stood in his driveway, his arms over his chest, and watched me lug his cooler out of the garage.

"For Pete's sake, will you help her with that?" Ansley barked from the front porch, Caleb in her arms.

"We don't even know this guy." Roger came around the other side and lifted the handle, the cumbersome job suddenly easy. "What if he's taking you out into the woods to rape and kill you?"

"He's not going to rape and kill her, Roger. He already had sex with her!" Ansley's voice, meant to carry across the impatiens and to our spot by the mailbox, was also easily heard by every house in a block radius. Roger glared at her and I stifled a laugh.

"It's true," I whispered. "He did have sex with me."

"Good sex," Ansley added, strolling down the sidewalk and brushing crumbs off Caleb's mouth. "Lots of orgasms."

Roger colored, and pushed the glasses up higher on his nose with precision. "He could *still* kill her."

"It's true," I agreed. "He could definitely kill me. If I don't come back tomorrow by two, call the police."

"It's not funny," Roger said, a bead of sweat dragging down his temple. "What do you really know about him?"

"Ummm... everything?" Ansley said. "You're being a pain. Go grab the bug zapper and shush."

His jaw tightened, and we watched as he walked up the driveway and toward the garage, which was a barely-contained pile of every item they had ever owned. Caleb squirmed and Ansley set him down, the stout three-year-old running after his father.

She lowered her voice and leaned into me. "He's so sexy when he's being protective."

I squinted in Roger's direction, trying to see past his khaki high waters and crisp plaid short-sleeve shirt, then shrugged. "Yeah. I don't see it."

"Did you pack condoms?"

"What?" I recoiled. "No."

"Bacon-flavored lube?"

I glared at her. "I'm going to personally tell Mr. Oinks that you said that."

"At least tell me you packed sexy panties."

I pulled up my T-shirt and looped a finger under the elastic of my size-too-big purple cotton granny panties. "Nope."

"Holy shit, woman. Did I not teach you anything?" She grabbed my arm and started to pull me in the direction of the house. "Come on. I've got a Fredricks of Hollywood set that Roger says gives him migraines. It'll look perfect on you."

I danced right, ducking behind her. Her arm twisted into an awkward angle, and she cursed, letting go of me. "You aren't listening. I'm NOT HAVING SEX WITH HIM."

"It's true." The deep voice from behind us scared the crap out of us, and we both screamed in reflex.

I blew out a burst of air at the sight of Declan, headed up the driveway, his hands tucked into the front pockets of his jeans. Behind him, at the curb, his truck idled. "Jesus, you are sneaky."

"She *might* have sex with you," Ansley offered as a way of greeting. "Don't let the adamant declarations scare you away from trying."

"Great," Roger remarked. "Encouraging aggressive behavior in the face of clear denial. Just what we want to teach predators everywhere." He tucked the giant yellow tennis racket shaped fly zapper under his arm and puffed out his chest. "I'm Roger. Autumn's brother." His voice was suddenly deeper, and when he held out his hand to shake Declan's, I watched the skinny veins in his forearms pop into action.

"He's my brother-in-law," I elaborated, unsure of exactly who Roger thought he was intimidating. I glanced at Ansley, who was absolutely no help, eyeing her husband with a gleam that spoke of ripped-off clothes and raw animal lust.

"Nice to meet you," Declan said. "Declan Moss. I'll take good care of Autumn."

He'll take good care of me? That's funny. The man talks on his cell phone while filling his car up with gas. He's lucky he'd lived to thirty-two without dying already. I poked him in the arm. "My bags are on the porch."

He glanced past me, his brow furrowing at the sight of the stack, three high and two deep. "We're just going for a night."

"Yep. Use your legs when you lift the blue one. It's heavy."

"I'll help," Roger offered, his chest still puffed up, and I watched as Ansley bit her lip in response. Weird married people. I elbowed her and she glared at me.

"What?"

"I put the instructions for Mr. Oinks on the dining room table," I reminded her.

"Yep. I know. Let him out four times a day. Check his water. Feed him crap. Got it," she said absentmindedly.

"And scratch his belly."

"The kids can do that. You know I don't like how sweaty he gets." She wrinkled up her nose as she watched Declan and Roger cross over the grass, my bags in hand. "Text me when you get there. And if he kisses you. Or anything else." She grinned at me and I rolled my eyes, pulling her into a hug.

"I can't believe you're wearing those underwear," she whispered against my ear.

"I can't believe you think Roger's sexy," I whispered back.

She laughed and squeezed me tight. "Go. Have fun. Live a little."

Live a little. It was strange that, in trying so hard to keep Declan from dying, I had kind of forgotten how to celebrate living. I thought suddenly of Mom, of her manic mood swings—full of happy energy one minute, and bitter and angry the next. When she was up, she was UP. It was like living in a disco ball of fun and love, the mood tampered with the constant fear that it was about to end. And when she'd gone down…we'd avoided her.

Ansley pulled away and kissed my cheek. "Go. Have wild passionate forest sex and tell me all the explicit details later."

I waved at her and met Caleb halfway across the lawn, bending to kiss him on the head. When I looked up, Declan was rounding the back of the truck, his gaze catching mine. "Ready?" he called, opening my door.

I wasn't ready, not with Ansley's words echoing in my ear, or the fact that Declan looked deliciously outdoorsy, in a long-sleeved T-shirt, worn jeans, and hiking boots. His sleeves were pushed up to the elbows, he had a golden layer of scruff on his face, and a baseball cap snug on his head.

"Roger," Ansley called out. "He's opening the door for HER."

I swallowed a smile at Roger's annoyed grunt and hoisted myself into the cab. "I'm ready."

"So, where exactly are we going?" I pulled my pillow out of the bag and rested it on my lap, readjusting the seatbelt.

"A hunting lease we have in Marion County. Outside Ocala. It's about two hours away." He glanced over his shoulder, waiting for a break in traffic so he could pull out.

"A hunting lease…" I picked at a stubborn hangnail. "How does that work? You rent the land?"

"Yeah. There's a group of ten of us who got together on it. There're a few small cabins on the property and a camp house. We all come down when we can."

"So, there'll be ten people here?" My fear quadrupled. Ten gun-toting idiots, all likely to be drunk and careless. I mentally flipped through the items I had packed. A gunshot wound kit, epi pens, the biggest first aid kit that Amazon provided, a foldable gurney and three books on wound care. It wasn't enough. I might be able to protect Declan, but what about all of the others?

"Nah. It's just us and Nate. Potentially our client, if he brings her along."

Our client. Her. I sat up a little in the seat, enthused at the idea of a second female. "Is she a hunter?"

He chuckled. "Benta? I wouldn't think so. Not unless you're the last designer dress on the rack." He reached down and picked up his phone. "But the jury is still out on her. I'm waiting for Nate to confirm it." He didn't seem pleased with the possibility and I dropped the subject.

"How do you know that no one else is coming? Do you have a booking system? Online calendar?"

He smiled. "Nope. We show up and if someone's there, we squeeze in. It works."

Great. We were driving two hours into a complete question mark of a situation. Technically, since he's bringing me, and Nick's bringing someone, all ten of the guys could be there, with girls, and how are twenty people going to share a few small cabins? I felt lightheaded.

He gently touched my arm. "Are you okay? You look a little pale."

"I'm fine." I found the window control and lowered the glass, gulping in some of the fresh air. "Is Nate pissed that I'm coming?"

He smiled. "Nate doesn't get pissed about stuff, especially not where women are involved. Plus, this was his idea."

That surprised me. "Really?"

"Yeah. And it's good for you guys to spend some time together. You can get to know each other better. His view of you is a little one-sided."

I pinned my lips together, uninterested in the idea of spending the next twenty-four hours explaining my erratic behavior to Nate Robb. I had seen Nate enough to know what sort of guy he was. The popular one. The sort who had women tripping over themselves. The kind who flirted as often as he breathed, broke hearts with wild abandon, and had probably spent the last six months making fun of me.

"Have you been to Marion County before?"

I tucked one foot underneath myself, grateful for the change in conversation. "No. Actually… I've only been outside of Tallahassee once, and that was to go to spring break at PCB."

He glanced over, surprised. "You're kidding me. The only place you've ever been is *Panama City Beach*?" He said the tourist destination as if it was crud in the bottom of a trash can.

"My mom didn't raise us to travel." That was an understatement on a nuclear scale. I thought of Mom's meltdown when she'd found out about my spring break trip, the way she had locked herself in her bedroom for three days straight, punishing me with a litany of facts about teenage pregnancies and date rape drugs. I had come back one weekend and a dozen missed calls later to find that she'd shaved her head, a result of her yanking out strands in patches.

"I can't believe you haven't ever gone anywhere else." He pushed back the brim of his baseball cap and scratched his head. "It seems like a waste of a trip, taking you to the middle of nowhere." He glanced over at me. "Where have you always dreamed of going?"

"I haven't ever really thought about going anywhere," I answered without really considering the question, but it was true. Even with Ansley and our new inheritance, we hadn't traveled ten miles outside the Leon County line. It was like we were still stuck in Mom's rules or would be violating her memory by stepping outside of them. Not that I felt guilty about tagging along with Declan on a sweaty and bug-filled camping trip. But if Ansley and I booked tickets to Tahiti, clinked champagne in first class seats, and read novels poolside, the ocean glittering before us—all on Mom's dime? I would hate every second of it. I'd feel like I was dancing in high-heeled shoes on her grave.

I tried to think of how to explain it all to Declan. But thoughts of

Mom, her impressions and impacts on us... it was like a tiramisu. Horribly intricate. Sweet with an almost bitter aftertaste. Good in small amounts only. I weighed different stories to tell him and finally, reluctantly, told the most impactful one of all:

The story of the HappyTie Corporation, and Mom's secret fortune.

28

Our mother was Debra Littlefield Jones. Graduated from University of Florida in 1984 with a degree in chemical engineering, and immediately hired to work for the HappyTie Corporation.

Declan hadn't heard of HappyTie, which didn't surprise me. Most people hadn't. For us, it'd been a household name, one typically muttered as a curse. Momma had been promoted through their ranks, and eventually landed on HappyTie's new product development team. According to her, and typically after four or five drinks, she'd invented the Happy Dye Tie, which was a head wrap that kept women from turning grey. She'd invented it, pitched it, and been shut down.

Years later, the HappyTie Corporation fired Mom, due in large part to her increasingly hostile behavior regarding every new product rolled out that wasn't the Happy Dye Tie. She never forgave them for it, never got over the slight, and never came in contact with an HTC product without lighting it on fire.

"She lit them on fire?" Declan interrupted the story. Tearing open a bag of peanuts, he offered me some.

I took a handful. "Yep. It was why we were—and probably still are—banned from Burger Kings. That one on North Monroe, just north of I-10?" I waited on him to nod. "When I was twelve, we were eating lunch there one Sunday when mom realized that the cup lids were Forth brand, which is owned by HappyTie. She snatched a lighter from a lady sitting in one of the booths and proceeded to light the entire stand of lids on fire." I smiled at the memory, which had been horribly traumatic at the time, but had eventually faded into a comical story. "It was a mess. They didn't light very well, and let off this putrid odor as they melted together. It was a pretty weak attempt at arson until the stack of napkins caught the flame. Then... *whoosh*." I raised my hands in a re-enactment of the blaze. "The sprinkler system went off, the police and fire department were called, and Ansley and I spent two days with a social worker before they agreed Mom was a fit parent."

Declan had an odd look on his face, a mixture of horror and sympathy, and I waved him off. "You have to understand, for us, chaos was normal. Ansley and I protected each other. We watched out for each other. Mom's activities... we just learned to avoid them. To do things that calmed her. To avoid things that didn't. Occasionally... like when I went to Panama City for spring break... or when Ansley got married, one of us would act out—but for the most part, we all worked as a cohesive unit. Ansley and I were a team, and Mom was the loose cannon that we worked together to control. Or..." I struggled to find a better word than *control*. "Manage. Pacify."

"And watch out for her?" He glanced over at me. "You mentioned ... when she was hit by the car, that you were supposed to watch her."

"Oh." I fiddled with the edge of my pillowcase. "She developed dementia in the last two or three years. Possibly, she'd had it even longer. It was hard to tell, because she'd always been erratic, so there wasn't a clear baseline of behavior to judge when she started losing her bearings. But it got to where she was wandering off. She'd leave the water running. Or the stove on. Or try to cook ballpoint pens for dinner. Her insurance provided a night nurse to watch her during the evenings, and Ansley and I would trade off days." *And it had been my day. A Tuesday. My day, and I had been too busy with selfish errands.*

"I'm sorry. I didn't mean to bring that back up—" He grimaced.

"It's okay." I watched as we passed a hitchhiker, his thumb

outstretched, a threadbare backpack hitched high on his shoulders. "It's not like I don't think about it."

"You were telling me about HappyTie," he prompted.

"Yes." I let out a breath and returned to the story.

When Mom passed, we'd opened up her checkbook to see our situation, in terms of funeral arrangements. To neither of our surprise, the balance was seven hundred and fourteen dollars—which, combined with a thousand of my money, and two thousand from Ansley, barely covered her cremation and burial. Her will, found in the top drawer of her desk, was entertaining. At some point, Mom had thrown away money she didn't have on a thirty-two-page document, which stipulated that her belongings would be controlled in a trust until her daughters were of 'intelligent' age to inherit her estate. We'd glanced around the rundown two-bedroom house that was half paid off and choked back a laugh, tossing the thick document onto the desk and continuing through her files.

We stopped laughing when we found the HappyTie files. There were twelve of them. Three pertained to bank accounts with institutions we had never heard of. Four contained lawsuit titles we were ignorant about. The rest were a collection of trust documents, patents and trademarks.

Mom, it turned out, wasn't so crazy after all. And HappyTie, despite her curses and impromptu fires, and badmouthing to anyone who would listen… HappyTie had never done her wrong. We sat down on the floor of Mom's office and read through every page, every bank statement, and then back through the previously tossed-aside will.

And then, as Forrest Gump said, I didn't have to work anymore.

There was a long silence, the tires thumping against the roadway, a country song ending and then another one beginning. Declan cleared his throat. "You didn't have to work anymore," he repeated.

"Nope. I mean, I could. There isn't a rule against working. I just don't need to." Ansley and I had been stunned. A little hurt. Confused as to why we'd spent our childhood taking two-minute showers to reduce the amount of our utility bills. Confused as to why I was paying twelve percent interest on six different student loans when there was enough in these accounts to buy our own university. Had it been to teach us the value of money? Or had she just been too damn stubborn to ever spend a HappyTie dollar?

"So, you're just never going to work?"

I frowned, his tone similar to Ansley's and Roger's, during family dinners, when they'd glare at me across the table and want to know *what I'm going to do with my life*. "I scrapbook," I said. "Plus, I haven't really had time to work anyway, what with everything I've been needing to do with you."

"And what did you do before?"

"I had a work-study at FSU that paid my tuition, and I babysat and waited tables at Ted's." I bristled a little, protective of the fact that I do know how to work. Just because I quit work and danced out the door of Ted's, swinging my apron around my head like a lasso didn't mean that I was lazy. I'd had a job ever since I was fifteen. Spent every year at FSU working two, sometimes three different ones. Granted, I was twenty-eight, and had the entry-level résumé of a high-school dropout, but our need to watch Mom during the day had prohibited me from having a normal desk job—one that made use of my degrees.

He rubbed his hand over his jaw. "So, when you had those bodyguards in your house, that was serious? You were going to actually hire them and pay for them to protect me?"

"Of course."

His face tightened, and I struggled to understand his expression.

"I have a lot of money," I pointed out. "It wouldn't have been an issue."

"Yeah, I got that." He slowed down behind a semi and glanced in the rearview mirror, then over at me. "But, you don't actually have the money. Not until you're a certain age, right?"

"Right. I have fourteen months to go. And there are a lot of hoops I have to jump through first. Like a quarterly meeting with a shrink. But I get an allowance now. And honestly, it's really all that I need." It was almost hard to spend money. With a paid-for house and my scant wardrobe, my expenses were limited to Declan-surveillance activities and safety gear. I'd considered buying new furniture for the house, but

Mr. Oinks just broke all of the old stuff in. With the exception of life-saving measures, I was still stuck in Mom's tight-fisted thinking, and the thought of throwing money away on crap just because I had it ... didn't make much sense.

Declan studied me for a long moment, before refocusing on the road, and it was strange, but it seemed like he was sad.

29

He shouldn't be upset. It was dumb to be upset, especially over something like this. He cared about her. He should be happy that she was financially stable and didn't have to worry about money. So, why was he suddenly pissed?

It was idiotic of him, to take her to a rundown cabin in the middle of the woods, with a cooler packed with homemade sandwiches, and expect to woo her there. He'd taken her to Tony's Subs, for shit's sake. How had he not realized from the expensive heels she'd abandoned downtown to the paid-for home they'd found on the tax rolls, that she'd been rolling in cash? Hell, even her staple gun was three times nicer than his.

She didn't need him to provide for her. She didn't need anyone. She had her pig, and her sister, and a bank account that must be packed as full as Scrooge's vault, and he was an idiot to think that he had any sort of chance with her. Hell, she had all but shoved him away anytime he tried to touch her. What was he doing? Holding his safety over her head for a chance to spend time with her? How much of a dickhead move was that? Chances were, she didn't even want to be here. She probably hated him. Right now, she was probably contemplating the easiest way to extract herself from this situation.

"Are you okay?" She peered over at him. "You seem upset."

Great. His thoughts were plastered across his face. She'd probably steal his truck at the next gas stop and hightail it back to Tallahassee. He forced himself to smile. "I'm fine."

"No, you're not." She turned in her seat, facing him, her knee bumping against his thigh, and crossed her arms over her chest. "What is it?"

Yeah, telling her the truth was definitely not an option. "I'm having some indigestion. I think it was something I had for breakfast."

She immediately launched into protective mode, unbuckling her seatbelt and springing across the cab toward him. "What kind of indigestion? Upper or lower intestine?" She crawled forward, examining him, and he took his eyes off the road for a split second to meet hers.

Damn. Those deep blue eyes, filled with concern… what was he going to do with her? He'd never seen someone care about him so … intently. How could he keep her in his life? She broke eye contact and spun to the rear of the truck, bending over the bench seat and messing with her bags.

"What are you doing?" He struggled to keep his eyes on the road, but her position was too tempting to ignore. Her torso hanging over the seat, her ass was eye-level with his, in cut-off jean shorts that were currently riding high on her cheeks. His hand tightened on the gear shift so he wouldn't reach over and grab her.

"Pull over." She stretched forward, one bare leg extending to help, and he watched as a flip-flop fell off her foot and down to the floorboard. Putting on his turn signal, he changed lanes and headed to the shoulder of the road. She emerged from the backseat, her hair astray, cheeks flushed, and triumphantly held up a huge yellow book, the words MEDICAL EMERGENCIES: STOMACH AND DIGESTION.

He came to a stop on the side of the highway and undid his seatbelt. "Look, it wasn't really—" His confession died on his lips as soon as she knelt on the seat next to him and tugged at the bottom of his shirt.

"Bite." She held the bottom of his shirt in front of his mouth and waited. He obeyed, taking a mouthful of the shirt and holding it up, his abs clenching the moment she brushed her hand over them.

"Where's the pain?" She walked her fingers up his bare stomach, from the top of his jeans to his ribs, the pads of her fingers gently pressing into him. "Here?"

"Lower," he grunted, and he was officially going to hell for this.

She slid her fingers lower, his abs tightening from the touch. Her bare knees were against his jeans, her hair brushing his shoulder as she bent over him. She turned away, flipping open the book and consulting an image of a dissected torso, different areas highlighted in various colors. She ran her fingers farther, hitting the top of his jeans. "Down here?"

"Yeah." The shirt fell from his mouth as he spoke.

She lifted her head. "Do you feel comfortable undoing your belt?" She was close enough to kiss. Her eyes were big and luminous, and her pale pink lips just begging for contact.

"Sure." He reached for his belt, undoing it and unbuttoning the top button on his jeans.

"And hold your shirt up so I can use both hands." She sat back on her heels, flipping through the book. "Are you having gas pains also?"

"Maybe?" He needed her hands back on him. He stretched his legs out and held his shirt up. "Should I take my shirt off?"

"Nah…" she said thoughtfully, running her finger over a column of text as she read, completely missing the view of his clenched abs that he was struggling to maintain. "You know," she said, looking up from the open book. "It might just be a stomachache."

"I'm having a little bit of a stabbing pain also," he said, desperate.

"Really?" She set the book to the side. "Where?"

He nodded toward his right side, and her hands followed the indication, her warm palms settling back on his skin, gently probing the area. "A little lower." She slid her fingers under the loose gap of his jeans, following the plane all the way to his hip.

"Here?" She looked up at him, and if he was ever going to kiss her again, now was the best time. She was so close, so concerned, her hands down his pants, and *God,* she smelled good. Like flowers. He dropped his shirt and reached for her, his eyes closing as he moved forward and completely missed her lips altogether.

He opened his eyes, surprised to see her settling back in the passenger seat, her phone out, staring down at the screen as she stretched the seatbelt across her chest and locked it into place. "I think we should get you to a hospital."

"No," he protested, his dick wilting and taking his self-confidence along with it. "It's probably nothing."

"Probably nothing?" She snorted. "Do you know how many cemetery plots are filled each year over *probably nothing*?" She tapped out a string of words on her phone. "Look, there's a hospital in Lake City. It says it's eight miles away."

"I'm not going to the hospital," he said loudly. "I'll stop at a gas station and get a Tums. If it doesn't go away in fifteen minutes, then I'll go to a hospital. Okay?"

"According to the book, your pain is near the beginning of your large intestine." She glared at him. "What if it's ruptured?"

"I don't have any abdominal distension or vomiting," he countered. "Put your phone away and relax."

"You're the one who mentioned stabbing pains." She slumped against the seat. "I'm just trying to take care of you."

"Which I appreciate." He thought of the last time he had thanked her, and the way she had launched herself at his mouth in response. "Thank you," he said, hopeful for a similar response.

"Uh-huh." She looked down at the floorboard, stuffing her feet back into her flip-flops. "I'll be sure to remember that when I'm giving your eulogy."

Apparently, that was a one-trick pony. He zipped his jeans back up and buckled his belt, letting out a groan at the missed opportunity. Reaching for the gear shift, he moved the truck into drive.

"Seatbelt," Autumn chimed in.

Despite himself, he started to smile. She was… just… everything.

30

The camp really *was* in the middle of nowhere. We pulled off I-10, took a smaller county road for fourteen miles, then stopped at a big metal gate with a padlock. Declan entered the combination, left it unlocked, and we pulled through. We took that path for another ten minutes. Twice, we had to drive over fallen trees, the truck barely making the climb over the trunks. Both times I looked to Declan in panic, and both times he reassured me with the words "four-wheel drive," like that meant diddly squat to anyone. One thing was for sure—there was no way an ambulance could get back here. Any emergencies would require a helicopter pickup, assuming there was a convenient landing pad in this forest of trees.

When we finally pulled up to the first cabin, I was relieved to see no other vehicles, my fears of armed strangers disappearing. He parked in front and nodded at me to get out.

He'd described the cabins as small, and it was an apt adjective. I stood in front of the tiny square structure, which didn't look much bigger than my garden shed. Declan climbed the steps to the skinny porch and twisted the knob, the door opening.

"Wait," I called out. "It was unlocked? What if someone's hiding in there?"

He grinned at me, the door half open. "It's a pretty small place. I'll see him." He stepped inside and I fretted in place, certain that I was moments away from a blood-curdling scream. He stuck his head out. "You coming?"

"It's safe?"

"Super safe." He disappeared back inside.

I gingerly climbed the steps and slowly stepped inside, relaxing when I saw the cozy cabin. It was actually really cute. There was a queen bed set in the middle of the back wall, and a rocking chair in one corner. A sink and toilet took up the other corner. I looked around for more. "Where's the shower?"

"There's an outdoor one around back." He crouched down next to the toilet and fiddled with something. "There. Water's on. Do you need to use it?"

"Uh, no." I shook my head. "I'm fine."

"Do you mind if I..." He nodded toward the toilet, one hand on his belt.

"Oh! Sure." I backed toward the door and almost tripped on the transom. Jumping down the steps, I stopped on an open patch of pine needles and tried to block out the incredibly loud sound of Declan Moss peeing. Sound insulation had not been a factor in construction.

He was a hand washer. I listened as he used the sink. When he stepped through the door, he dried his hands on his shirt as he came down the steps, glimpses of abs showing with each step. My examination in the car had been a test of wills, his skin warm and tense under my hands, our proximity a little too close for professional comfort. Once, I'd felt certain he was about to kiss me, my body leaning into the action, begging for the touch, and I'd catapulted to the other side just to keep from crawling into his lap.

Ever since that moment, the thought of kissing Declan had been heavy on my mind. I glanced back at the path, hoping that Nate and their client would get here soon.

He stopped before me and looked down at my feet. "You brought other shoes, right?"

I nodded. "Should I get them?"

"Better put them on now. The critters are going to run right past those flip flops."

My snake boots, hardly used since I went all Crocodile Dundee on the backyard, were stiff. I sat on the tailgate of the truck and pulled on a pair of thick socks and worked them on, watching Declan carry my bags into the cabin. He shook his head each time he picked up a round of duffel bags, a slow smile stretching over his face as he trooped back and forth, wearing a path in the wet leaves.

"What?" I demanded, hopping off the truck and grabbing a lantern out of the back.

"Your propensity to prepare for the worst is entertaining. Think you'll be disappointed if someone doesn't get hurt tonight?"

"That's morbid." I followed him into the cabin and looked around to see where I should set down the lantern. The cozy space was suddenly a little tight, my stuff stacked along the wall and eating up any spare floor space. To get to the toilet, I was going to have to use the bed as a steppingstone.

"Here." Declan held out a hand and I passed him the heavy lantern, watching as he reached up and hung it from a nail on one of the rafters. "I'll move it down before you go to bed."

There wasn't enough room for him to pass me, so I stepped back outside, watching as he took the steps and headed to the truck. He glanced my way. "I'm going to open up my cabin now. You coming, or you want to rest here?"

"Coming." I opened the passenger door to the truck and got in, glancing back at the cabin. "When is Nate arriving?"

He glanced at his watch. "He might be at the camp house now. We can swing by there on the way and see."

It took four minutes of treacherous driving to make it to the camp house, and I blanched a little at the realization of how far away everything was. Why didn't they put the cabins closer together? It seemed incredibly antisocial to be so spread out. I voiced my opinion and Declan chuckled. “I think the guys who built this place valued their privacy. And it helps if there are different groups using the land. Sometimes you don’t want to see or interact with anyone.”

“If no one knows where anyone else is on the land, how do you keep from shooting each other?”

He came to a stop at the fork in the road and pointed to the glove box. “Open that up and grab me the yellow map.”

I did as he asked, and watched as he unfurled the map, pinning it against the steering wheel and pointing to the different landmarks on it. “This is where we came in.” He showed me a dotted line, coming in off the highway. “Here’s your cabin.” There was a blue X helpfully labeled as Cabin 1. I leaned forward, interested. “We’re here now.” He moved his finger a millimeter over, stopping at a place between Cabin 4 and a square labeled Camp.

“Wait.” I reached out and stopped his hand, my fingers curling around his hand as if I was holding it. I let go before he got any ideas. “That’s all we’ve gone? Just that short way?” I scanned over the entire map, seeing a stream, a lake, and a dozen areas labeled and shaded across the parcel. “This is huge.”

“Four thousand acres.” He nodded to my boots. “I hope those things are comfortable.”

I grimaced and he smiled. “Just joking. But yeah, it’s big.” He circled the cabins with his finger and I noticed a checked pattern over the area. “All this is a safety area. No guns or bows. If anyone gets shot in these three hundred acres, then someone is doing something wrong.”

“But it could happen,” I pointed out.

“It’s not going to happen,” he assured me. “Not with anyone in our club. And again, chances are that it’s just us using it tonight. Most of the club is from Orlando, and they’re not stepping away from their televisions during football weekends.”

I relaxed a little at the clear rules that seemed to be in place, the map both reassuring and terrifying in its size. I scanned it again and noticed the area labeled Skeet. "Is that where you are going to shoot today?"

"Yep." He passed me the map and grabbed the wheel, taking a right at the fork and continuing down the path. "Assuming Nate gets here quickly. There's a fair amount of prep we have to do first."

"But you told me you *aren't* shooting skeet."

"Right. Because you don't want to hurt them." He shot me a wry smile. "I'm about to change your mind on that."

It didn't matter what he showed me. Skeet could be bloodthirsty bats that eat kittens in their spare time, and I still wasn't letting him shoot them. We had a deal, and I was here, boots on in the humidity, so he needed to keep his end of the bargain.

His phone buzzed and he pulled it out of the cupholder and glanced at it. "Looks like Nate is still in Tallahassee, so we've got plenty of time." The truck rounded a turn and stopped by a wide screened-in lean-to, a chimney rising from its back. Before it was a fire pit, surrounded by logs, and a large stack of wood. "Come on." He put the truck into park and stepped out. "I want to show you something before he gets here."

Curious, I followed him, picking my way through some overgrown brush and around to the back of the structure, where a large padlock held two double doors shut. He twisted the combination on the lock, tugged, and then opened it up, revealing a surprisingly neat storage area with a dozen shelves stacked with boxes, containers, bottles, and tools. Everything was labeled, and he pulled out a box under a heading marked 'clays'. He pried open the lid and pulled out a round clay disk. "Here." He held it out for me.

I took it, turning it over in my hand. "What's this?"

"A sporting clay. What do you think?"

What did I think? I studied it, confused. "It's nice."

"Are you emotionally attached to it?"

I laughed. "No."

"Throw it against the wall." He nodded at the side of the lean-to.

"What? Why?"

"Just get your aggression out on it. See if you can get it to break."

"What if I damage the wall?"

"That's not going to happen. Just fling it with all your might."

I stepped back a few paces and cranked back my arm, heaving the small disk forward in my best impression of a pitch. It hit the wooden side and smashed, breaking into a dozen pieces and falling to the ground. I frowned, aware of the mess I had made.

He laughed. "Good job."

"And… *what* was the purpose of that? To show my brute strength?"

"To prove you wrong." He bent down, picking up the shards and collecting them in his palm. I crouched beside him and started to help. "There is no such thing as a skeet."

"What?"

He nodded to the destroyed remains of the disk. "Skeet shooting is shooting clay targets, like the one you just massacred."

Well, I felt *stupid*. I picked up a broken piece and recalled my declaration of love for skeet and loud insistence they be kept alive at all costs. My cheeks warmed, and my knees bumped against his as I settled back on my heels. "Oh."

His hand reached out, cupping my cheek and pulling my chin up to meet his gaze. I expected to see scorn, a cocky smile pulling at his mouth, but he wasn't smiling. He was studying me, his dark brown eyes kind as his gaze moved across my face, drawing to my lips and staying there. He pulled gently, asking for more, and I wavered, weak in my position, weak in the force of that worshipping look. I shouldn't, but I wanted to, could still feel the ache of that missed opportunity in the car. He pulled me forward and I let him, our lips meeting.

It wasn't a crash. It wasn't confident. It was a tentative brush, our contact whisper soft and quick. We parted, and his hand moved into my hair, gripping the strands and pulling me back to his mouth. The second kiss was stronger, heavy with need, my mouth opening beneath his, his tongue moving in as my hands found him. I hung on for balance, my nails digging into the shirt on his chest and bicep, needing more. We broke and rejoined, my eyes closing, our kiss deepening, my body coming alive, every spark firing, need flaring, my recklessness growing bolder with every confident swipe of his tongue.

In that moment, I didn't want to protect Declan Moss. I wanted him to want me. To take my heart as his own. I wanted to feel, and be unafraid, and to trust in him to protect *me*.

31

Declan kicked at the screen door to the base camp, and it swung open, the familiar smells of burnt wood, citronella candles, and grass hitting his nose. He ignored it, his attention focused on the woman in his arms, their legs tangling as he maneuvered them toward the picnic table in the middle of the room. Their mouths fought over the kiss, the taste of her imprinting on his mind as he gripped her waist and lifted her onto the table, bringing her face almost level to his. Her knees parted and he moved in between them, pulling her ass to the edge of the table as he deepened their kiss.

She was addicting. Not just her mouth, or the way that her body fit perfectly in his hands and against his body. It was more her reactions. Her smiles. Her lovable comments. The concern she had—for him, for the non-existent skeets, for the random events in life that she thought she controlled. He pulled at the thin straps of her tank top, getting them halfway down her forearms and exposing her bra, tan and practical, the conservative choice as much of a turn-on as her lace one had been. It was a front closure, and he undid the clasp, weakened by the sight of her breasts, falling loose, her nipples red and pert. She groaned, and when he lowered his hands to her breasts, brushing his palms over her nipples, she shuddered into his touch. He tightened his grip, his thumbs moving reverently over the taut tips, and watched her response, the heavy lids of her eyes, the way her legs parted, hips thrusting forward. God, if only she was naked right now. He would take his time, tease her senseless, and coax a half dozen orgasms from those lips. Fuck her money. Fuck her worries. He knelt, dragging his fingers down her shirt and thumbed open the clasp of her shorts. No belt. Easy access. He glanced up, meeting her eyes, and held the contact as he brought himself to standing. "What do you want, Autumn?"

She panted softly, her breasts heavy and hanging, eyes wild, her hands reaching and making tight fists in the cotton of his shirt. "What do I want?" Her words wobbled on the question.

"I want to rip off these shorts, spread your knees, and bury myself in you. I want to take you on this table, and then over it, and then on that chair. I have a long list of the ways I want to enjoy every inch of your body, but I need to make sure, before I lose control, that that is what you want to do." He tried to keep his voice level, but his dick heard every word, swelling to full attention as the ideas clogged his head.

Her eyes dropped to the crotch of his jeans, and she inhaled sharply. "What I want…" she mumbled.

He started to speak and she held up a hand and shushed him. "Let me think about this for a minute."

His dick scowled, contemplating retreat, and flexed in protest against the seam of his jeans. His hands tightened on her breasts, lifting them to his mouth, and he gently kissed a line across the deep dip of her cleavage, waiting for her to decide. He trailed the kisses up over her collarbone and along her neck, gently nibbling on her cheek before he ended with a soft kiss on her lips.

"What do I want…" she repeated when he pulled away, her eyes half shut.

He carefully re-clasped her bra and pulled up her tank top, covering her beautiful cleavage and positioning the straps over her shoulders, leaning forward to kiss a freckle he spotted on her collarbone. "Let's go open up my cabin."

"Wait." She grabbed his shirt, pulling to keep him in place. "I haven't decided what I want."

It didn't matter. Uncertainty was a no in his book. He shook his head. "Maybe it's better for us to take a step back."

She blinked, focusing on him. "A step back? Sure. Yeah. Good." She pinned her knees together and pushed off the table, coming to her feet. "Excellent idea."

Excellent idea? No. It was a fucking awful idea. She was supposed to argue with him, and certainly didn't have to be so cheery about it. He frowned, watching as she wandered the room, exclaiming over the wood stove, the double fridges, and the full bath, as if she'd never seen modern plumbing before. She lingered in the living room section, trailing her hand over the wicker couch, then finally completed her tour of the space. Adjusting himself in his jeans, he swung open the door and waited for her to step out.

"It's fancy," she said, stepping through the door. "There's a bookcase with board games and movies. I haven't seen a VHS in years."

"Super fancy," he intoned.

"Maybe we could play Pictionary tonight. I'm awesome at it. You could be on my team." She walked ahead of him, swinging her arms as she went, her back rigid, voice high. "I once won a pecan pie in a Pictionary game, which is funny, since I don't even like pecan pie. Want to know the word I won on?" She swung to face him, and almost tripped over the root of a pine tree.

"Careful." He steadied her, taking her around to her side of the truck and opening the door.

"Water Buffalo." At his quizzical look, she continued. "That's what the word was. Have you ever tried to draw a water buffalo?"

He struggled to keep from smiling. "Can't say I have."

"It's pretty impossible." She twisted into place on the seat, reaching for her belt.

"Congratulations." He made sure her feet were inside, then carefully shut the truck door.

Rounding the front of the truck, he fought back a smile at the paradox of the woman inside. Incredibly passionate, yet guarded. An open book, but also a complete mystery. Any other woman he'd pursued would have been on her back right now, yet she fought to keep her distance. It should have driven him crazy, but instead, he couldn't get enough. His phone rang and he paused by his truck door, fishing in his pocket and pulling out his cell. Seeing Nate's name, he answered the call.

"Bad news."

"What?" Declan watched Autumn through the front windshield. She had the yellow medical book back in hand and was flipping through the pages.

"I can't make it. Something came up with Benta."

"Something?" He frowned.

Nate let out a low laugh, his voice dropping. "You know how it is."

Yeah, right now, looking at Autumn, he knew exactly how it was. And he couldn't say that he was disappointed to hear he'd be alone with Autumn. Nate, while entertaining, had a habit of dominating the room with his charisma. It'd be nice to have some one-on-one time with her.

"I'm sorry," he said. "I feel bad, given that it's your birthday."

"No need for that." He could hear the smile in Nate's voice and winced at the thought of all it could mean.

"Are we still going to have a job come Monday?"

Nate scoffed. "Give me some credit."

"Just ... don't piss her off." He hung up the phone and pulled at the handle of the door.

Assuming this news didn't cause Autumn to want to go home, it'd be just the two of them out here. Which sounded pretty fucking perfect to him.

32

Declan's cabin was a twin to mine, with plaid sheets instead of blue. His backpack took up considerably less space than mine had, and I started to rethink everything I'd packed. Surprisingly enough, there were fire extinguishers mounted on the walls and first aid kits visible, proof that someone with two brain cells had had input in the outfitting. He pulled a bag out from under the bed and then a variety of camo-colored garments. "I'm going to head out to the range and work through a box or two."

"I'll come." I shifted my weight on the light brown linoleum. "If you don't mind."

He grinned and pulled his shirt over his head. "I hoped you would. Without Nate, it's going to be a little lonely."

I wasn't prepared for a shirtless Declan. That night we had met... the room had been dark, body parts slapping and entangling, my hair flinging, kisses interrupting my views of his body. But here, with the afternoon sun blaring through the open window, his abs bunching as he worked open the top of his jeans, I was getting the full effect. Long sinewy muscles connecting strong shoulders, beefy biceps and toned chest muscles. He had those V muscles, which I do remember scraping my nails along as I'd taken him down my throat. I blushed, whirling to face the door as his pants fell to the floor, the belt buckle clanking loudly upon impact. I covered my eyes as an additional precaution, a move which earned a chuckle from behind me.

"I've got underwear on. There's nothing to see."

Nothing to see? I half choked on the concept, my mind permanently fried with the view's imprint. I was already rethinking my brain fart from the camp house. You know, when he asked what I wanted—namely, *did I want his beautiful penis inside of me*—and I had stuttered along like a crackhead. There was a rustle of clothes and the sound of a zipper being drawn.

"There. Fully covered."

I turned slightly, not trusting him until my peripheral vision showed him clothed, in a head to toe getup that instantly sent my vagina into Sahara territory. "Huh." I dropped my hands from my eyes. "Sexy."

"Don't laugh." He held up a smaller version of his own overalls. "I got one for you, too."

"I'm *not* wearing that." I made a face, and did a convincing job of waving my hands in the air in an emphatic gesture that clearly communicated the concept.

"We'll be going through some high brush and wet areas. That, combined with the bugs and the snakes…" He thrust out the garment. "Just wear it. It'll make me worry less."

As a fellow worrier, I took the item out of professional courtesy. Plus, if I looked half as ridiculous as he did, then that was one more brick in the Not-Having-Sex and Keeping-Things-Platonic wall. Apparently, I needed to build that bad boy high enough to keep my libido at bay. I held the outfit against my chest and nodded at the door. "Can I have some privacy?"

He winced. "You know how to smash a guy's hopes and dreams." Moving past me, he paused by the door, glancing down at my boots. "Mine had built-in footwear, but the smaller sizes don't. Just tuck the bottoms into your boots."

"Sure." I waited until the door shut behind him, then quickly undid my boots and stripped out of my shorts. The outfit was huge below, my socks swimming in fabric as I stepped in and pulled the giant straps over my shoulders and clipped them to the front bib. I found a big plastic zipper along the side and pulled it up, the outfit tightening a little. I made the mistake of glancing in the small mirror over the sink. *Wow*. I'd thought the potato dress was bad. This made that look like a Dallas Cowboy cheerleader uniform.

"You're killing me..." Declan called from the front porch.

"You can come in." I sat down on the bed and lifted up my first boot. "I'm dressed."

He cracked open the door, testing the waters, then stepped inside. When he saw me, he didn't react, making me wonder exactly how many women he'd seen in this getup. A sharp pain hit my gut, one I recognized as jealousy. I pushed it away and pulled my hair into a ponytail.

He peered down at me. "Let me get you a better shirt."

I glanced down. "What's wrong with this one?"

He ignored the question, fishing through the big bag and finding a long-sleeve tee covered in a leafy print, just like the one he had on. Passing it to me, he turned away. "Go ahead. I'm not looking."

I grimaced, unhooking the overalls and quickly swapping my tank top for the scratchy long-sleeved tee. Re-hooking the clasps, I stood. "Okay. Thoroughly covered." I held out my arms for his inspection.

He turned, gave me the once-over, and then flashed me a thumbs up. "Perfect."

Perfect? This guy needed to get his eyes checked.

We were ass deep in the woods when the skies opened. I smiled when the sprinkles began, appreciating the cool dots of them on my face. But then, without warning, it was a monsoon, torrential rain soaking us the moment it hit. Declan grabbed his gun and threw a cover over the skeet shooter, waving me toward the truck. I scrambled to grab my bag, struggling with the heavy tote as I splashed through the downfall toward the truck. Declan rescued me, reaching out and grabbing the tote's handle. "I got this!" he called over the rain. "Go!"

I abandoned the bag and ran, climbing into the truck and slamming the door. Wiping rain from my eyes, I searched for something to dry off with. It was a hopeless situation, my hair a portable water bucket, one that was leaking water all over the place. I leaned forward over the floorboard and tried to wring out the thick blonde strands, grateful for the rubber floor mats. Through the blurry downpour, I watched as Declan ran around the front of the truck and opened the back door, tossing the heavy gun into the back where he'd put my bag. A moment later, he joined me in the front seat.

"Damn." He took off his baseball cap and shook the head of it out. "That came from nowhere."

"The clouds were there. I should have realized it was growing." I peered out the window, looking up at the sky, now dark with cloud cover. At least there wasn't any lightning. "Can we make it back through this?"

"It'll pass over in a little bit. Let's wait it out. We can eat those sandwiches."

My stomach instantly cheered at the idea, even as a cold shiver vibrated through me. He noticed the tremor and nodded to me, his brow pinching. "You need to get out of those wet clothes." He reached for the keys and started the ignition, turning the dial to start the heat. "This'll help, but not if you're sitting there in that soaked shirt."

I was well aware of the dangers, and wasn't ready to court disaster with a cold. I squeezed the right sleeve, testing the viability of wringing it dry, but it was a useless endeavor. I glanced at the back. "I don't have another shirt."

He undid the top of his coveralls, then skinned the wet cotton off, over his head. "I'd offer you this one, but it's worse than yours."

I weighed my options, watching as he left the top of his overalls undone, the cut of his hip visible, the edge of his black underwear showing. The cold seemed to be sinking into my bones, and I felt the annoying click of my teeth beginning to chatter. I made my decision and moved quickly, the soaked material suction-cupping itself to my skin as I peeled it off. I got the long-sleeved shirt over my head and dropped it onto the floorboard with a wet splat.

Leaving my bra on, I angled the vents toward me, almost moaning in pleasure as the warm air hit my bare skin.

"Better?" Declan's voice was a little husky, and I glanced over to see him watching me, his own skin goosebumping along his chest muscles.

I looked away, rubbing my hands over my arms. "So much better." I did a foot check, my toes nice and dry, thanks to my boots.

He twisted around, reaching into the backseat and grabbing the small cooler from the back. We'd stopped at a little deli in the last town before the camp, getting Pepsis and some ham and cheese hoagies. He passed me one and I unrolled it, spreading the paper across my lap and picking up the sub. A clap of lightning hit, and I jumped, the strike bright enough to light the interior of the cab.

"That felt close." Declan peered out the front window, looking up at the sky.

I nodded and took a big bite of the sandwich, surprised by how hungry I was. Thinking back, it had been five hours since we'd eaten, and that had just been a banana and one of Ansley's blueberry muffins, the snack passed through the window right before we'd pulled away from her house. He seemed similarly famished, and we fell into a companionable silence, save the crack of a soda and the steady cadence of rain.

I turned the heat down, my body temperature back to normal, and relaxed against the seat, slowly chewing a bite of the sandwich. They'd put pickles on it, which I normally wasn't a fan of, but honestly—it wasn't bad.

"So… No Nate?" I opened the sub and picked through its ingredients, pulling the remaining pickles off and depositing them on the white wrap. "What happened?"

"He didn't exactly say." He wiped at his mouth with a napkin. "But chances are, it's something to do with our client."

"A romantic something?"

He chuckled. "Yeah."

"So, he's single?"

He nodded, finishing a sip of his soda before speaking. "Obsessively so."

I took a sip of soda and watched the water streaming down the windshield. I hated to admit it, but I was almost glad they weren't coming. While their presence would have helped my stronghold of virtue, it was nice to be alone with Declan. It had been fun to watch him shoot and hear his stories. His dad had taught him everything he knew about guns, and hunting and—after Declan's mom died—about life. He sounded like a really great man, even if his love was hidden behind what sounded to be five layers of prickly exterior. Declan had shown me the proper safety techniques to handling a gun, though I had drawn the line at actually firing it.

It was kinda sexy, I had to admit, watching him out in the woods, his shirt sleeves pushed up, hitting each target with unwavering precision. And I'd be lying if I said my mind hadn't been skittering all over the place with thoughts of what we were going to spend this alone time doing.

I nodded to the rain. "How long do you think this will last?"

"Ten, maybe fifteen minutes, tops."

Two hours later, I rested my head in his lap and stared up at the truck's ceiling. The rain was unrelenting, the beat of it against the roof unwavering and constant.

"And her current boyfriend, according to Nate's sister's snooping—which, by the way, rivals yours—is a shrink. Which"—he tilted his head to one side with a rueful grin—"Isn't such a bad thing. Maybe he'll understand her more than I ever did."

I watched his face, looking for hurt or longing, but it was … amused? If someone had cheated on me, it would have left deep emotional scars, but he seemed to be fine with the fact that his ex-girlfriend had humped her way across the capital city. I squinted and did the math. They had broken up the day of the plane crash… which had been almost seven months ago. Thinking back over my time watching Declan, he had changed, his mood more somber at the beginning, and lightening up as time had passed. I'd barely noticed the subtle transformation, but I'd been going through my own mourning and healing process. I looked away, and played with the back of his hand, which rested on my bare stomach.

He looked down at me. "What about you?"

I pretended to misunderstand the question. "Oh, God no. My shrink is a complete tool bag." I made a face at the thought of Dr. E in a sexual scenario. "Plus, he knows all about my undying love for you."

He crooked one brow and I laughed. "Okay, not love. Obsession? Possessive twerk?" I tried out the different titles, then shrugged. "Let's just say he knows that you and I are inexplicably bound by circumstance."

"And he hasn't committed you yet?" He tilted his hand back and I threaded my fingers through his. "No offense."

"None taken." I smiled. "He doesn't believe that I have extraordinary guardian angel powers, but he *does* think that my attempts to protect you are helping me heal from my mom's death." It was surprising how comfortable I felt telling him that. I hadn't even shared that fact with Ansley, though she'd often accused me of channeling my guilt over Mom into my Declan crusade.

"That makes sense." He tightened his fingers, squeezing my hand, and I risked a peek upward, into his face. It was kind, non-judgmental, despite the *guardian angel* mention that always sent Ansley into a tizzy.

"I mean," I said quickly. "I'm still crazy. Obviously."

"Obviously," he repeated with mock severity. "But beautifully so."

I hiccupped out a laugh, closing my eyes when he reached across his body with his left hand and tucked a loose tendril of hair behind my ear. "Yeah?" I asked, lulled into a dreamy state by the gentle brush of his fingertips across my face.

"And it's sweet how you watch out for me. How you worry over me." He leaned forward, and his face came into focus, my eyes drinking in every high-definition detail. His short-clipped beard. The flecks of hazel in his eyes. The concerned pinch of the muscle between his brows. The pale tint of his lips. "I don't mind it."

"Thank God, since it seems to be the only thing holding my sanity in check," I quipped, surprised when he shifted on the seat, his hands sliding under my shoulders and pulling me up into his lap. *He was going to kiss me*. I could feel it, the crackle of expectation, that heady moment where I wanted it and he wanted it, and I was probably giving him bedroom eyes and all of the signs, and *oh my god, I think I'm leaning into this*.

And then, Declan Moss kissed me. He kissed me and I forgot about Dr. E. I forgot about his ex. I forgot about my duties as a guardian angel, and any rules I should be following, and I responded as any red-blooded woman would.

I grabbed at the back of his head and, with the rain drilling a romantic cadence along the roof, kissed him back.

33

"Well."

Declan watched as Autumn cleaned out the backseat of his truck with the efficiency of a deranged woman.

"That can *NOT* happen again."

He smiled as she slung a Pepsi can into a trash bag as if it had personally wronged her.

"I mean, what is *wrong* with us?" She spun to him, her face flushed, hair wild, and God, he could fall in love with her. He realized it in the same moment that she stabbed the air between them with her finger. "We need to get our act together!"

He closed the distance between them, pinning her back against the side of the truck, a surprised squawk coming from her in the moment before his lips closed on hers. She argued against his mouth, her hands attempting to shove him back even as her mouth fought for more. He slid his hands down her body, cupping her delicious ass and pulling it against him, branding her as his own. *Fuck,* he couldn't get enough of her.

When he finally came up for air, she was clinging to him for support. He ensured that she had stable footing, then gave her a quick final kiss. He smiled at her. "Let me clean the truck out. Go get those boots off and relax."

She scowled at him. "I'm not going to *relax*, Declan. You obviously aren't taking this problem seriously."

He moved around the open door and took her spot, pulling the gun bag out. "What problem? Us being attracted to each other? That's not a problem."

She followed him toward the camp house. "You realize what just happened right? We had *sex* back there." She whispered the word as if there were anyone around to hear it.

He smiled and set down the bag by the door. "Yes, I remember." And that was a memory that would be branded on him for a while. Stripping her down in the front seat. Reclining back, her bare feet settling next to his thighs, his hands lifting her up and down atop him. He'd never be able to grab that roof handle again without remembering her holding onto it for balance, her eyes shuttering closed, her mouth opening in a silent O of pleasure.

"...and all the *kissing*, and the *looks*..." She was ticking items off on her hand, her focus flipping to him as he turned to head back to the truck. "Hey!" She jogged next to him. "This is important!"

"I'm not going to stop kissing and looking at you." He pulled at the tailgate handle, lowering the door and frowning at the kindling he'd collected before shooting, now too wet to do anything with. The same went for the charcoal he'd brought for the grill, which was now a damp mess, the bag weakened and split from the rain. He'd have to chop up some of the logs they had and get to their dry centers. He closed the tailgate.

"I came here to keep you safe, not to bounce around on your penis," she said plaintively, and he couldn't stop the laugh that fell out of him.

Coming to a stop, he turned to face her. "I'm sorry I had sex with you."

She fidgeted. "Well, it wasn't *all* your fault. I was a pretty willing participant."

"Yeah, the whooping and hollering kind of gave you away." He smiled, expecting her to react and was rewarded by her irritated eye-roll.

"We both know there wasn't whooping and hollering. Not this time." She held up her hands in surrender. "I can't be held responsible for what happened that first night."

His dick twitched at the comparison. She was right, there hadn't been any loud cries of pleasure this time. Instead, he'd experienced an entirely different set of Autumn sounds. Soft inhales. A quiet mew of pleasure when she'd settled down on him. His name in a dozen different ways—panted, begged, whispered, and worshipped. It had only gotten better when he'd laid her across the bench seat and settled on top of her.

Thunder rumbled and her neck snapped toward the sound. "We should get inside."

"I'll get the rest of the stuff out of the truck. You go on in."

She listened to him, going into the building without an argument. By the time he brought the last box of clays in, she had the cooler lid up and half the contents out on the table. He pulled the screen door shut and her head popped up.

"What are you thinking about for dinner?" She gestured to the items. "You kind of have a hodgepodge of stuff here."

"I packed it thinking Nate would be with us." He came closer, looking over the items. "You want steaks or burgers? There's a grill on the side we can use."

She winced when a strike of lightning hit nearby. "Outside? No way." She gestured to the stove. "I could do burgers in a skillet, if you have one."

"There's a ton of pots and pans inside the oven. Feel free to go nuts."

She smiled, and he felt his heart flip a little in response.

There wasn't Pictionary, much to Autumn's disappointment. There was a Scrabble board, and they spent a couple of hours bent over the board, competing over words. She cooked burgers, he opened up a bag of chips, and they worked their way through most of Nate's beer.

The more she drank, the more she talked, and the more layers that unfolded.

"Most embarrassing death," he prompted.

"Too many to name," she shot back, sitting sideways in the wicker chair.

"Cop-out."

She gave a confident smirk, which might join his list of top five favorite Autumn expressions. "I can give you five without thinking twice about it."

He spread his hands. "I'm waiting."

She stuck her thumb out and rattled off the first one. "Kenneth Pinyan, who died from internal injuries after having anal sex with a stallionnnn."

Her word slurred, the final syllable given extra attention, and he smiled at how quickly the alcohol had hit her, the last hour a quick downward turn into clumsy Autumn. Still, he nodded, giving her the point and waiting to see if she had anything else.

"Number two. The owner of Segway was killed when his Segway drove off a cliff."

Not really embarrassing, as much as ironic, but he let it slide.

She counted the third one out. "Three. Dayton, Ohio. 1986. A couple was having sex in a car. He died mid-thrust, and she was stuck underneath him. Died of hypothermia and dehydra..." She paused, her brow furrowing.

He waited for her to continue. She didn't, and he guessed at the word. "Dehydration?"

"No, I'm fine." She lifted the bottle of beer as proof. "What were we talking about?"

"That's it." He swiped the beer from her fingers. "No more alcohol for you." Pouring out the bottle in the sink, he reminded her of the task.

"Oh. Right." She started to launch into a fourth and he tossed her bottle in the trash and held up his hands in surrender.

"You know what? I give up and stand corrected. I will never question your Guardian Angel knowledge again."

"Thank you." She stood up and did a little bow, her right leg buckling, and she swayed before sitting back down. "God, I'm drunk." She lifted a hand to her head. "I think the alcohol is making my headache worse."

He came to her chair and bent over to get a kiss. That was another great thing about drunk Autumn. She seemed to relax her stiff stance against affection, a position he would eventually decimate altogether.

She gazed up at him, her lips parting, back stiffening, and her arms folded, limp-wristed, into her chest. He froze at the sight, his chest tightening, and examined her more closely. In his chest, threads of panic began to pulse. *What the…*

"Autumn?" he said quietly, trying to keep his voice calm while his heart galloped against his chest. "What's wrong with your eyes?"

She looked at him, confused. Leaning forward, she tried to push at his chest and then, without warning, vomited all over the floor.

34

He drove, his hand on her chest, keeping her upright, and dialed 9-1-1. The truck bumped hard, and she mumbled out a curse, her body curving around his hand. The operator answered, and he explained their situation, cursing the camp's lack of physical address.

"We're off Chat Franklin Road. If you can have an ambulance at the gas station by the boat ramp, I can be there in ten minutes. Maybe sooner."

"You shouldn't be driving," Autumn said quietly. "You've been drinking."

Yeah, well. The ambulance wouldn't be able to get down the camp's roads. He gripped the wheel tightly, answering the emergency operator's questions and trying to keep the F250 on the muddy path. What the *fuck* had he been thinking, bringing her out here? Why couldn't he have been a normal man and taken her on a romantic getaway to a beach resort, with a hospital and modern conveniences readily available?

"I really think you're over..." Her voice dropped off and he looked over to see her head loll forward, heavy on its axis.

He cursed, jerking the truck into park and trying to lift her head. "She's unconscious," he told the operator grimly.

"Is her posture still decorticated?"

Decorticate posture had been a term taught to him in his EMT classes —the posturing characterized by a stiff frame, arms bent in toward the body, the wrist and fingers held on the chest. Autumn's exhibition of the signs had been his first indication that something was seriously wrong. When his gaze had darted from that to her eyes, one of her pupils dilated, he had started to piece together the other symptoms. The confusion. Incoordination. Headache. It hadn't been the alcohol. Something was seriously wrong with her—and her symptoms were getting worse.

He checked her. "Yes. Her legs are stiff also, they're sticking straight out." He racked his memory, trying to remember what decorticate posture had meant. It wasn't a stroke, but it had been serious. Something with the brain.

"I've got an ambulance on its way, but it's important that you get there as soon as *safely* possible."

The woman didn't need to repeat herself. He slid back over into the driver's seat and jerked the truck into drive, flooring the gas and praying, desperately, that he wouldn't be too late.

The ambulance was waiting at the closed gas station, lights flashing, the back doors open, paramedics ready. When he came to a stop, they were already pulling open the passenger door and rolling up the gurney. He launched out of the truck and to their side, barking out symptoms and timeframes, giving them everything he knew about her.

"Contact her next of kin," the closest EMT said. "We'll need medical history and to know if there are any health surrogates or advance directives in place."

Advance directives. The words stopped him in his place, the thought of life-prolonging procedures, or Autumn's incapacity... he raked his fingers through his hair, wanting to rip out every strand by its roots.

He ran beside the gurney, grabbing her hand, but it was limp, her features slack, void of life.

"Where are you taking her?" He choked out.

"Ocala Regional. You can ride with us or follow."

He warred between leaving his truck or driving after the three beers, Autumn's concern echoing in his mind. "I'll ride with you."

They began to load the gurney and he ran around to the truck, grabbing his cell and finding Autumn's in the cupholder. Making it back to the ambulance, he gripped the handle and stepped up into the clinical space.

"You aren't supposed to be calling me," the female voice drawled. "You're supposed to be having vigorous outdoorsy sex and taking notes to tell me about later."

"Ansley, this is Declan Moss." In another world, another moment, he might have seen the humor in her greeting. Now, he could barely speak without breaking down.

"Oh." She paused. "Declan. Hello. Is everything okay?"

"No. I need you to come to the hospital in Ocala. Something's happened with Autumn. Do you know if she has any medical problems?"

She inhaled sharply, then spoke to someone in the background. "She doesn't have any medical problems. She's perfectly healthy, aside from a sugar addiction."

He didn't know whether to be relieved or more concerned. If they knew what this was, at least they could do something to fix it. For it to come out of nowhere… his hand tightened on the phone.

"Declan, I need to know what happened. You've told me just enough to freak me the fuck out. Did she get injured? Shot? What's going on?" Her voice grew harder with each question, and he wished he had more to tell her.

"She started to have a headache. She grew confused. Uncoordinated. I thought—we thought it was the alcohol, but it started to get worse. Much worse."

"Headaches?" She let out a strangled laugh. "She always has headaches. That's normal. And she's... Autumn. She's always a little uncoordinated and confused. Maybe this is nothing. Like you said—"

"It's something. I need you to come here as soon as possible. They're asking for a health surrogate or advance directives."

She fell silent, then he heard her scream at her husband to get the car.

35

Autumn died at 10:12pm.

It was a short death. They brought her back to life as Declan watched, paddles shocking her heart back into action, her pulse spiking to life on the monitor. But it was weak and the issue was her brain.

Now, he huddled in a waiting room chair, Autumn's family beside him, and tried to sort through his feelings. It seemed unfair that he had spent six months running from her, when he could have been holding her. Loving her. By the time they had finally met, he'd only had a week with her. A combined twenty-four hours, tops. That wasn't enough time, not when those hours had been the best of his life. Anger spiked through him at the unfairness of it all. She had spent so much time protecting him and he—in the moment when he could have protected her—he had been the one to put her in danger.

If she'd been home, she would have seen the signs. Realized something was wrong. Called an ambulance.

And … if she'd never seen him that day of the plane crash, she never would have attributed her head pains to his safety. She would have gone to a doctor. Followed normal protocol instead of wasting all of her time following him around, worrying about him, when *she* had been the one at risk.

A colloid cyst had been the cause. All of those sharp pains she had associated with his danger—that had been her brain screaming for help. And now, it had progressed to the stage where the cyst had blocked the flow of cerebrospinal fluid. Declan had been searching every site on the Internet to educate himself on CSF and colloid cysts, and the more he learned, the more his stress rose. The only solution was the one they were taking now—a complicated and high-risk surgery to attempt to remove the cyst.

The three potential outcomes were all bleak. First: potential paralysis of her entire left side. The second: coma. And finally… and the most likely of the three: death. He asked what the chances were of a complete recovery, but was only given a regretful frown. *"At this point, those chances are too slim to measure. This is the time to set realistic expectations."*

The "realistic expectations" were that he would not leave her side. If she was paralyzed, he would take care of her. He'd build her a beautiful home with ramps and unique design features to accommodate her limitations. If she was in a coma, he would sit beside her bed every day until she woke up. And if she died… at that point of the thought process, was when Declan normally broke down into tears.

Ansley and Roger were used to it. They had all spent the last two days in varying states of grief. Autumn's niece and nephew had been shielded from it, a carousel of babysitters soon replaced by Bridget, who stepped in and offered to keep them at her house. She'd been filling their time with trips to the zoo, movies, junk food and fun. At the moment, all they knew was that Autumn was "sick" and had the general impression that it was something as simple as a cold.

Four and a half hours had passed since they'd taken her into surgery. It should have been over by now. Ansley had worn out the path to the reception desk, her constant requests for updates yielding no new information. Declan pinched his palms together and, for the hundredth time since loading her into the ambulance, began to pray.

Finally, more than two hours after the surgery was supposed to be over, the door to the ER swung open. The doctor came out, slowly pulling off his gloves. Declan looked into his face and saw all he needed to.

OCTOBER

ONE MONTH LATER

"Mr. Moss." The man stood, extending his hand, a leather portfolio pressed tightly to his breast. "I've heard so much about you." He gestured to the empty seat across from his desk. "Please, sit. Unless you'd prefer we move to the couch?"

"No, this is fine." Declan took one of the high wingback chairs. "Where would Autumn sit?"

The man thought it over. "She liked to wander. Touch things. She moved around a lot. I suspect the majority of her seating decisions were designed to irritate me." He almost smiled, the edge of his mouth twitching before settling back into place.

"She liked to irritate you?"

He set the portfolio on the desk and opened it to a blank pad of paper. "She didn't like me very much, I'm afraid."

His memory was fuzzy, but he believed the term she had used was *tool bag,* so the shrink's powers of perception were capable. Declan smiled. "That's okay. She spent half of our interactions shoving me away from her."

The man sat down in the heavy leather chair, taking his time to arrange himself into place, one thin knee crossing over the other. Picking up a polished black pen from the desk, he uncapped it and studied him. "I was told by the trust that she is in a coma, is that correct?"

Declan nodded, his throat tightening at the simple four-letter word, one he had never given much thought to before. Now, it was his life. Wake. Shower. Work. Autumn. Coma. Sleep.

"If you're here to find out things about her, I'm afraid I can't help you with that." The man rolled the pen over in his hand. "Whether Ms. Jones is incapacitated or not, she is still considered to be living, and our conversations are protected by confidentiality laws."

She is still considered to be living. Of *course* she was. She was less than a mile away. Skin warm. Heart beating. He'd just eaten lunch with her. For this prick to even suggest anything else… he gripped the arm of the chair tightly and forced himself to calm down.

His emotions, during the month since her surgery, had been all over the place. He was wound up, jittery. Prone to anger one moment and anguish the next. Autumn's entrance and sudden exit from his life had left him with a mountain of feelings that he struggled to process and didn't know how to handle.

The man's gaze focused on his tight grip on the chair and he sat back a little in his seat. "Grief is a very powerful emotion, Mr. Moss. There are ways to work through it, if you'd like some help."

"I'm not *grieving*," he said tightly. "I'm fine. She's fine. I'm here because …" His mind floundered. Why *was* he here? He had made the appointment without thinking, desperate for contact with anyone and everyone who had known her and chasing… searching for some sign of her life. He'd walked in this office with a glimmer of hope that this man might say something, anything that would help. But maybe he had had the right mindset from the beginning—and kept psychology in the garbage bag of events that weren't for him.

So far, he'd walked dogs with Mrs. Robchek, then sat down in her floral-covered living room and received in-depth tours of every scrapbook Autumn had ever made her.

He'd driven south and had dinner with Mr. Clevepepper, who had griped about politics, the heat, and the wax jobs of The Villages' women, all the while saying little about Autumn, other than complimenting her coffee.

He'd taken Mr. Oinks to his vet appointment and met Adam, who had expressed sharp concern for Autumn while giving Declan the exciting news that Mr. Oinks' reluctant testicle had finally dropped.

He'd eaten a dozen meals with Ansley and Roger, taken Paige and Caleb to the playground, and wandered through Autumn's empty house like a lost puppy.

He'd run out of places to go, and this session was only five minutes in and the prick was already making everything worse. *She is still considered to be living.*

"Autumn had a singular focus and that was on you," the doctor said, peering at him through tortoise-framed glasses. "Don't consider it a burden of guilt. As I told Autumn in our last session, I believe that watching out for you was helping her recover from the loss of her mother. She was a strong woman, Mr. Moss."

"She *is* a strong woman," he gritted out. "Stop talking about her as if she's gone."

The man nodded. "I understand."

He understands? What kind of bullshit response was that? He didn't understand anything about this situation, and he sure as hell wasn't fixing it. Out of every loose end he'd followed, this had been the biggest mistake.

He stood, moving to the door, the plush Oriental rug silencing the sounds of his steps, and he shoved the door open and breezed past the receptionist without saying a word.

Talk about a waste of three hundred dollars. No wonder she hated that man.

He jabbed at the elevator button and swallowed the wave of emotion that threatened his composure.

NOVEMBER

"Can you build me a dollhouse?" Paige threaded her fingers together and begged, her pigtails bobbing as she danced in place before him. "Pretty please?"

"Hmm…" Declan mused. "I don't know. I'm *very* expensive. Do you have money?"

"No." She shot out the word with such cheerfulness that he had to laugh.

"Do you have any ideas?"

"YES." She reached forward, turning a page in his pad and tugged at his pen, pulling it out of his hand. "Let me *show* you."

"Wait." He stopped her, carefully pulling the latest Aldrete drawings out from the book and opened his leather binder, sliding them into the pocket. "Okay, show me."

The little girl bent over the page, her pen working, the tip of her tongue stuck out in concentration. He closed his eyes for a moment, tired. He'd been at the office late, going over items with Nate, Benta's parcel finally picked out and purchased. Now, with the smells of pumpkin pie and turkey heavy on the air, and the soft couch enveloping him, the desire to settle back on the leather and sleep was overwhelming.

The sound of heels on wood floors woke him. He turned his head and watched as Ansley walked through the doorway and stopped, an orange dishtowel in hand. "Paige. Wash up for dinner."

"WAIT," she said plaintively. "I'm working with Declan."

"It's true." He smiled up at Autumn's sister and felt a stab of pain at the familiar features, the glimpse of what she would look like in five or six years. "We may have a new associate on our hands."

He thought of his secret project, one he was working on during late nights in Autumn's room and between Aldrete project drafts. A house, designed for her. One with a scrapbook room with giant windows that overlooked a garden. A giant doggie door, big enough to accommodate a getting-bigger-every-day pig. A master suite with room enough for two.

Ansley wandered over and looked over his shoulder at the sketch Paige was creating. It looked like a scribbly blob that could double as a doctor's signature. "Oh, yes." She leaned forward, her hand resting on her knees. "I see. Very intricate. Is there going to be a living room?"

Paige looked up at her with a blank expression. "OF COURSE." She jabbed the tip of the pen on the right side of the blog. "It's right here."

"Ah." Ansley nodded. "And your bedroom?"

"Here." Paige added a curly-Q of a circle to the top of the scribble.

"And what's this?" Declan pointed to a big looping area, filled in with a bunch of dots.

"That's Auttie's room." She smiled. "It's bigger so it can hold all of her machines."

His chest squeezed painfully and he glanced at Ansley, their eyes meeting over the top of the little girl's head.

"And these"—the tiny glitter-tipped finger tapping at all the little dots in the area—"these are her angels, watching over her until she wakes up."

Ansley's eyes brimmed with tears and she leaned forward, pressing a kiss to the top of Paige's head and bringing her into her chest.

"So?" Paige wiggled out of her mother's arms and fixed Declan with a stare that was impossible to run from. "Will you design it for me?"

He swallowed and gave her his best smile. "Yeah, sweetie. Of course I will." He met Ansley's eyes and she smiled, taking a deep breath.

"Now," she said. "Who is ready for turkey?"

He wasn't. The thought of food and family, of sitting down at their table without her ... it made his stomach cramp. But he couldn't look into Paige's beaming face, her sweet ability to include Autumn in all that she did, without putting on a mask and playing along.

He smiled. "I'll be right behind you guys." Picking up Paige's drawing, he ran a hand over her room for Autumn, then carefully opened his notebook and tucked it into place.

DECEMBER

Dear Autumn,

It doesn't seem right, celebrating our first Christmas in a hospital room. Still, I did the best I could. A drunk girl in a karaoke bar once told me that I had a sexy singing voice, so I tried a few lines of Have Yourself a Merry Little Christmas. It wasn't half bad, honestly. Had your panties been anything other than hospital-issued Teflon, they would have combusted. Also, small confession: I peeked at your panties. Then your breasts. I couldn't help myself. I missed them. I kissed them. I promised them all sorts of filthy activities by the time next Christmas rolls around.

You can't see the lights, but they're strung all around the room. Janice, your night nurse, is a real bitch when it comes to most things, but even she smiles when she walks in and sees the colorful glow. We snuck in a tree, which is hidden in your closet, but is dripping with every ornament that Paige and Caleb could find, and more than a dozen that they've made.

I went to my dad's for dinner. He's dating this woman who reminds me a little of you. She's quirky. Loveable. Caring. Extremely messy, which Dad has somehow managed to overlook with a smile, and that's a new look on his face. I gave them all of your updates, and the latest doctor's report. You probably don't know, but he comes in with me sometimes. He's real quiet, so if you've heard a lot of stoic grunts, that was him.

I miss you. It sounds crazy to miss a person after such a short time together, but I do. I miss you in a way that hurts my gut. I've beat myself up for every missed opportunity with you, but promise you—swear to you—that I'll make it up to you. You're going to be so sick of me when you wake up. You're going to be researching restraining orders and privacy fences and you better lock up your trash cans at night, because I have it on good authority that stealing someone's recycling is a straight ticket into their heart.

I opened your gift earlier and set it next to your bed. Spoiler alert: it's a baby monitor. The best they sell. It has a range of six miles, which easily covers the distance between my house and your room. During the day I leave it in my living room, so you can listen in on all of the interesting sounds that Mr. Oinks creates. I apologize in advance for his assortment of farts, but I know that each one will bring a smile to your face. And at night, you can listen in on the super exciting sounds of me cooking dinner, and watching TV with him, and going to sleep. I'd let you listen in on my more erotic activities (all solo of course) but Nurse Janice is already eyeing me like a prize pie in a county fair, so I don't want to fan that flame any brighter.

I don't ever want you to be alone and I hope this helps. I hope it gives you a sense that we are in your life, because you are always in ours.

I love you, Autumn.

Merry Christmas. Next year is going to be our greatest one yet.

JANUARY

The engagement announcement was buried on the third page of the Lifestyles section, right next to the obituaries.

Mr. and Mrs. Jeffrey Capp of Orlando, Florida are pleased to announce the engagement of their daughter Nicola Capp, to Dr. Frederick Stokes, originally of Waco, Texas. Ms. Capp, a graduate of Florida State University, is a beverage curator for a local restaurant. Dr. Stokes is a graduate of the University of Florida, and practices psychiatry at his office in Tallahassee, Florida. A March wedding is planned.

Declan read the announcement twice, then he tossed the paper back on the top of the trashcan, dumping his coffee cup into the can and heading for the door.

"So, that's it? No reaction?" Nate grabbed the paper and followed him out the door, weaving around a group of suits and jogging to catch up.

"I'm happy for her." He stepped onto the crosswalk and glanced over, meeting Nate's worried eyes. "Honestly." He glanced at his watch. "Now, come on. The cupcake store closes at two."

"I'm not going to lie, I'm a little freaked out by your laissez-faire attitude about this. And maybe I wouldn't be if we weren't heading to the birthday party of your unresponsive girlfriend."

Declan stopped suddenly and turned on him. "She's responsive. Last week there was a spike in her brain activity. I told you this."

"Right, the spike." His face softened. "I just don't want you to get hurt. Again." He lifted the paper. "Nicola's moving on. Maybe—"

"Don't even fucking think about finishing that statement." He snatched the paper from Nate's hand and shoved it into a trashcan. "I don't want Tinder, or to screw Jenn from the reception desk, or to go out and get drunk with a bunch of sorority girls you saw on Instagram. I want to eat a fucking cupcake and sit with Autumn, and tell her what a complete dipshit you are."

"You don't want to date other people, fine. But have you thought about what will happen if she does wake up? What might really happen?"

Nate's words cut deep into his biggest insecurity. "You think she won't be interested in me."

Nate lifted his shoulders in a shrug. "It's just that you've immersed yourself into this world where she is your everything, and I'm worried that she might wake up and..."

"And I'll be nothing to her."

"Yeah." Nate's face softened. "I'm just watching out for you. You know that."

He knew that. He just couldn't face that reality. Not right now. If and when it came to that—he'd deal with it, and accept whatever role she wanted to cast him in. Even if that role was just as her friend.

Nate reached forward and hugged him, the contact brief and strong. "Look. Forget I said anything. And tell her about Nicola, okay? Maybe she can work some voodoo magic and get the bitch to choke on her wedding cake."

"Deal." Declan pushed away from him and glanced at his watch. "But we need to—"

"Get to the cupcake store. Yeah. I got it. Let's carpe diem the shit out of some icing-topped chocolate ones."

FEBRUARY

Dear Autumn,

I've never been a big fan of Valentine's Day. But it's provided me the opportunity to write you a letter, so I'm secretly enjoying it on the inside, much as Mr. Oinks and I enjoyed an entire pan of heart-shaped ravioli last night, courtesy of your sister.

Mr. Oinks misses you. He likes to chase me in the yard. Eats everything in sight. Accepts belly scratches without complaint, and has no problem sleeping on my chest (he's getting really heavy) but I can see it in his eyes. He watches the door a lot. Perks up at the sight of Ansley, but then seems to deflate when he realizes it isn't you. I've got a plot to sneak him in here one night, but it's going to take a little more buttering up of the staff before I can make it happen.

Tonight, I have big plans to drown you in gushy stuff. Not that roses can compare to your garden, but I swapped out your normal vases for a set of long-stemmed roses. Don't worry, I'm still spending my Saturdays at your house, keeping all of your plants alive. The gardenias are looking a little sad, but everything else is surviving. Getting back to tonight's big event… I brought two movies that Ansley swears are your favorites. One is The Proposal, and the other is While You Were Sleeping. The latter seems a little morbid, seeing the similarities between your condition and his, but Ansley says it has a happy ending, so I'm game if you are. I've also got the biggest box of chocolates that Godiva sells, and I have big plans to eat any that you don't, so I hope you brought your appetite.

I miss you. I love you. I hope, wherever you are, that you come back to me soon.

Love, and Happy Valentine's Day…

Declan

MARCH

"Did you see the article?" The blonde nurse, the one who normally worked days, came to a stop in the middle of the hall, blocking his way.

Declan's first thought was that the article was about Autumn. His gaze dropped to the Tallahassee Democrat in her hands, and he wondered how long she had been standing there, waiting for him to arrive. The headline read COMING TO TOWN and showed a photo of him, Nate and Benta, at her new site. He took the paper from her and flipped it over, surprised that the article ran past the fold and onto another page. It detailed their work and showed a digital rendering of the complex. Six months of hard work, and they finally had a complete set of plans. From now on, the execution of the plans would be in the contractors' hands. The article would be good for business, though their calendar had filled up already with referrals Benta had sent over. She had barely set foot in this town, yet already seemed poised to take it over.

"You can keep that copy. I brought it for you." She followed him as he walked toward Autumn's room. "I've got another one in the break room that everyone's reading. You're a local celebrity!" She giggled.

A local celebrity? The piece had been an advertorial, the placement bought and paid for by Benta's company. He passed the paper back to her. "Here. I'm sure my office has some of them." A press piece with Nate's photo on it? He'd probably wallpapered the office with it. "How's my girl?"

Her face faltered, and he came to a stop, imagining the worse.

"Did something happen?"

"Oh, no. Nothing has changed. Nothing." She gave him a soft look. "Have you spoken to her doctors? Her condition is—"

"Strong." They hadn't used that word, exactly, but that was the sense he got. "She could wake up at any moment." Dr. Jeffers *had* said that. When Declan had pressed, he had confirmed that possibility.

"Right." She paused by the nurses' station, and he hated that look on her face. It was as if she'd already written Autumn off in her mind. Didn't she see? Didn't she realize, as she cared for her, that there was a *person* inside that body?

He moved past her and opened the door to Autumn's room, stepping inside and pulling it shut behind him.

She wasn't the first woman who had been friendly. The hospital staff had taken him under their wing, some in a more predatory fashion than others. He seemed to be a combination of sympathy case and prized acquisition, the dynamic unsettling. But not in her room. In her room, everyone seemed to leave him alone. In here, it was just the two of them.

"Hey, baby." He sat by her bed and lifted her hand, bringing it up to his mouth and kissing the inside of it. "I heard the craziest thing today. Back in 1998, a sixteen-year-old died from a heart attack brought on by a buildup of butane and propane in his bloodstream. Want to guess how that happened?"

He gave her a moment to think, studying the quiet lay of her features. "Excessive use of deodorant sprays. He had an apparent obsession with personal hygiene." That would have been a good story for her list of most embarrassing deaths.

Reaching over, he turned off the baby monitor, silencing the sounds of Mr. Oinks soft snores. Leaning forward, he rested his head on her stomach and closed his eyes, inhaling deeply and trying to find her scent. It was there, hidden behind all of the hypoallergenic soap and medicinal scents. It was there, but faint. He fought to remember her laugh. He hadn't really ever made her laugh. There had been chuckles. Some giggles. But a hard belly laugh was definitely in order, once she was up and about.

He tightened his grip on her slack hand and listened to the machine's comforting sounds. The steady beep of her heart. The whoosh of her ventilator. The hum of her circulation compresses.

"I love you," he whispered.

But, like always, she stayed silent.

APRIL

Declan & Autumn's list of to-dos

Uncontrollable, cramp-your-cheeks laughter
A Pictionary battle
Cooking dinner together
Making love in the morning
Skinny-dipping
A dance by a campfire
A confession of all of our secrets
An early morning ~~run~~ walk
Stolen kisses
Giving Mr. Oinks a bath
Building window boxes for more flowers
Saturday morning laziness
A candlelit dinner
Cuddling in a hammock
Kissing away tears
Swimming in the ocean
Smores at midnight
A kiss at Niagara Falls

MAY

They ran, side by side, his stride easier than hers. When they made it to the top of the hill, Ansley pulled at his arm, shaking her head. "I need a break."

He slowed to a stop and stopped the timer on his watch. "You're getting faster. Down a minute on your mile compared to last month."

"Really?" she wheezed. "I feel slow as ever."

He watched as she leaned forward, her hands on her knees. "You okay?"

"Yeah." Ansley grimaced and straightened, twisting to the left, then the right. "Just getting old." She nodded down the hill. "Mind walking for a bit?"

"Sure."

Out of reflex, he glanced down the first cross street, the damage from the plane still visible. The damaged home had been scraped, and a new frame was already in place.

Ansley stayed quiet, looking down at the road. He reached back, stretching his pec, enjoying the warmth of the sun on his face. It'd been a cold winter, unseasonable for Tallahassee. He'd had to cover all of Autumn's plants and bring in all the pots. He'd even gotten a sweater for Mr. Oinks, much to Ansley's disgust.

He smiled at the memory, the sweater now in a landfill, Mr. Oinks enthusiasm for the piece rivaling Ansley's. Apparently pigs don't like to wear things. And, as Ansley so irritably pointed out, he had a *lot* of fat to keep him warm.

"I'm pregnant." Ansley stopped short and turned to him, shielding her face from the sun with her hand. "I haven't… I haven't told anyone yet, other than Roger."

He struggled to process the feelings that came, his surprise and elation for her mixed with a wave of sadness. Over the last eight months, they had grown close—bonding over Autumn, united in their fierce protectiveness of her fight—and she felt like a sister to him, one he felt honor-bound to.

"So, you haven't told her yet?" He watched Ansley's face as it crumpled, her shoulders rounding in and he reached out, pulling her into his chest in a hug.

"I can't. I tried. Three times I've tried. But I need her to *know*. To understand. Not to just *lie* there." She choked out the words and looked up into his face, her eyes red and filled with tears. "I just…"

"I know," he said gruffly. "She'll be so happy." He held her against his chest, feeling her shake with quiet sobs, and wished he could take away that pain. She should be happy. They should be celebrating. He squeezed her tighter and tried to find the right thing to say.

Autumn would know. Autumn would have a joke, and dance around, and spout off morbid statistics in the most adorable fashion possible. She would christen this baby as hers, and whisper against Ansley's stomach, and meet Declan's eyes with a playful and happy smirk.

He pulled away from Ansley and fought his own tears at her grief.

36

JUNE

In the afternoons, he read to me. We went through a dark period two months ago, when he took us through The Shining. I was torn between hating the book, and wanting to know what would happen next. Now, (thank God) we'd moved on to lighter reading material. Ansley recommended a new contemporary fiction novel, and though he pretended to hate it, I knew he was dying to find out what secret Jocelyn's husband was keeping.

This hadn't been easy for him. He acted like it was. His greeting to me was always light-hearted, and he always had a funny story to tell. At this point, I felt like I knew Nate and Bridget well. She seemed like a lot of fun and had continued to babysit Paige and Caleb on the occasional weekend date night. And Nate was dating Benta, which shocked both Declan. He didn't think their relationship would last a year, but I was secretly rooting for them. Behind all of Nate's humor and cockiness, there seemed to be a real sweetheart hidden away. Just like under Declan's stoic and dry exterior, there was gold in his heart.

Even Roger loved Declan. He came by last week, on his lunch break, and sat quietly by the window, eating his sandwich. He didn't say much, but Roger never was a talker. He told me all about his meatball sub, and that he had really wanted a BLT, but that Ansley thought the bacon would offend me, given my love of all things pig. I'd smiled at that. He'd also told me that Declan had invited him to play on his softball team. Roger hadn't had the heart to tell him no, which was unfortunate for Declan, since Roger's attempt at sports typically looked like a seizure victim. Their first game was in a week, and I wished I could be there, for the comedic view of Roger swinging a bat, if nothing else. Poor Declan. I hoped he didn't have anything riding on this season.

The door opened, and I waited for a hint as to who it was. They'd already checked my vitals this morning, so it had to be a visitor, but it was too early to be Declan. I heard a cadence of clips across the floor and my throat grew thick, emotion swelling when I recognized the sound. *I'd heard that sound before*. Hundreds of times. I'd heard it when I was sleeping on the couch, the clicks across the wood floor my only warning before a wet snout would nudge my face. I'd heard it barrel down the hall, clippity-cloppiting, whenever the doorbell rang. I'd heard it jump beside my bed, the floor creaking in protest, in an attempt to get me to lift him up. It's Mr. Oinks! He's *here,* in the hospital!

My entire body strained to reach for him, to touch him, to hug him. I heard Ansley and Declan's quiet voices as they worked together to lift him onto the bed. "Easy," Declan murmured. "Watch her cords." The bed creaked and shimmied, and I could hear the gentle puff of his breaths. He was smelling me, and I hoped he could recognize me. I couldn't possibly smell the same. I wasn't wearing my perfume. My hair was washed by clinical hospital soap and not my normal Herbal Essence. I hadn't just finished baking. I hadn't been out in the yard, or wearing his favorite sweatshirt. I wasn't *me* anymore, and it would *break my heart* if he couldn't recognize me through the tubes and mask and hospital gown.

Suddenly he grunted, excited, and I *knew* that grunt. That grunt was the sound of his happiness. It was the sound when he got close enough to something to recognize it, and I've never loved this half-blind pig more. I could hear the sheets rustling, the bed shaking, and Ansley started to cry. If I could move, if I could reach him, I would have done the same thing. I would have bawled. Inside, I was. I was sobbing and hugging Mr. Oinks, and both of them in turn. I was squeezing them tight and never letting go.

Declan's voice was suddenly in my ear, and he was whispering all the things that he always says to me just before he leaves. How much he loved me. How much he missed me. How, once I was able to get up, we had so many wonderful things to do. He had such big plans for us. He saw me in a way that I didn't deserve to be seen, but that if I ever got out of this bed, I would strive to be.

"Declan." Ansley's voice sounded different, and I stopped breaking down long enough to listen to her. "Declan," she repeated. "*Look.*"

I wished I could see what she was pointing at. Was it Mr. Oinks? Was he okay? Was it my monitors?

Hard steps moved out of the room, and Declan didn't say anything. Did he leave? Mr. Oinks was still happily grunting, and Ansley was saying my name, over and over again, and I couldn't tell if she was happy or sad. Was this *it*? Was I *dying*? I struggled to move, struggled to do *anything*, but I couldn't.

More sounds came. A door slammed. Wheels rattled. More people, more voices, more steps. Mr. Oinks squealed, and I heard him hit the floor, his steps moving away as he squawked in protest. Everyone was saying my name—a chorus of voices—and I'd never been so frustrated. I wished someone would shut up with my name and TELL ME WHAT THE HELL WAS GOING ON.

I fought for movement, strained to open my eyes and then, suddenly, I couldn't breathe.

37

She was here. It was only for a moment, but it happened. Ansley saw the tear first, the lone drop of moisture running down her cheek. By the time Declan got the doctors, she had started to breathe on her own. They removed the tube and then put her back under. But she was *here*. She was coming back.

There were few certainties in life. Declan knew every degree of angle it took to build a house. He knew that the Yankees, no matter what, weren't ever going to put Chase Stern back in pinstripes. And he knew, *had* known from the very beginning, that Autumn Jones would wake up. Screw what the doctors had said. Screw every nurse who had gently urged him to "go out and live your life." He had *never* stopped believing in her.

And today, finally, it happened.

She was as beautiful as ever, especially now they had removed her mask and tubes. Her hair had grown a lot in the last nine months. And she was thinner. Once she was out of here, they'd need to put some weight back on her bones. Lots of protein-rich meals were in order. Lots of stories to tell, things to catch up on, backrubs to give, feelings to share. And kisses. Lots of kisses.

If he'd ever wondered about his feelings for her, about whether it was purely lust or a fleeting attraction, his resolve had been strengthened during the nine months of her coma. Every day had been a prayer. A plea. He'd fallen for Autumn Jones on a downtown street, over a deli sandwich, and in the woods. But he'd given her his heart during those nine months, and he would have sat by her bed for another nine years.

Now, watching her through the glass, Ansley's hand gripping hers, the two sisters talking, he was filled with the panic that he might lose her again, in a different way this time. *Rejection.* Ansley leaned over, hugging Autumn, and then glanced at him, smiling. She moved out to the hall and held open the door for him. "She's all yours."

If only she was. He stepped in and quietly closed the door behind him. She watched as he approached, her gaze holding his, and he couldn't hold back his smile as he got closer. *She was alive.* In the light of that fact, it didn't matter if she ever grew to love him.

"Hey." Her voice was raspy, and he was reminded that they weren't supposed to tax her. The doc had given strict orders to keep conversations to a minimum and to give her time to rest.

He sat beside her bed and fought the urge to pick up her hand. He had to remind himself that, though he had spent nine months falling in love with her, she was still stuck, one week into their relationship. Back then, she'd fought tooth and nail over anything other than a platonic relationship. Although… his mouth tugged into a grin… that hadn't exactly been their MO. He schooled his thoughts away from the memories and back to the present. "Did the doctor tell you about your brain?"

She nodded. That morning, they had performed an MRI and discovered that her brain had healed, fresh tissue filling the divot left by the cyst removal. It was a miracle, one assisted by her unlimited funds and world-class care. He had tortured himself endlessly over his selfish frustration at her inheritance and his insecurities around it. That inheritance had saved her life, and he was eternally grateful for its existence.

"Don't cry." She reached out for his face and he leaned into her,

her touch soft as she brushed away his tears. He swallowed at the gentle contact, and struggled with his emotions, the urge to kiss her, to squeeze her, to tell her all of his feelings ... it took every ounce of his resolve to stay in place, and he let out a shudder of breath, his hand tightening on her bed's rail.

"So..." she said quietly. "No Guardian Angel superpowers."

He watched her closely. "No. Just normal Autumn Jones awesomeness."

She smiled weakly. Started to speak, then gestured for the cup of water beside her bed. He tried to hold it for her and smiled when she batted it out of his hand with a scowl. She took a sip, then swallowed, passing it back to him. "Doesn't sound nearly as cool."

"It's way cooler," he responded. "But it wasn't bullshit."

She raised her brows at him in question.

"I think you did have Guardian Angel superpowers," he said gruffly. "At least for a short period of time." He set down the cup and picked up her hand, bringing it to his mouth and kissing the back of it. "You saved me."

She rolled her eyes and he squeezed her hand, getting her attention.

"You did." He turned her hand over and kissed her wrist. It was an act he had done almost daily, his lips brushing over the delicate skin as her hand had hung, limp and unresponsive. Now, her fingers curled around his, tugging, and the simple act broke a dam in his control. He swallowed hard, fighting back tears, and leaned forward, trying to hide the emotion behind another kiss to her wrist.

She *had* saved him. She had created *them*. She had wormed her way into his life, and then his heart, and broken him open in a hundred different ways. Gave him love and chaos and color in a world that had always been precise angles of gray.

She surprised him by patting the bed beside her. "Come here."

"I don't think it's big enough for both of us." His voice cracked, and he cleared his throat, fighting for control. She patted the bed again, and the look in her eye didn't allow for argument.

He was careful, getting into the bed, taking the time to gingerly move her to the edge before cautiously climbing in. The minute he got into place, he gathered her against him. "I just want to make sure you don't fall off."

She didn't respond, resting her head against his shoulder, and it was a good sign.

He curled his arm around her and closed his eyes, desperate to tell her everything of the last nine months and yet, not ruin a second of this perfect moment. "Did you know…" he said slowly, "that a lawyer in Toronto once fell to his death from the twenty-fourth floor of a building while demonstrating that the building's windows were unbreakable?"

She turned her head, looking up to him. "I did."

"Oh." He sighed, crestfallen.

She gently poked at his chest. "*You* told me that."

"I did?" He frowned, his propensity to collect useless death stories a habit picked up after she fell into her coma.

She curled against him, one weak leg wrapping over his, her arms stealing around his waist. "Can I ask you a favor?" she whispered.

He swallowed a thick lump that rose in his throat. "Anything," he said huskily.

"Read to me."

He glanced over, their paperback in its normal spot on her bedside table, his dry-cleaning receipt holding their place. Careful not to jostle her, he reached over and picked up the worn novel, flipping back to the first chapter and clearing his throat. When he started on the first line, she stopped him.

"No." She ran her fingers over the spine, working open the book to the place where the receipt was. "Here."

"But you won't understand it," he protested.

"I want to know the secret," she whispered.

The secret? He looked at the book dumbly, the new release still topping the bestseller charts. She couldn't have read it before, wouldn't know about a secret unless… hope, that evil and cruel mistress, sprang in his chest. "You know this book?" he asked carefully.

She nodded, her eyes on his, the corners of her mouth tugging upward. She looked like a child on Christmas, one dying to open a present, their anticipation spilling out. "I heard you… reading it to me."

He thought of the story of the lawyer's death, her declaration that he had told her the fact. Of course he had, months ago, in this same room, to her prostrate form.

She had heard him. He blinked, trying to focus on her face, as all of the possibilities locked into place. His arms tightened on her and she wheezed in protest. "I'm sorry," he whispered, planting a kiss on her head. "I just… do you remember?" He looked at her and her mouth widened into a slow and happy smile.

"Yes," she whispered. "Everything."

"So, you know that I love you." He felt shy saying the words, his mind tripping through all that he had said, all that he had *confessed,* during these months.

"Not a big deal." She lifted one shoulder in a weak shrug. "I'm easy to love."

He chuckled, pulling her head toward him and kissing the top of it. "Yes, Autumn, you are."

She dropped her head on his shoulder and nudged the book in his direction. He picked it back up, his mind ricocheting in every direction as he opened the paperback and tucked the bookmark into the back cover. Settling deeper into the bed, he found their place on the page and cleared his throat, preparing to read. *She knew everything.* The events of the last nine months. The project he'd finished with Nate. Paige's missing tooth debacle. His dreams and hopes and love for her.

"Wait." She gripped his shirt and looked up at him. She tried to pull up higher on his chest, but was too weak to do so. He tilted down, toward her mouth, a question in his eyes. She nodded, and he gently pressed his lips to hers, his body trembling in an attempt to keep his feelings in check. It was a soft, sweet kiss, four or five mini-kisses in one, and when they parted, she smiled. "I love you, Declan Moss."

She loved him. Could she? Could her own feelings have developed at the same time his did? Maybe this was drugs—a cocktail of chemicals they were pumping into her IV to keep her brain in check. Would she remember this, or all of the last nine months, when she woke up tomorrow?

He swallowed every fear and looked into her eyes. God, he'd missed those eyes. "I love you, too." His voice broke a little on the words, and he swallowed, holding back every other thing he'd ever said to her. They had the rest of their lives for those confessions, and chances were, she'd already heard them from him a hundred times before. He pressed a soft kiss on her forehead and then brought her into his chest, relaxing back on the bed.

Then, together, they discovered Jocelyn's husband's secret.

EPILOGUE

"I'm not putting a penis on a cake. I don't care what sort of significance you think it has." A very pregnant Ansley glared at me, a spatula in hand.

"I'm not asking you to put the penis *on* the cake, I'm asking you to put the penis *in* the cake." I turned from the counter and looked to Declan for moral support. "Tell her she has to put a penis in it."

He raised his hands in surrender. "I'm staying out of this. I have a strict policy against touching any penis that isn't my own."

"Ew." Ansley crinkled her nose.

"I suppose you'd prefer that he touches other people's penises?" I asked dryly.

"Can you all stop saying that word? Please?" Roger stood in the doorway, a bag of party decorations in hand, and gave us a pained look.

"*I* can say the word penis. I was in a *coma,*" I informed him primly, and everyone in the room groaned. "*Whaaaat?*" I glared at them.

"You can't pull out the coma card anymore." Declan tugged at the back of my jeans, pulling me into his arms. "Remember? We all voted and agreed."

"*I* didn't agree," I reminded him. "Maybe you couldn't see my weak little hand raised in the anti-vote, but it was up there. Hospital band on and everything."

He wrapped his arms around me and bent over, pressing a kiss against my collarbone. "Your vote didn't count."

"That's bull crap," I said indignantly. "I—"

He silenced me with a kiss, spinning me around and pressing his lips to mine in a fierce lip lock that sucked every relevant thought out of my head. Someone threw a party hat at us and Declan blocked it with one hand, using the other to keep me tightly gripped to him. When we came up for air, I couldn't remember my middle name, much less what we'd been discussing.

"So, it's decided," Ansley said. "No penis in the cake my children are going to have pieces of."

I whirled around to speak and Declan clamped his hand over my mouth. "I have another place you can put a penis," he whispered, his breath tickling the edge of my ear. "I'll give you three guesses where."

"GROSS," Ansley said. "WE CAN HEAR YOU, you know."

"The garbage disposal?" I guessed, painting my face into a mask of innocent inquiry.

He winced, his hand moving to protect my favorite organ in the entire world. "Nevermind. I rescind the offer."

I grinned at him, and he straightened, his teeth sawing over his bottom lip as he eyed me. That's all it took between us. One long look, and a playful smile could ignite into wet panties and stiff arousal. He tugged me to him and I ducked around his hold, jogging down the hall and laughing as he took up the chase.

He caught up to me in the laundry room, and backed me up against the dryer, his hands hooking around my ass and pulling me into his kiss. "I love you." His words slipped out between deep kisses, our heads angling for better positions, mouths frantic, hands groping and skating over every piece of each other we could access.

"I love you too." I had my hands in his hair, fisting the thick strands, when someone knocked on the door.

"Auttie?" Paige's plaintive voice rang out from the other side of the door. "Declan?"

I yanked my shirt back into place. "Just a second!" I called out, giving Declan a quick zipper and bulge check before opening the door and offering my niece a breezy smile.

"Mom says to tell you no cardinal activities are allowed in our house."

"An excellent rule." I reached down and tickled her stomach, moving aside to let Declan sweep her off her feet and into the air, her shoes narrowly missing the hall lamp as he swung her around and onto his shoulders. "Should we see any cardinals, I'll shoo them out."

Caleb ran in, holding his hands up to Declan and begging for the same. I watched as he scooped up the boy with his other hand and carried them both through the back door, their shrieks of laughter increasing in volume when he launched them onto the trampoline.

I struggled to silence my inner thoughts on trampoline injuries, and the likelihood of broken necks, and enjoyed a moment where I watched them. Declan curled into a ball in the center of the circle, holding his knees as they bounced all around him, their arms swinging through the air, determined to break his popcorn.

He cracked, dramatically bursting out of his ball, his arms and legs springing open, and they piled on him, pulling at his limbs, their grins as big as my own. I recalled Ansley's *conversations* with me when I was in the coma, telling me how Declan had become part of the family. It was true, he had. *How had I found such an amazing man to love?*

I felt my sister's arms wrap around me and she squeezed me tightly, following my gaze.

"Damn, I love him," I whispered.

"You should." She smiled at me, and gave me a squeeze. "He's a keeper. But you already know that. Hence the no-penis cake engagement party."

I looked at my hand and stared at the diamond, surrounded by baby blue stones, the ring more precious to me than anything I had ever owned. "Yeah," I said, smiling. "He is."

"I think there's a weight limit on this thing." I listened carefully to the soft squeak of the rope and imagined the three of us plummeting to our death when it broke.

Well, maybe not death. But plummeting at least three feet. Bruises and sore backs were a definite risk factor.

"Are you trying to say that we're overweight?"

I could feel the curve of Declan's grin against the side of my forehead and I laughed, turning into him and rubbing the giant belly between us. "Well, not all of us." Mr. Oinks lay flat on his back in the double hammock, his legs open in a most immodest way, his junk on full display to every star in the sky. I ran my palm over his warm tummy, and he let out a sigh of gratitude.

"This wasn't exactly what I had in mind when I built this." Declan leaned forward and pressed a kiss to my forehead, then dropped his head lower and found my mouth.

"So you thought you'd build a big comfortable bed out in the middle of his yard and he wouldn't want to get on it with us?" I gave him a knowing glance. "Sure."

There was the faint hiss of pig flatulence, and Mr. Oinks jerked, as if surprised by the action. Declan laughed, then struggled to sit up, the hammock almost dumping us out before he got his feet on the ground and stabilized us. "Out you go, buddy." He hoisted Mr. Oinks onto the ground and settled back down next to me, watching as the pig waddled over to the flower bed and collapsed on top of my fresh plantings.

I groaned and rolled into the crook of his arm, hooking one leg over his. "I'm going to have to replant that bed."

He pressed a kiss to my lips. "I'll help."

We lay there for a long moment, swaying under the moon, a chorus of crickets humming from the bushes.

"You know what I *had* envisioned when I built this?"

"What?" I played with my ring, the feel of it still foreign on my finger.

"This. You and me. Planning our future. Discussing our dreams. Making sweet love to the faint smell of Mr. Oinks' farts."

I laughed, and wrapped my arm around his side, pulling him tighter to me. "There's no way that you and I are coordinated enough to have sex on this hammock."

He scoffed and I grinned, watching as Mr. Oinks rolled onto his back and thrashed around, destroying hundreds of innocent tulips.

"Then let's talk about our future. Your dreams." He ran his hand gently across the top of my head. "I want to make all of them come true."

My heart swelled and I blinked rapidly, trying to contain the emotion that threatened to spill out in tears. "It's a big list," I said, aiming for a light-hearted tone and almost nailing it. "It's going to take you a long time."

"That's okay," he said quietly, and damn if he wasn't intent on trying to make me cry. "I've got the rest of my life."

"I want a wedding in the woods," I started, imagining our wedding party in camo, with a bonfire and steak reception.

"Done." He nipped at my neck.

"And maybe we could go to Daytona Beach for our honeymoon? To that surfing competition?" I looked at him hopefully.

He made a face. "Sure. Not exactly shooting for the stars, but whatever makes you happy."

"And build that house you designed." He'd shown me the plans in the hospital, the sprawling one-story being exactly like every fantasy I never knew I had.

"And babies," I pressed. "Lots of fat and happy babies."

"Human babies?" he asked, concerned. "Because I love Mr. Oinks, but I can't take—"

"Human babies," I assured him. "But only if they have my sense of humor and your good looks."

"Lots of babies…" he mused, grinding his hips into me, his readiness hard and apparent. "That seems like something we could start on now."

"*Right* now?" I lost a breath when he rolled on top of me, my sleep shirt bunching up as he settled in between my legs. "Because I have a lot of other items on my list."

"Right now," he muttered, one hand pushing down the drawstring waist of his pajama pants. I got a brief glimpse of his dick, stiff and thick and beautiful, before his knees slipped on the hammock and he fell forward. His elbow hit my side, and I jerked right, the combination of factors causing the hammock to swing upside down and unceremoniously dump us out onto the grass.

I started to laugh and Declan wheezed out a cry.

"Not my finest moment," he said.

"Right now," I mimicked his deep drawl, and another laugh bubbled out of me. "I told you we weren't talented enough for that."

"I blame the failure on the hammock and not our bedroom skills." He rolled onto his knees and crawled across the grass and above me.

"Yeah?" I said, smiling up at him.

"Yeah," he said, his gaze focusing on my lips before coming back to my eyes.

And there it was. Another look. Another flame lit. A crackling of need that flamed between us and lit every pore in my body on fire.

"Declan?" I said, my voice husky.

"Yeah?"

"Let's make some babies."

And there on the damp grass, under the cover of a faulty hammock, we did just that.

Want more? Get a better peek at Benta Aldrete in Love Chloe - a fun and sexy romance about trying to find love in the big city. Continue reading for more!

Someone was trying to break in. I sat up with a start, pushing up my sleep mask, the sunlight coming in through the windows too bright, my drunk stumble into bed last night neglecting the blackout curtains. I found my phone and peered at it. 9:48 AM—an odd time for a robbery. There was more pounding, the sound coming from the living room, then the splintering of wood. I yanked at the cord of my cell and unplugged it, gripping it tightly, pushing the covers aside, my bare feet hitting the floor just as my bedroom door swung open, a stranger in the opening.

My search for a weapon stopped as I stared at the man, clad head-to-toe in tactical gear, a walkie-talkie at his mouth.

"Chloe Madison?" he asked.

"Yes?" I said weakly, praying my grandma underwear didn't show underneath my baggy tee, a Versace number that barely hit mid-thigh.

"I'm from the FBI. As of now, this apartment is the property of the US Government. We're going to have to ask you to leave, or you will be arrested."

"But … I own this apartment," I said weakly, my gaze darting around the bedroom, a Monistat box open on my dresser. I closed my eyes in embarrassment, two more men appearing in the doorway.

"Your parents *did*," he corrected me. "Not anymore." He glanced at his watch. "I'm going to need you to get dressed."

There was a time in my life when I found FBI agents sexy. Let me assure you, they aren't.

ONE MONTH LATER

I stood in the afternoon sun, my eyes stretching up the Central Park brownstone, counting the stories out of habit. Five. Double-checking the address on my phone, I rang the bell, my toes tapping a nervous beat, my eyes tracing over the decorative ***B*** that was carved into the heavy door before me. I wasn't used to being nervous. Or anxious. Or desperate. And that's what I had become. Desperate. It didn't wear well; it itched along my skin like a T.J. Maxx clearance sweater.

I should have been in South Beach, with Cammie and Benta, lying on a beach and celebrating our NYU graduation. They'd flown out yesterday and hadn't stopped Instagramming since. If I could have reached through the Internet and throttled them, I would have. Instead, I gave them the ultimate passive-aggressive snub: no likes.

A pathetic move on my part, but the best I could manage from my reduced social state. Anyone who'd seen a television in the last month knew about my family's downfall. The Madisons—a filthy rich financial advisor couple who pocketed a hundred million bucks from insider trading—were front-page news. My mom had befriended all of the Fortune 500 wives, prying business tidbits from their martini-stained lips and passing them on to Dad. Daddy Dearest had used the information wisely illegally, steering his clients (and our portfolio) through a hundred highly profitable deals. I'd gotten a new Range Rover for my sixteenth birthday and didn't think twice about it. My parents got arrested in the midst of their Christmas party and laughed it off. Told me it was a 'minor mis-understanding.'

They weren't laughing now. Not since last week, when the easy wealth I'd enjoyed my whole, pampered life ended faster than a Taylor Swift relationship. Our accounts were frozen, cars taken, assets seized. Including my NYC apartment. Thank God they had let me keep the clothes. I might be homeless, but I was rocking it in Marc Jacobs.

The biggest issue was my tuition. Half of my last semester was due, NYU being absolutely uncool about it, holding back my degree until it was paid. A month ago, I'd have swiped my AmEx and not thought another moment about it. Now, the huge bill seemed impossible. What good was four years of undergrad without a degree? Worthless when it came to the cutthroat job market that was NYC. So while Cammie and Benta were toasting their futures with mojitos in the sunshine, I was alone in New York, praying that this interview would go well. I'd had three interviews so far, submitted my résumé to twenty-two jobs, and had gotten zero callbacks. I was getting desperate.

The door swung open, and Nicole Brantley stood there.

Nicole Brantley. Sole heir to the inventor of the latex condom. Every time a foil package got pulled out of a pocket, Nicole Brantley got paid. At sixteen, she played a blonde bimbo on a *Party of Five* knock-off and had humped the Lifetime movie circuit ever since. My mother met her at a charity golf luncheon last year, and they'd stayed in touch. Mother promised that "Nicole was a doll" and "would be a pleasure to work for." This all coming from a woman who hadn't worked a day in her life. Regardless, I couldn't be picky. I needed money, and Nicole Brantley had piles of *that*.

"Yes?" she asked, her bright blue eyes skipping over me, darting from my heels to my handbag, a critical appraisal that ended in approval. "Can I help you?"

"I'm Chloe Madison. My mother said you were looking for an assistant? I have an interview scheduled for one." A pathetic opening. *My mother*? But, remarkably, the woman's face curved into a smile, the Madison name still having some pull in the lowly area of hired help.

"Thank God," she drawled, dragging me through the front doors. "This week has been a *disaster*. Come inside and let me track down

Clarke." She turned on her heel—a hot blue Louboutin—and clicked a rapid path through the foyer.

I'd been in New York for four years. Enough time to realize the mansions of my Florida youth didn't exist on Manhattan's streets. Pools and guest homes, tennis courts, and country clubs—those niceties were in the Hamptons or New Jersey. In the city, wealth was spoken through garages, Central Park views, and square footage. The Brantleys had all three. I spied a housekeeper, uniformed in the white and black attire that a sliver of the upper-class demanded. Saw the Picasso and Kandinsky in the hall. Noticed the views of the park that dominated the room we moved into, and the man who stepped away from the window, a phone to his ear.

He nodded to me, a curt smile passed over before he refocused on his conversation, his voice sharp as he spoke into the phone. I watched his hand come up to the window and press, the lean of his body against the glass stretching his suit tight across broad shoulders and a tight ass, the drop of his head a masculine, sexual gesture. I watched him and felt a pull of longing, the Chloe romance channel devoid of excitement for a very long time.

"That's Clarke." Mrs. Brantley's voice rang out loudly, no concern given about his call. "Sorry about his lack of greeting," she said airily, snapping at me and gesturing for me to follow, her ability to move in five-inch stilettos admirable. "His hand is permanently attached to that phone." She rounded a staircase and headed up and glanced down at me. "Chanel is up here." She took the steps two at a time, her calves ridiculous, my follow more laborious in execution. I tried to respond and managed a wheeze, glancing around for the elevator that surely existed. *Chanel.* Mom hadn't mentioned any children, and I prayed this girl would be old enough to be potty-trained.

Nicole glanced back. "As far as pay, it's a thousand a week. I'll need you from nine in the morning until four, Monday through Friday. Chanel will be a large part of your job. Does that work for you?"

My breath was short as we finally hit the top of the stairs, my mind working overtime. A thousand a week? That should be enough for food and rent, with a little extra to pay down my tuition until NYU coughed up my diploma and allowed me to get a real job, one that would make use of my real estate development degree. I frowned. My original plan, after graduation, had been to work in commercial and residential real estate, a non-salaried, straight-commission job. A job that—in the wake of my newfound poverty—was now unfeasible. I refocused on the conversation, my mind stuttering a little at the second mention of the child. I'd never been around a baby, my knowledge of infants restricted to sporadic episodes of *Teen Mom*. "Yes, great. That sounds perfect."

She stopped on the landing, holding up a red-tipped finger and pressing it to her lips before turning the handle, pushing open the door to a nursery. I silently groaned at the crib, set in the back of the pale pink room, CHANEL on the wall in block letters. I followed slowly, reluctant to meet the baby. A smile fixed into place, I leaned over, glancing into the crib, and—helpless to stop myself—gasped at the body that lay there.

A *dog's* body.

I stood at the side of the crib and fought to keep my expression normal as I took in the pink outfit that encased a body not weighing more than five pounds. It lay on its side, brown poufs of hair spilling out of each opening in the ensemble, a fur-lined hoodie loose across its back, and snored, little purrs as it stretched out across a duvet.

"She's sleeping," Mrs. Brantley whispered loudly.

Duh. I attempted a polite smile and looked back at the pup. *This* was a large part of my job? To dog sit? Everything turned more appealing, diapers and runny noses no longer part of the equation.

"When can I start?" I whispered, careful to give the proper respect to sleeping Chanel.

She glanced at her watch, a diamond-studded timepiece. "Can you work today 'til four?"

"Absolutely." I smiled brightly.

Mrs. Brantley patted my arm in what seemed to be approval. "Tomorrow, I'll go over my needs. Today, I'd rather you focus on getting to know Chanel and introducing yourself. I've got to hop on a call. If you have any questions, hunt down one of the help."

The Help. A group I was now part of. I nodded politely, watched her exit, and performed a cursory sweep of the room. Decorated in three different shades of pink, the en suite included a miniature treadmill, a puppy closet that rivaled my own, and dressers stocked with supplies and toys. Unsure of what exactly *Getting to Know Chanel* meant, I settled into a leather chair and waited for her to wake up, the gentle snores from the crib creating a soothing lullaby.

I may or may not have fallen asleep. But we could pretend that I diligently watched over Chanel's sleeping form without a single head droop. That was me. Best New Assistant EVER.

At 4:05 PM, I nodded a goodbye to the maid, pulled on my coat and stepped onto the street, the afternoon sun minimizing the chill as I pulled the door tightly shut behind me. *Success*. I wanted to dance—right there on the street, strangers brushing by—in celebration. I wanted to wave my arms and revel in the fact that I, Chloe Madison, was officially independent. I had my own job. Would not become homeless. Would not fail. It was liberating, exciting in a way that my privileged upbringing could never afford. Yes, a thousand a week would barely make a dent in my mountain of debt. Yes, I'd be eating Ramen noodles and taking the subway. But still! I was on my own and, for the first time, it didn't feel scary; it felt manageable.

I moved down the street, swinging my purse from my shoulder and dug for my cell, the phone to my ear by the time I hit Park Avenue.

"Hey beautiful!" Cammie's voice rang through the phone, her greeting seconded by Benta, and I could imagine the two girls, faces together over a pitcher of margaritas, the phone held between them.

"Hey you tan goddesses," I teased. "Enjoying the Florida sun without me?"

"We'd be lying if we said we weren't." In the background, I heard music start. "How'd the interview go?"

I delivered the good news, the girls squealing with an excitement that rivaled my own, a laugh spilling from my mouth at their reaction. "I wish you guys were here to help me celebrate."

"Woman, hop on a plane and get down here! We'll save one of these beautiful men for you."

"Don't tempt me," I warned. "I'm so sick of New York men I could scream." A vision of Clarke Brantley appeared in my mind's eye, his hand against the window, his masculinity screaming through every line in his body. I closed my eyes briefly and fought the urge to check my lower lip for drool. "Anyway, I've got to run. I'm going to check out apartments, try and find a place to live. I just wanted to let you guys know the good news."

"That's great news, babe," Benta called out, her voice overshadowed by the background noise. "Go have fun tonight! Celebrate without us!"

I smiled at her order, said my goodbyes to both of them and ended the call before dropping my phone into my purse and jogging down the subway steps, the mild warmth of the afternoon sun fading as I stepped into the dark underground.

My phone rang as I hit the bottom step, the muted song chiming from my purse. I stepped out of the way, digging frantically as my ringtone neared its end. I followed the glow of the screen, pulling out my cell just in time. My finger froze mid-swipe, and I stared down at my screen at the name.

I smirked. Straightened the strap of my gown and looked out the window. "Shh. The driver will hear you."

"The driver's job is to hear me. Now, get on your knees." Vic's hand landed on the back of my neck, pulling me toward him. I twisted away, shooting him a warning look.

He leaned over, whispered in my ear, his breath tickling the wisps of my chignon. "Do it, and tomorrow I'll fly us to Paris."

That *got my attention. I turned, sliding across the seat, his hand immediately traveling up the slit in my dress, teasing the skin on my thighs, my legs obediently parting as he did what he did best and ran his fingers over the silk of my panties. "Private?" I asked, the negotiation eliciting a chuckle from him, his eyes darkening when my hips curved into his fingers, the steal of a digit sliding under my panties turning everything—for one exquisite moment—beautifully black.*

"Yes, we'll fly private, you spoiled woman. Now, let me feel that delicious mouth." His fingers gently played on my neck, a light reminder, and this time, I didn't resist, sliding down, the limo's carpet stiff against my knees, the beaded dress snagging on the edge of the seat before breaking free.

I unbuckled his belt and looked up into his eyes, dragging the zipper down. Heavy and hooded, they stared at me as if drugged, his handsome mouth opening slightly when my hand stole into his tuxedo pants and wrapped around him.

The car took a turn, my left hand gripping his thigh for balance, his finger tapping at the window control, a sliver of cold night air and city sounds pouring through the now-open crack, my eyes narrowing as I placed his cock in my mouth, showing my teeth, threatening him with my eyes.

"Easy princess." He smiled, his perfect grin white in the dark space. "Just adding a little atmosphere. Not enough for anyone to see in. Now, suck."

His order excited me, the dominance in his tone making my thighs clench, arousal growing. Arousal, which, knowing Vic, he'd light into a full-fledged fire by the time we hit his elevator. Arousal he'd put out with his fingers, his mouth, and his body. I closed my eyes and concentrated.

I loved the power of having him in my mouth. I took my time, taking him deep and feeling him stiffen against my tongue, in the course of seconds, my oral ability proven in eight inches of reaction. I smiled around his cock and buried it down my throat.

Fifteen blocks later, only minutes before we pulled up to his Fifth Avenue residence, he moaned my name, his hand tugging at my hair, the shudder of his body the final warning before he thrust into my mouth and came. Hot satisfaction of which I swallowed every bit, the small aftertaste well worth the worship in his eyes as he pulled me into his arms and kissed me senseless.

"I love you," he whispered, brushing the hair off my shoulder, the hair that had come undone somewhere around SoHo. "Oh Chloe. I love you so much."

And that, in a cum-filled nutshell, was my ex. Vic Worth. His family's name was plastered on buildings all over Manhattan. A billionaire trust-fund baby, we met sophomore year at NYU. Dated eighteen months before I walked in on him mid-thrust into his maid. I dumped him, and he popped the question with a six-carat ring amid a flurry of exorbitant gestures. I said "no" in about four different combinations, most paired with an expletive or immaturely presented middle finger. He wasn't deterred, his pursuit impressive in its effort, a pursuit that I had hoped, with a two-month hiatus since his last contact, had finally ended.

Yet that afternoon, my high from my new job draining with every note of my ringtone, he called. I hesitated, then, despite my better judgment, dragged my finger across the surface and raised the phone to my ear.

I barely had time to speak before Vic's voice came through the cell, his words barking out with some degree of urgency. "Don't get on that filthy thing. The subway? God knows what you'll catch."

I spun around, peering up into the bright white square of sunlight, a swell of bundled New Yorkers pouring over its edge and hurrying down the steps, the vibration of the oncoming train pulsing under my feet. "Are you following me?" I hissed into the phone.

"Hell no. I'm at the Bellagio about to clean house in blackjack. But Jake just texted me that he saw you going down to the six. What the fuck are you doing?"

"Is this seriously why you called me?" The train approached, its brakes screeching as it came to a stop and was immediately surrounded, the crush of bodies swelling like a sea of maggots around a prize. I tapped my MetroCard against my leg, in no hurry to join the party.

He sighed into the phone. "According to Jake, you're in heels—and I know your heels. They aren't built for actual use. Trot your sexy ass up those stairs and get in the warm car; let Jake take you home. *Please*. Then I'll hang up and never bother you again."

"Never?" I challenged, the promise one I'd heard before.

"I'll try my best."

I twisted back and forth, my purse swinging with the momentum, from darkness to light. Though, in this twisted scenario, they were flip-flopped: the dark and dirty wheeze of the subway was where I *should* be going, the light and sunny street the path I should avoid.

"Come on, baby. Let me do this one thing. Just one." The beg in his voice, the crack on the word *baby*. It reached up my skirt and teased my skin, probed into my brain and lured out all of the times his gorgeous mouth had whispered the words.

Come on, baby… his hand pulled me into a coat check closet, parting furs and pushing me back against the wall.

Come on, baby… his tongue, soft on my inner thighs, the scrape of his five o'clock shadow tickled as his hands spread my knees apart and his mouth moved higher.

Come on, baby… his hands up my dress, fingers digging into the meat of my ass, his mouth on my neck as we—tucked into the shadows of a club, music thumping, bodies everywhere—let passion override sense.

Come on, baby…

That was the problem with love. There was no OFF switch.

I ended the call and hurried down the steps into the cold darkness.

ALSO BY ALESSANDRA TORRE

Looking for another sexy read?

Hollywood Dirt. (Now a Full-length Movie!) When Hollywood comes to a small town, sparks fly between its biggest star and a small-town outcast.

Love, Chloe. (First created for Cosmpolitan.com) A fallen socialite works for an heiress, dodges an ex, and juggles single life in the city that never sleeps.

Hidden Seams. A billion-dollar fashion empire is surrounded by secrets, sex and lies.

Blindfolded Innocence. (First in a series) A college student catches the eye of Brad DeLuca, a divorce attorney with a sexy reputation that screams trouble.

Black Lies, the New York Times Bestseller. A love triangle with a twist that readers couldn't stop talking about. You'll hate this heroine until the moment you love her.

Moonshot, the New York Times Bestseller. Baseball's hottest player has his eye on only one thing—his team's 18-year-old ballgirl.

Tight. A small-town girl falls for a sexy stranger on vacation. Lives intersect and secrets are unveiled in this dark romance.

Trophy Wife. When a stripper marries a rich stranger, life as a trophy wife is not anything like she expects.

Some suspenseful Alessandra Torre novels:

The Ghostwriter. Famous novelist Helena Roth is hiding a dark secret – her perfect life is a perfect lie. Now, as death approaches, she must confess her secrets before it's too late. An emotional and suspense-charged novel.

The Girl in 6E. (Deanna Madden, #1) A sexy internet superstar hides a dark secret: she's a reclusive psychopath.

Do Not Disturb. (Deanna Madden, #2) Fresh from prison, an online client's casual interest quickly turns the corner into obsession.

If You Dare. (Deanna Madden, #3) Love turns deadly in this cat and mouse game where police grow closer to the internet's biggest star.

ABOUT ALESSANDRA

Alessandra Torre is an award-winning New York Times bestselling author of nineteen novels, and is the Bedroom Blogger for Cosmopolitan.com. In addition to writing, Alessandra is the creator of Alessandra Torre Ink: a website, community, and online school for aspiring authors.

Learn more about Alessandra at alessandratorre.com or join 40,000 readers and sign up for her popular monthly newsletter at nextnovel.com.

facebook.com/alessandratorre0

twitter.com/readalessandra

instagram.com/alessandratorre4

ACKNOWLEDGMENTS

With every book, a team effort is involved. I wanted to take a moment and thank the following individuals:

Marion Archer - for your care and attention to this plot, characters, and the hundreds of little moments we worked through in these pages. Thank you so much!

Tricia Crouch - for all of the support and friendship you give me, the pep talks when I was ready to abandon this plot, and for reading a dozen different versions and loving them all. Thank you!

Janice, Perla, and Erik - it is incredible how three sets of eyes can find so many flaws! With over a hundred catches, I am reminded, over and over again, how valuable you each are and what a difference you make in my novels. Thank you!

Sommer from Perfect Pear Creative - you nailed this cover on the first try, then made it even better. Thank you so much for sharing your talents with me!

Yulanda B, Jenny V, and Karen L - thank you for reading early bits and for your quick and insightful feedback!

Maura and Flavia - thank you for taking this new baby under your wing, let's get it in bookstores around the world!

Made in the USA
Middletown, DE
09 January 2019